A NOVEL OF INDIAN JUSTICE FROM THE SPUR AWARD–WINNING AUTHOR OF *AMONG THE EAGLES*

As a boy, he was called Raven Feather . . .

He was only ten when the Plains Indians gathered at Horse Creek to ratify a treaty of peace among their peoples and the whites who had begun to sweep across the West.

But peace would not come. And the boy would become a man—a man called Wolf Running, who would watch as his beloved plains were marked with blood. He watched as the white men's Army was ordered to kill Cheyennes on sight . . . and as the last unspoiled hunting grounds of the Sioux and Cheyenne peoples were lost as forts sprung up in the Powder River country. And with each act of vengeance, his fighting spirit was fueled as he led his people down the road of courage and survival . . .

WARRIOR'S ROAD

An unforgettable novel of the changing American West . . . and one man's brave struggle to save his people . . .

WARRIOR'S ROAD

G. CLIFTON WISLER

BERKLEY BOOKS, NEW YORK

WARRIOR'S ROAD

A Berkley Book / published by arrangement with
the author

PRINTING HISTORY
Berkley edition / May 1994

ISBN: 0-425-14229-9

BERKLEY®
Berkley Books are published by The Berkley Publishing Group,
200 Madison Avenue, New York, New York 10016.
BERKLEY and the "B" design
are trademarks belonging to Berkley Publishing Corporation.

PRINTED IN THE UNITED STATES OF AMERICA

10 9 8 7 6 5 4 3 2 1

Remembering
Eddie Boyle

1

RAVEN FEATHER ROSE slowly from his sleeping pallet. It wasn't his habit to rise early. The soft rabbit and elk skins beckoned him back to their comforting warmth, and he almost allowed his weariness to overwhelm his eager heart. Instead he bit his lip and let the pain bring a sharp edge to his senses. Outside his father's lodge the first traces of dawn were already brightening the Omissis camp.

It's time, he thought as he gazed at the sleeping figures in the dimness of the lodge. Close to the door, Red Hawk, his father, lay intertwined with his mother, Burnt Willow Woman. His small brothers, Little Hawk and Willow Boy, rested on the opposite side. Nothing was as comforting as family, Raven Feather's uncle, Raven Heart, had said a few days earlier.

"Here is the continuing of our people," the Heart had observed. "From me to you, Nephew, our blood and our traditions pass."

"Yes," Raven Feather whispered as he dressed himself. He inhaled deeply, allowing the fragrant mixture of sage and cedar that filled the lodge to flood his being. Had there ever been such a clear, bright morning? How many boys had greeted their eleventh summer with higher expectations?

The Feather was tempted to howl with joy, but he held himself in check. It wouldn't do to wake Red Hawk, and if the brothers stirred, they would insist on following him to the creek. Raven Feather had no intention of herding children—not this morning!

Quietly he slithered across the lodge and made his way through the narrow opening. Outside, he drank in the cool, damp air and glanced out beyond the lodge circle to the shallow waters of Horse Creek. Downstream, pony boys were watching over the horse herd. Upstream, the smoke of morning cook fires was already rising from the Oglala Lakota camp.

The sound of a meadowlark drew his attention to a tall cottonwood that hung out over the creek. In the shadow of that towering tree stood his Omissis cousin, Three Toes. Alongside Three Toes, Curly, their Oglala relation, paced impatiently. Raven Feather crept across the Omissis circle and marched out through the gap that marked the entrance to the camp. He then scrambled around the back of the lodges until he joined his cousins beneath the cottonwood.

"It's a good day," Curly announced in his odd mixture of Tsis tsis tas and Lakota words. For many winters the northern Tsis tsis tas and the Lakotas had hunted and camped together, and many young men now carried the blood of both tribes. Red Hawk had been born to the Oglala band, but his own father had been Tsis tsis tas.

"Yes," Raven Feather said as he clasped the arms of his cousins.

"As good as yesterday?" Three Toes asked.

Curly tried to conceal a grin. The afternoon just past, he had accepted the challenge of a boastful Crow horse racer. That Crow and others were now poorer, for Curly had outwitted them and won a celebrated victory.

"You have enough horses to buy a wife," Raven Feather said, grinning.

"What use has a boy of ten for a wife?" Curly answered.

"Wrong question," Three Toes said, laughing. "What use has a wife for a husband of ten summers?"

Raven Feather stepped back and allowed his cousins to face each other. The two of them barked and snapped like a pair of camp dogs.

"Wives," Raven Feather grumbled. "Women. They're always leading to quarrels. I thought we came here to swim."

His cousins grinned, exchanged a glance, and turned on the Feather.

"Nooo," Raven Feather said, backing a step toward the creek. His cousins howled wildly as they pounced on him. The three boys grappled a moment. Then they rolled onto the sandy bank and on into the shallows of Horse Creek. Immediately the cold bite of the stream sent them splashing back to the bank.

"Ayyyy!" Raven Feather exclaimed, shaking off the icy water.

"It's as cold as winter," Curly remarked.

"As cold as the eyes of an angry woman," Three Toes said, laughing.

"He knows all about women, after all," Curly whispered to the Feather.

"Yes, I do," Three Toes insisted. "As you will, cousins, when you're older."

Raven Feather laughed, and Curly grabbed Three Toes's shoulders and threw him back into Horse Creek. Soon the sun peeked out over the ridge to the east, offering comforting warmth to the swimmers. Other boys hurried down to the creek, followed afterward by their older brothers and fathers.

"Fools," an old Oglala muttered when he noticed the

cousins. "You'll be sorry you didn't remove your breech-clouts when the skins tighten."

Raven Feather dropped his eyes. He hadn't even kicked off his moccasins. He dragged himself onto the bank like a whipped pup and silently removed his clothing. He then draped the skins over the branches of the cottonwood to dry and set his moccasins on a nearby boulder. Three Toes and Curly did likewise.

"What does anyone need a wife for when there are so many grandfathers about?" Curly complained.

"He was right," Raven Feather observed. "Wet hides can give you trouble. What if our fathers send us out riding later?"

"What for?" Three Toes asked. "They're too busy listening to Wihio promises and accepting presents. That's why we're here, after all. To be fed and flattered and lied to by the whites."

Raven Feather scowled. Three Toes was only a year older, but sometimes he seemed as ancient as the nearby bluffs. Years before, the boy had been walking along Red Shield River when a Wihio trap closed on his foot. The two smallest toes of his left foot were sliced off as cleanly as if by a steel knife. As Three Toes stared at his mutilated foot, his eyes filled with unrelenting bitterness.

"You can't be certain they'll lie this time," the Feather argued. "Broken Hand, the trader Fitzpatrick, is speaking the treaty words. Look at all the bands that are here. Not Lakota and Tsis tsis tas only, but Arapaho, too."

"And Crows," Curly noted.

"They at least fight a man," Three Toes declared. "The Snakes are here from the north, too. And Pawnees."

Raven Feather followed his cousins' eyes out across Horse Creek toward the hundreds of lodges erected by the many tribes. Some said there were a hundred hundreds there.

"There can't be peace among us all," Curly insisted.

"Who would want it?" Raven Feather asked. "How can a warrior earn honor if he has no enemies? It's only to reach agreement with the Wihio on what's right that we've come here."

"And to trade for good guns like the Snakes and Pawnees use against us," Curly added. "As for peace, the Wihio can have it. All they must do is keep out of our country."

"You three must know everything," their uncle, Raven Heart, observed as he joined their small circle. "Soon enough you'll sit in the councils and grow fat, chewing words. Now you should be running and wrestling and swimming. Go on now."

Raven Feather laughed at his uncle's chiding. Raven Heart was certain to tell them about the Wihio and treaties himself before the great encampment disbanded. Ah, their ears would ache with his many words!

"Go!" Raven Heart urged.

The boys sprang to their feet and charged the river. Soon they were splashing across to the far bank, chasing friends, racing, and wrestling with age-mates. It was the way to grow strong and confident, to prepare for the more difficult tasks that lay ahead on man's road.

For Raven Feather, it was a good time. He was growing. Like his father, he would stand tall among the Tsis tsis tas. Already he excelled at running and riding. Even boys who had seen fourteen snows come and go had difficulty keeping pace, either afoot or mounted. And while he lacked the size to defeat his elders at wrestling, he was quick and elusive.

"More smoke than raven," Curly told him.

"It's having brothers," Raven Feather declared. "The eldest learns early he must run fast or have them forever hanging on his heels."

"I have brothers," Three Toes pointed out.

"But only one good foot," Curly observed.

"If I had four feet, I couldn't catch *him*," Three Toes muttered, growling at Raven Feather. "Besides, not everyone must run hard to strike his enemies. Mine often find me. In that case, it's not running that matters."

"No," Curly agreed. "And no one here can move Three Toes when he makes his stand."

The cousins stood solemnly in the shallows a moment as the thought settled over them. No one spoke much about fighting and dying, but even the youngest boy knew that was what a warrior faced daily once he came of age. Each recalled a day when a war party returned with news of some good man's death.

"Without dying, life is meaningless," Red Hawk once told his son. "It's knowing each day may be the last that makes it precious. We must always walk with honor and be prepared for death."

Raven Feather took those words as a powerful truth, even the first time he'd heard them as a small boy. Now, with all the tribes gathered around, a sense that a great moment was at hand heightened his awareness of reality.

The cousins finally left Horse Creek shortly after midday. Raven Feather was seized by a great hunger, and he led the way to the cottonwood. Once they had dressed, Curly led them to a party of young Oglalas who were roasting a freshly slain buck.

"Welcome, brothers," a broad-shouldered young man of twenty snows told them as he made a place beside the fire. "Join us."

"Thank you, Claw," Curly said. "These are my cousins, Three Toes and Raven Feather."

"Welcome," the Oglala said, grinning at the youngsters. "Have some meat. It's good."

Raven Feather let his cousins help themselves. He then tore a strip of venison off the crackling carcass and began chewing. The Oglalas were still talking about Curly's victory over the Crow, and they were glad to have the young rider among them.

"You ride well," Claw said, turning to Curly. "We always thought you part white. Your hair . . . and light skin."

"I, too, have light skin," Raven Feather pointed out. "Are you saying Red Hawk, my father, is Wihio?"

"Your hair is dark, like midnight," Claw noted. "And your skin isn't very light for a Sahiyela—Cheyenne."

The Oglalas stared at Curly, who shrank from their gaze. The boy's hair had always been reddish brown, and his skin *was* lighter than most Oglalas. Raven Feather knew that troubled his cousin. Even now, after the boy had won his people a victory over their Crow enemies, someone had to mention it.

"You shouldn't let that bother you," Claw argued. "You can't change it. We've had whites among us many times. Some have good hearts."

"Most don't," Three Toes barked.

"Ah, they're just crazy," Claw insisted. "They're strangers to the sacred path. Their medicine comes from their good guns, but it's nothing against a man with real power."

"No," the others agreed.

After satisfying their hunger, the cousins left the Oglalas on the hillside and returned to Horse Creek. The shallows were full of boys and young men. Arapaho, Lakota, Tsis tsis tas . . . it was hard to tell which were which. Near the cottonwood a handful of Wihio youngsters gathered. As they undressed, Raven Feather couldn't conceal his amusement. No sensible person would wear so many garments. And nothing was as humorous as a naked Wihio!

"Look how white they are," Curly whispered.

"Soft and fat, all of them," Three Toes pointed out.

Raven Feather didn't speak. He was too busy studying the strange ones. Their hair wasn't black like his own. It came in many colors—yellow like winter grass or red like berries. Even the darker shades were lighter than his own.

"Come," Three Toes urged. "Let's race them."

"In the water?" Raven Feather asked.

"There or on the hillside," Three Toes replied. "Anywhere. We should show these Wihio they should go back where they came from."

Although the Feather lacked Three Toes's bitterness, he nevertheless followed his older cousin to the cottonwood. The Wihio boys had scattered their clothes along the bank, and Three Toes paused long enough to spatter them with water. Then the cousins placed their own garments in the branches of the cottonwood and splashed into the creek.

"Hau," Curly called to the tallest of the whites, a yellow-haired boy of fourteen or so.

"Hey," the yellow-haired boy answered, raising his right hand in the accepted gesture for peace.

Curly spoke to the whites in his mixture of Lakota and Tsis tsis tas words. The whites didn't respond.

"You try," Curly said, turning to Raven Feather.

The Omissis camps had been near the Wihio soldier fort on Platte River, and Raven Feather had learned something of the Wihio language. Three Toes understood as well, but he didn't like to speak the tongue of his enemy.

"We race," Raven Feather suggested. "You, my cousins, me." He then motioned to the far bank and back. Several of the Wihio boys had already started back toward the bank. The older boy now turned to join them. A younger yellow-haired boy laughed.

"They can't swim," he explained to Raven Feather. "And they're scared of you. I'll race you, though. Over and back?"

Raven Feather told his cousins, and both agreed.

"My brother Andy there can start us," the white youngster suggested. "Me, I'm Walker. Walker Logan. My pa came out with the freight wagons."

"I'm called Raven Feather," the Feather explained. He then introduced Three Toes and Curly. Walker nodded and offered each his hand. Raven Feather, who was accustomed to the Wihio habit of touching each time they met someone, clasped Walker's hand. His cousins somewhat reluctantly did likewise.

Walker turned and explained things to his brother, who nodded.

"You be careful, Walk," Andy warned. "Them's tricky, you know."

Young Walker laughed and turned to his brown-skinned opponents.

"We just racin', or you got a wager in mind?" he asked Raven Feather.

"Just racing," the Feather answered. "Later maybe we make bet."

"Fine by me," Walker declared.

The swimmers then readied themselves. When Andy shouted, "Go," Raven Feather plunged into the water and began thrashing his way to the far bank.

He wasn't certain just when Walker Logan went under. The Feather's eyes were misted over by water, and the sound of his cousins slapping and splashing the water at both elbows obscured any possible shout. Even so, when Raven Feather reached the far bank and turned to head back, he spied a frantic Andy Logan jumping and gesturing.

For a brief moment Raven Feather continued swimming. Then he realized there were only two others atop the surface. The Wihio was gone!

"Ayyyy!" Raven Feather shouted, but his cousins didn't hear. Although two Wihio boys were racing along the bank, shouting with alarm, their confused pleas for help weren't understood.

Nothing else to do, the Feather told himself. Taking a great mouthful of air, he dove beneath the surface and began an underwater search.

Fortunately Walker wasn't in the shallows. A hundred feet had churned the sandy bank, and the water there was clouded. In midstream, the creek was deep and clear. And it was there that Raven Feather saw a frantic whitish blur. He bobbed up on the surface, took a second gulp of air, and dove down once more. This time he shot out into mid-channel. Once there, he searched the bottom. Only a few feet to his left Walker Logan's limp body lay. His foot was snagged by the branch of a dead tree, and he had ceased motion.

The Feather darted to the branch, freed the foot, and grabbed the Wihio boy by his hair. The two of them bobbed to the surface together. There, jolted by the shock of regaining the surface, Raven Feather coughed and trembled. He almost lost his grip on the Wihio. He recalled how Raven Heart had once driven the water from a young swimmer's lungs. The Feather dragged Walker into the shallows, grasped the boy below the belly, and pushed upward with both hands.

Walker spit out a mouthful of water and sand, and a second later choked his way back to life. By then Andy had marched over to take charge of his younger brother.

"What sort of redskin trick did you use on him?" Andy cried. "You close to kilt him!"

Raven Feather staggered back, stung by the words.

"Come," Three Toes urged. "You can't expect a Wihio to make sense."

Raven Feather turned away, but Andy called him back. Walker sat up, holding out a shivering hand.

"Thanks," the younger Wihio called. "Come here. I got something . . ."

"Come," Three Toes urged, pointing to where their clothes hung in the cottonwood's branches. The Feather nodded, but instead of following, he turned back and knelt beside the trembling Walker Logan.

"Sorry," Andy whispered. "Didn't understand."

"There was a . . . branch or something," Walker stammered.

"You caught your foot," Raven Feather explained.

"You didn't have to," Walker noted. "Andy, my pouch!"

Andy brought his brother a small buckskin pouch, and Walker fished out a small silver eagle attached to a rawhide thong.

"For you, Raven Feather," Walker whispered.

"No, you . . . not . . ."

"Please, accept it," Walker urged. "Not as a reward, but as a gift of friendship. In return for your gift."

"My gift?" Raven Feather asked.

"My life," Walker explained.

2

NEWS OF RAVEN Feather's actions spread among the Wihio, and even the old trader, Broken Hand, had kind words for him.

"Here's a boy who understands that there can be peace between our peoples," Fitzpatrick declared.

Raven Feather did his best to avoid the Wihio and their flattering words. He could read the anger of his age-mates and the confusion of his cousins.

"Why save one of them?" Three Toes asked. "It's just another who will cause us trouble later."

As for the eagle charm, Raven Feather placed it in a rawhide bag and left it beside his bed. It would only remind the other Omissis boys of his actions, and he wanted to put the whole episode behind him.

It was Raven Heart who first noticed his nephew's confusion and drew the boy aside.

"You're troubled," the Heart observed. "Why?"

"I don't know," Raven Feather told him. "At first, I was

glad I was able to save the Wihio. I didn't seek any reward. I only wanted to prevent bad feelings."

"And now?"

"The others say I did wrong. Na khan, Curly avoids me. He fears the Oglalas will think I acted because our family has Wihio blood. Three Toes complains Wihio are only for killing—or tricking."

"Each has reasons for his feelings," Raven Heart said, frowning. "And you, Na tsin' os ta, what do you feel?"

"I wouldn't have the boy drown."

"No, that would disturb the harmony of this good place."

"Then I did right, Na khan?"

"Don't you know?" Raven Heart asked. "What were your intentions?"

"I didn't have any," the Feather confessed. "I wasn't thinking. I only knew the Wihio needed my help. I gave it."

"Naturally," Raven Heart said, resting a weathered hand on the boy's shoulder. "Listen to me, Na tsin' os ta. The day a man has to consider whether to save another will be a sad day for us all. We are bound here, in this place, all of us. Tsis tsis tas, Lakota, Wihio, even our old enemies, the thieving Pawnees and the hated Crows. Our chiefs have spoken strong words here. A death would have turned many good hearts away from the sacred path.

"Feather, you know a man must do more than hunt and sleep. He must see to the welfare of his brothers, or his people."

"As you and my father do."

"A man of the people must always ensure the safety of others," the Heart explained. "It's a great responsibility, but much honor comes of it."

"Is that what I did?"

"Yes, Na tsin' os ta. So now you, too, carry the obligation."

"I don't know that I'm strong enough."

"You are," the Heart declared, clasping Raven Feather's arms.

"I'm not very big," the Feather said, dropping his eyes. "I still carry a boy's bow."

"It's not the size of a bow that indicates a man's strength," Raven Heart argued. "It's the power he holds here."

The Heart then placed his hands over Raven Feather's heart.

"Never be afraid of being generous," the Heart whispered. "Some may consider it foolish, but more can be won with a gift than with a hundred battles. See what the Wihio will obtain by giving away a few wagons full of blankets?"

"You don't think this treaty will be a good thing?" Raven Feather asked. "Even the Oglalas say it will keep the whites out of our country."

"I don't know, Na tsin' os ta."

"Will we have peace?"

"It would be a good thing. I watch these strange ones, the Wihio, though, and I see how blindly they walk the world. They live outside the sacred circle, and they don't understand anything. Everything they touch is torn from the harmony we once knew."

"As I was?"

"Yes, Na tsin' os ta."

"Then there won't be peace," Raven Feather declared.

"Not even strong men like Broken Hand can change coyote into raven. Even the wisest chief can be blinded by silver medals and promises."

"The chiefs will touch the pen, though, won't they?" Raven Feather asked. "There will be a treaty."

"Yes, the paper will be signed, but papers hold no power. The wind can carry the good words away as easily as the brown leaves of a cottonwood. What's needed are speakers who hold iron in their heats. I see only hope in the eyes of the treaty makers. It won't be enough."

Raven Heart's sobering words remained with the Feather

the last days of the Horse Creek encampment. Each morning he joined Curly and Three Toes at the creek, but only after accompanying Raven Heart and Red Hawk into the hills to make the morning prayers.

Before first light he helped Raven Heart prepare a small fire on a nearby hillside. Then the boy stood with his elders and bared himself before the rising sun. When his father made the pipe ritual, Raven Feather touched his lips to the sacred pipe when it was his turn. Afterward, he watched his father and uncle thank Heammawihio, the Great Mystery, for the gift of another day. The Feather seemed to hear the words of their prayer for the first time.

> "Give us struggles to make us strong,
> Heammawihio.
> Brave up our hearts,
> Heammawihio.
> Show us the sacred path,
> That we may walk within the harmony
> Of the Hoop,
> Heammawihio."

When they had finished the remembered song, Raven Heart held out his arms toward the east and sang a second song. Afterward, he glanced at Raven Feather.

"Heammawihio, you've given us strong sons," Raven Heart added. "Give them eyes to see the truth. Give them strong hearts to withstand the coming pain. Help them remember who they are—and what!"

"Ayyyy!" Red Hawk added.

Raven Feather warmed with the knowledge that he had such good men to guide him upon man's road. How could he be other than strong and wise?

The treaty council at Horse Creek concluded with a great giveaway. There were many celebrations—much feasting and dancing. Young men took wives from allied bands,

forging stronger links between Tsis tsis tas and Lakota and
Arapaho. Afterward the Snakes and Crows and Pawnees
departed. The Omissis broke camp and rode south toward
Red Shield River to hunt Bull Buffalo.

Raven Feather busied himself tending his father's ponies.
Too young to ride with Red Hawk on the hunt, he remained
in the main encampment. Three Toes, just a year older, rode
with the men. And Curly had ridden north with the Oglalas.
The Feather felt more alone than ever.

He wasn't, of course. His brothers were never far away.
Little Hawk, at eight, was a particular torment for his
brother, and Willow Boy, a year younger, was eager to join
in any prank.

"Our uncle had taught me how to cut away a boy's skin
and leave him alive!" Raven Feather warned the morning
after the brothers had painted his bow with honey, attracting
an army of ants. "I thought to practice the skill on some
Pawnee pony boy, but I suppose a brother would do just as
well."

Four days later, when the younger boys followed the
Feather down a ravine, he turned, trapped them near the
mouth of a small cave, and bound them tightly with rawhide
strips.

"It's well known a bear lives there," Raven Feather
explained as he turned to leave. "To him, you'll prove quite
tasty."

"You don't intend to leave us?" Willow Boy cried. "Nah
nih, don't abandon us!"

"Ne' hyo will be angry," Little Hawk warned.

"No, he's a man and understands tormentors must be
punished," the Feather explained.

"We won't bother you again," Willow Boy whimpered.
"You're our brother. Aren't you supposed to shield us from
danger?"

"I can't protect you from your own stupidity," the Feather
insisted.

"We'll do whatever you say," Little Hawk promised. "Anything!"

Raven Feather laughed. He then walked off into a nest of willows and waited. His brothers shouted and raged, but there was no one to hear them.

"Brothers," the Feather said, sighing. "Has a man ever known a greater trial?"

Still, he knew he couldn't leave them. They were right. He was pledged to guard them from harm. He didn't believe their promise, but he soon pulled his knife out of its sheath and walked out to free them. They were only being themselves, after all. A coyote would always howl, a young brother would always be a nuisance.

When the men returned from the hunt, the women worked to dry the buffalo meat so that it could be saved for winter's need. The warrior societies then met in council. Young men who had proved themselves at the hunt were then called to join the Elks or the Crazy Dogs or the Bowstrings. Raven Feather looked forward to the day when he, too, was summoned. He wouldn't be a pony boy forever. Although Red Hawk rode with the Foxes, the Feather secretly hoped his uncle, Raven Heart, would invite him to ride with the Elks. The Heart was a famous fighter, and he now rode to battle with one of the two sacred Elk lances.

"A lance carrier accepts a dreadful burden," Red Hawk had once explained. "When the Elks ride out against an enemy, the lance carriers pledge to sacrifice themselves if retreat becomes necessary. They halt their horses, dismount, and drive a stake into the earth. Their legs are then bound to the stake. They vow to fight and hold the enemy on that spot."

"Can't they untie themselves after the others escape?" Raven Feather had asked. "The enemy will surely swarm over them and bring their death!"

"They can never free themselves, Naha'. Only a brother Elk can release them from their obligation, and then only he who has distinguished himself that day with many coups."

"He pledges himself to die then," the Feather had said solemnly.

"In order to give his brothers their lives," Red Hawk had added. "It's our way. Life always flows from death."

That winter, as he sat with his brothers beside the fire in their father's lodge, Raven Feather listened intently to the many stories his father told of the Tsis tsis tas and his own father's people, the Oglala Lakota. It was often difficult to distinguish the one from the other. Like Curly, Red Hawk would mix his Tsis tsis tas words with those of the Lakota people. It sometimes brought a smile to Burnt Willow Woman's face.

"You just said your uncle was a goat," she would whisper.

"You weren't listening," Red Hawk usually objected.

"I *was* listening," she would argue. "You were careless with your words again."

That winter the snows came early, but they didn't bring with them the numbing cold of past years. The Omissis had made camp in a protected valley above a winding stream. There was plenty of game nearby and good wood to keep the fires burning. The ponies were let loose to spread out and chew the leaves of berry bushes or eat tall grass.

For the pony boys, it offered a chance to engage in boys' games, to shoot small game for the supper pot, or work hides into new moccasins, breechclouts, or shirts. Raven Feather crafted moccasins for his brothers. Burnt Willow Woman prepared buffalo robes, for a good robe required a skilled craftswoman. As for the men, they sometimes carved bows, made arrows, or repaired horse equipage.

"Mostly men pass the winter smoking and talking," Winter Fawn Woman, the wife of Raven Heart, complained.

Raven Feather thought there was truth in her words, but of course he would never confess it, even though he was particularly fond of his aunt. It was her misfortune to be heavy with child. Infants born in winter faced a difficult challenge, and many failed to see their first spring. Twice before, Winter Fawn Woman had given birth. The small daughters had cried out, grown sick, and died.

"This time it will be a son," she boasted daily. "He'll grow tall and strong like his father. Like you, Feather."

Raven Feather always glowed when she spoke such flattering words to him. His own mother had been too occupied with his brothers to dote on her eldest child. His grandmother, who would certainly have scolded him for enjoying Winter Fawn Woman's praise, had long since started up Hanging Road. She was now on the other side, removed from the turmoil of earthly life.

While Winter Fawn Woman sang and worked hides into a cradle board, Raven Heart passed those first days of the Big Wheel Moon alone, on the snow-covered hills above the Omissis camp. Sometimes Red Hawk would walk out there, too. More often, Raven Feather would join his uncle.

"Why don't we shoot a rabbit, Na khan?" the Feather suggested one afternoon. "Fresh meat would give strength to the Fawn, and the fur would make a good warm coat for the child."

"We have meat enough," Raven Heart replied. "As for clothing, this new son of mine could swim in it. Our friends and relations have been generous."

"Then what makes you so sad?" the Feather asked. "Soon you'll have a son. Before long, he'll be tall enough to watch your ponies. Then you'll craft arrows for him, as you have for me and my brothers. You'll ride together to hunt Bull Buffalo, and you'll . . ."

"Perhaps," the Heart said, frowning heavily. "I worry if he will be strong."

"He'll be your son," Raven Feather declared.

"I've seen two children die, Na tsin' os ta. Winter's a bad time to be born. The Big Wheel Moon sends snow and wind to torment us."

"Na khan, I was born under the Big Wheel Moon," Raven

Feather argued. "Look at me. Aren't I as tall as any my age? Can't I run and swim and wrestle as well?"

"You have a strong heart, Na tsin' os ta," Raven Heart observed. "Even so, I worried for your survival. Winter's a hard time."

"Then we'll make prayers," the Feather suggested.

"That would be good," the Heart agreed. "Red Hawk and I passed three nights on a hillside, seeking a dream when you were born."

"Ne' hyo has many responsibilities," Raven Feather noted. "Maybe I could come with you."

"Yes, that would be good. Maybe the Big Wheel Moon favors your dreams."

"Maybe," the Feather agreed.

Two mornings later Raven Feather rode out with his uncle to the nearby hillside. They made a camp near an empty cave, and the Feather built up a fire to keep them warm. For two days and nights Raven Heart chanted and prayed, seeking a dream. He cut flesh from his wrists and chest. The bleeding invited a fever, and the Heart collapsed. He awoke early the third morning to discover Raven Feather steadfastly tending the fire.

"Did you find a dream, Na khan?" the boy asked.

"No," Raven Heart answered, frowning. "It is as before. I fear for the child."

"Maybe you should make a vow."

"I've already told the chiefs," Raven Heart explained. "I will make the New Life Lodge this year."

Raven Feather nodded gravely. There wasn't a greater vow possible. The remaking of the earth was a sacred responsibility. All the ten bands, Tsis tsis tas and Suhtai, gathered to renew life and invite the favor of Heammawihio.

"I, too, should undertake a vow," Raven Feather said. "I'm only a boy of eleven snows, but I can . . ."

"Be quiet," the Heart barked. "You're too young to suffer.

Don't seek something you'll later come to regret. It's for me
to do this thing."

"I want to share the burden, Na khan."

"You shared this praying, Feather. When more is required, I'll ask it."

That afternoon they both noticed a commotion in the
camp below. Women shouted and ran about. The medicine
chiefs hurried to Winter Fawn Woman's lodge. Finally Red
Hawk rode out toward the hillside.

"Ne' hyo!" Raven Feather shouted when he spotted his
father. "It *was* a boy, wasn't it?"

Raven Heart eyed his brother-in-law soberly. He smiled
expectantly. Then he dropped his eyes.

"The child was born dead," Red Hawk explained. "He
never knew the pain that is life."

"Ayyyy!" Raven Heart screamed, tearing his shirt as he
wept bitter tears.

"Ayyyy!" Red Hawk howled, throwing off his buffalo
robe and clawing at his chest.

"Ayyyy!" Raven Feather cried in his high-pitched voice.
He, too, tore at his flesh and shirt. Together they lamented
the child who would never know man's road. And the
Feather did his best to share his uncle's grief. To ease his
suffering. But, of course, that wasn't possible.

3

WINTER GAVE WAY to spring. Life returned to the hills and rivers. The wind carried the sweet scents of flowering plants and greening trees across the land. Birds flooded the morning with their songs while newborn fawns steadied their wobbly legs.

All around him Raven Feather saw rebirth. Another year it would have gladdened his heart. He was growing taller himself, and he felt an eagerness to take his first steps upon man's road. And yet a sadness hung over the Omissis camp.

"Na khan, the horses are growing fat," Raven Feather told his uncle.

"Yes," Raven Heart replied. The Heart's hair was cut short in mourning, and he remained bent and broken with grief for the little son born without life.

"This summer I will ride to hunt Bull Buffalo," Raven Feather announced. "I've made many good arrows, and Red Hawk has crafted me a new bow."

"It was my obligation to do those things," Raven Heart

said, frowning. "It's as well you've learned to make your own arrows. My hands couldn't manage it."

"Na khan, I know you're sad, but someone must teach me a warrior's obligations. I have no grandfather to do it, and my other uncles are far away."

"Yes," the Heart muttered. Raven Feather didn't know whether his uncle was agreeing to do it or merely noting the task needed doing.

"Na khan, once, when I was very small, I saw a dead sparrow," the Feather remarked. "You explained life was just one road that led to another. You told me not to be sad, for the sparrow had climbed Hanging Road. Now it flew on the other side, in the shadows."

"That's right, Na tsin' os ta."

"If I wasn't to be sad then, why are you sad now?"

"A boy isn't a sparrow," Raven Heart pointed out.

"But isn't it wrong to let your grief hold him here, in this world? Shouldn't you give up his ghost and let him begin the long walk?"

"Walk? He never learned to walk, Na tsin' os ta. Or to speak. I never held him. We should have ridden many summers, but instead we had none."

"It's a sad thing, Na khan, but the snows have melted. It's time to hunt. Soon all the people will gather for the remaking of the earth. You haven't forgotten your vow?"

"My vow," Raven Heart said, pondering the words as though they were heavy and required effort to lift. "Yes, I pledged to make the New Life Lodge."

"Red Hawk would help if you asked. I will, too."

"There's not much you can do, Feather," the Heart said. A trace of a smile came to his lips, but grief soon drove it away.

"Maybe I'll ride out with the pipe carriers and summon the other bands," Raven Feather suggested. "I can certainly help cut poles. Maybe I can—"

"Enough," Raven Heart barked, waving the boy silent.

"There is much to do, but I'm the one to do it. First I must send word to the Arrow-keeper. He's among the Hevataniu down south."

"I suppose it's too far for me to ride then."

"Too far, yes," the Heart agreed, drawing Raven Feather closer. "But there are other things that need doing. While I'm busy with my new burdens, Winter Fawn Woman must not starve. You might shoot something for us to eat."

"My bow's eager, Na khan."

"And you, Feather?"

"Also eager."

And so Raven Feather occupied himself that spring hunting and fishing. Sometimes he rode out with Red Hawk and the other men in search of deer and elk. Other days he led his brothers up the creeks north of Red Shield River. There, the boys would set out rabbit snares or throw stones at prairie chickens. When not hunting, they would run and swim and stretch themselves taller.

It was a good time to be alive. The Horse Creek treaty-signing was still fresh on the minds of the Plains peoples, and even the horse-stealing Crows seemed reluctant to stir up trouble. As for the Tsis tsis tas, all nine bands and their northern brothers, the Suhtai, were converging on Red Shield River. It was time to remake the world.

Among some neighboring tribes, the New Life Lodge ceremony was called a sun dance. The dancing was but a part of the Tsis tsis tas ritual, though. It was firstly a gathering of all the ten bands from their scattered winter camps. There were whole days devoted just to assembling the people. Then the sponsors of the renewal met with the medicine chiefs and old men to plan the ceremony.

It was impossible for Raven Feather to learn anything of the sacred preparations his uncle and the others made. The old men guarded their secrets well. Inquisitive boys and their prying eyes met with frustration and failure.

"You should keep to our lodge, Naha'," Red Hawk finally scolded Raven Feather. "Heammawihio might grow angry."

"Why did he make boys curious then?" the Feather asked.

"Didn't I tell you about the foolish rabbit?"

"I don't think so, Ne' hyo."

"Come along then. Let's sit by the fire, and I'll tell you." They walked together to Red Hawk's lodge. Outside, by the cook fire, they sat side by side. Red Hawk waited a bit. Then, stirring the fire with a stick, he began the tale.

"Once, not so many years ago, Rabbit was exploring a thicket. Not too far from here perhaps. As he was walking along, he'd stop and chew the soft grass or nibble a plum. Then he heard something move just ahead. 'What's there?' he cried. 'Is that a fox?'"

"Was it, Ne' hyo?" Raven Feather asked. "Had Fox come to eat Rabbit?"

"It wasn't a fox. Or a dog, or a horse. Instead Rabbit saw the strangest creature he'd ever set his eyes upon. It was no bigger than he was, but it moved about as unafraid as a bear. 'You there!' Rabbit called. 'Don't you know there are animals around who are sure to eat you?' The odd creature ignored Rabbit and went on as before. 'You! Aren't you afraid? Do you have sharp teeth or deadly claws to fight off your enemies?' But the odd creature only laughed. 'I don't have either,' the stranger told Rabbit. 'But I'm not afraid, like you.'"

"He should have been," Raven Feather argued.

"That's what Rabbit thought, too," Red Hawk explained. "Just to show the strange creature how foolish it was to go about so carelessly, Rabbit hopped over and pounced on it. 'Ayyyy!' Rabbit howled as he hopped away. The stranger had shot little arrows out of its back into Rabbit's soft fur."

"It was a porcupine," the Feather observed.

"Yes," his father agreed. "And Rabbit learned how painful it can be when you're too curious."

"Like I am?" Raven Feather asked, grinning.

"As you were while stalking the Medicine Lodge."

"I only worried about Na khan, Ne' hyo. The Heart's so sad."

"Maybe as he remakes the world, he'll renew his own heart."

"I hope so, Ne' hyo."

"We all do," Red Hawk said. "Your mother's brother is a great man. He leads the young men wisely, and his eyes always find game. It would be a sad loss for the people if he lost his way."

After his father's story, Raven Feather paired himself with Three Toes. They busied themselves tending their father's horses, hunting small game, engaging in contests, and avoiding their younger brothers. Sometimes the cousins raced ponies or fought mock battles with their age-mates at the river. Mostly, though, they swam and sang and laughed away the warm afternoons.

When the preparations for the New Life Lodge had been completed, Raven Feather and the other boys were summoned to their camps. Suddenly everyone became serious. It was vital the earth be remade. Otherwise there would be hunger and suffering.

Eight days were required for the earth renewal. On each of the first four the Tsis tsis tas and Suhtai camps were moved short distances. On the fourth day, when a permanent camp was made, the soldier societies paraded through camp, singing brave-heart songs and wearing their best clothes.

It was a wonderful thing, seeing so many good men together. To Raven Feather, the people appeared stronger than ever. He looked forward to the day when he would ride with the young Elks or Foxes. Yes, that would be a remembered time.

The principal parts of the New Life Lodge ceremony occupied the second four days. Most of the fifth day was spent erecting a Medicine Lodge and performing the sacred rituals required for the placement of every stick and pole. The lodge consisted of a circular framework dominated by a tall cottonwood pole. All manner of plants and hides were added to represent the world. Toward the end of the day women brought presents of food to the New Life Lodge. Others provided hides on which the lodge-makers and dancers could rest. Finally, the young men who pledged themselves to suffer arrived. They danced and sang while the people gathered outside and watched.

The sixth day began when the criers roused the camp. Long before sunrise Red Hawk roused his sons.

"Come, dress yourself," the Hawk told Raven Feather. "The dancing will be starting. Hurry your brothers."

Raven Feather obediently stirred his brothers to life while his mother prepared something for them to eat. Little Hawk and Willow Boy were far from eager to leave the comfort of their beds for the chill that awaited them outside.

"I wish you wouldn't hurry," the Feather whispered to them. "Ne' hyo said if you don't get dressed quickly, I can drag you naked to the river and throw you in."

The notion of splashing into the frigid waters of Red Shield River had an immediate effect. Both younger boys sprang to life.

Even as the people set off through the darkness toward the New Life Lodge, drumming began. Dancers sang and blew on eagle-bone whistles. It was hard for Raven Feather to see much. A few men entered the New Life Lodge. Outside, female relatives sang. All the others were gathered around, but there were far too many people for a boy to get very close.

The drumming and dancing continued until just before sunrise. At that time the lodge-makers, medicine chiefs, dancers, and their instructors left the New Life Lodge. Raven Feather smiled approvingly as he gazed at his uncle. Raven Heart's eyes held a new fire. He seemed at peace.

The dancers were painted brightly. They joined their elders in a long line and turned toward the sun. As the horizon grew lighter, they sang and motioned their arms toward the bright yellow brilliance radiating from above the eastern hills.

Once the sun had emerged from the hills, most of the dancers returned to the New Life Lodge to rest. Others smoked and spoke personal prayers. Inside the New Life Lodge the ceremonies continued. What had once been a bare framework was now blossoming with life. The earth was being reborn!

The singing and dancing resumed later, and the ceremony continued two more days afterward. On the last night the dancers sat silently while their instructors cut the flesh of their chests and inserted small slivers of bone. These, in turn, were attached to rawhide thongs tied to the center pole. In this way the dancers were linked to the lodge itself. They sang and blew their whistles, all the while moving first toward the pole and then back away from it. As they pulled away, straining the rawhides, blood trickled down their chests.

Raven Feather watched in awe as the young men suffered. Their instructors would offer encouragement, and relatives would sing medicine chants to provide strength. It was needed, for the young men ate nothing those long four days. After a considerable length of time, the instructors began urging the dancers to break away. Each in turn leaned back and fought to tear himself free. First one and then the other sliver of bone cut through the flesh, releasing the dancer from his pain.

The instructors howled approvingly each time a dancer freed himself. For while suffering brought a dancer great power and promised prosperity for the people, it had its limits. Sometimes a dancer would simply lose consciousness. His instructor would then free him. Such dancers never owned the chest scars of their companions, though.

"There is suffering and there is suffering," one young man had told Raven Feather. "Just as some men own great power and others have little."

The Feather watched the young men and prayed each would find the strength to endure. Their suffering would prevent calamity. He both admired and appreciated them.

Mostly he watched his uncle, though. Raven Heart appeared weary, but often exertion was the only cure for grief. For a time Winter Fawn Woman sat with him..

"Will he be better now?" the Feather asked.

"He's given our son up to Heammawihio," she answered. "I hope my husband will now be restored to the harmony of the sacred hoop."

"That's my hope, too," Raven Feather said.

It was later, after the earth had been remade and the chiefs sat in council to plan the buffalo hunt, that Raven Feather had a chance to speak with his uncle.

"Things will be better now, Na khan," the Feather argued. "Many have suffered. They kept their vows, and so did you."

"A man can't remake the world if he is not in harmony with himself," Raven Heart explained. "It's not an easy thing, letting a part of your heart float free. The welfare of the people required it, though."

"Only a man of the people thinks that way," the Feather observed.

"Yes," Raven Heart said, nodding. "You'll be one yourself one day. So, will you ride with me to hunt Bull Buffalo?"

"Am I invited then?" Raven Feather asked excitedly.

"I believe I just asked you. Red Hawk says you have proven you can look after the horses. Besides, I think you should have some time away from your brothers."

"I welcome it, Na khan."

"I'll speak of it with your father, but I don't think Red Hawk will have any objection. He made you a man's bow, didn't he?"

"Yes, and I can pull it."

"I should have made the bow myself, Na tsin' os ta. I have failed my obligation to you."

"Your heart was heavy," Raven Feather said. "A man has many obligations."

"He should never neglect his relations, though. Rest long and well tonight. Tomorrow we'll craft more arrows. New, better ones with sharp points to drop Bull Buffalo. We'll speak of rising to the hunt, and other things besides."

"Many things?"

"There are many hills a boy must climb before he steps onto man's road."

"Ne' hyo says all of them are steep."

"Some are," Raven Heart admitted. "Others aren't. All are easily climbed in time."

"When you have a proper guide."

"I'll show you what I can, Feather. Teach you what I know."

"No one could ask more."

"I'm glad you didn't grow tired waiting for me to come back, Na tsin' os ta," Raven Heart said, swallowing hard.

"I'm glad you came back, Na khan," the Feather whispered.

Raven Heart drew the boy to him, and they embraced. Then Raven Feather hurried back to his father's lodge, filled with dreams of hunting Bull Buffalo, hanging from the pole, and standing tall among all the people.

4

ALL BOYS LOOKED upon their first buffalo hunt as a chance to prove themselves. So it was with Raven Feather. Although he was younger than many of the pony boys invited along by their fathers and uncles, he greeted the coming test with confidence. Raven Heart had devoted every morning since the making of the New Life Lodge to the sharpening of the boy's skills. Even before, the Feather had been a competent horseman. Now boy and mount were one.

More importantly, the Heart had introduced his nephew to the warrior prayers a hunter sang when approaching Bull Buffalo. The two had gone together to the sweat lodge to purify themselves for the hunt. Afterward they had sat side by side, crafting good arrows.

"It's a fine thing, hunting," Raven Heart explained the morning the scouts left camp. Raven Feather had followed his father and uncle to the river that morning when they set out to bathe. "Just remember. Our task is to bring meat to the defenseless ones. Some men's hearts burn with a fire and are eager to kill anything. Bull Buffalo, yes, but even a rabbit or prairie hen. Even other men. A man of the people must keep his eyes to the task ahead, to the needs of others."

"Yes, Na khan," Raven Feather replied.

"Our task is to see hunger satisfied and our brothers saved from their own foolish notions," the Heart continued. "If we don't strike a single bull, we'll find honor if no one is hungry, and all the hunters return unharmed."

"Yes, Na khan," Raven Feather said, sighing with disappointment.

"Don't look so disappointed, Naha'," Red Hawk said, lifting his son's chin. "Raven Heart has rarely failed to strike Bull Buffalo. Your chance will come."

"Last summer Three Toes rode with Swift Antelope," the Feather noted. "Neither made a kill."

"Swift Antelope's task was to scout the herd. Three Toes was young and small besides," Raven Heart pointed out. "He was instructed to stay behind with the spare mounts. Now he's taller and will have a chance."

"And me?" Raven Feather asked.

"Your arrows fly into the heart of their targets, Na tsin' os ta," the Heart said. "You ride with the wind. Others can watch the ponies. You will ride with Red Hawk and myself. Ayyyy! We are three now!"

"Ayyyy!" Red Hawk howled. "We are three!"

Two days later, when the scouts sent word a herd had been found a day's hard riding to the north, the men made a camp beyond the lodge circles. They assembled in soldier groups, made the sacred prayers, and shared stories of past successes. The oldest men began by recounting coups. Then younger men told of more recent events. Finally the hunters feasted and taunted the youngsters.

"Don't wet yourselves with fear," a twenty-year-old named Yellow Horse told Three Toes and Raven Feather. "Bull Buffalo is big and strong, but we men are here to protect you."

Others boasted they would slay five beasts the very next day, even though the scouts warned two days would be required before proper hunting parties could be organized.

"It's good you've come along this year," Three Toes whispered to his cousin when the two spread their hides on the ground that night near the river. "We'll show the others who's afraid!"

"Ne' hyo and Raven Heart are riding with the Elks," the Feather explained. "Is your father coming to join them?"

"No, but he said I could ride with you," Three Toes explained. "Swift Antelope is leading the scouts."

"You could have gone with them. The scouts will find the herd. It's they who will make the first kills!"

"They would have kept me back, though," Three Toes grumbled. "Last summer I held horses. Now I want to hunt."

"Raven Heart may hold us back, too."

"He might urge caution, but he won't order us back. It's always been his way to ride fast and strike hard. We're his nephews. He'll expect us to do the same."

Three Toes had never been so prophetic. The Heart wasted little time giving the boys advice. Instead he rode out ahead. He expected them to heed his example, and they did. When scouts approached the Elks with word Bull Buffalo was near, Raven Heart merely glanced at his nephews. Both Three Toes and Raven Feather knew to follow.

The Elks broke into smaller parties as they approached the herd. Raven Heart and Red Hawk led a band of eight along the herd's left flank while others turned to strike the right and rear.

"Always give the herd a direction to run," Raven Heart said, pointing toward a ridge to the west.

"Those hills will prevent their escape," Raven Feather noted.

"Ah, they'll be turned before that," Red Hawk explained. "Naha', see how Bull Buffalo, too, sends out his children to scout? Those are the ones we must strike first. Then the lead bulls."

The Feather watched as his father pointed to several beasts that stood out from the herd's main body. The Elks approached with great caution. Then they galloped hard.

Raven Feather was trailing his father and uncle, and the dust obscured his vision. Even so he noticed one of the buffalo turn its nose to the wind and snort a warning. The herd stirred. Before it could begin its run, though, Red Hawk was notching an arrow. The Hawk turned his horse and raced toward the sentry buffalo. The beast, too, turned, keeping its head to the charging rider.

"Ayyyy!" Red Hawk shouted as he made a swift turn, then another, and raced along the beast's side. The arrow flew from his bow and tore deep into the buffalo's vitals.

"Ayyyy!" Raven Heart thundered. "Red Hawk is first. I will be second."

As the buffalo began to run, a great blackish brute of a bull emerged to take the lead. It was toward that bull that Raven Heart directed his attention. He seemed to ride on a cloud of dust as he charged the bull. The Heart, too, notched an arrow. An instant later the arrow was dispatched, and the lead bull was dead.

"Ayyyy!" Raven Feather shouted as he kicked his pony into motion. "Raven Heart was second. I'll be next!"

Silently, as his heart beat a thunderous tempo in his chest, Raven Feather recited the old prayer his uncle had taught him.

> "Heammawihio, give me this test,
> That I can grow strong.
> Bull Buffalo, give me your life,
> That the people's hunger may pass.
> Nothing lives long,
> Only the earth and the mountains."

The Feather screamed fiercely as he urged his horse through the choking dust that followed the buffalo. He picked out a large bull and drew an arrow from his quiver. His horse eased its pace when he abandoned the reins, for both hands were required to notch the arrow and shoot it. Steadying himself by squeezing the pony's ribs with his knees, Raven Feather let out a long breath and blinked his eyes clear. The bull was alongside now.

"Give up your life to me, brother," the boy whispered as he took aim. Then he pulled back the bowstring and released the arrow. It flew savagely downward, piercing the bull behind the shoulder and ripping into the creature's vitals. The bull raced onward five or six steps before its front legs gave way. It went down hard, rolling to one side, and Raven Feather had to jerk his horse back to avoid the stricken buffalo. Then, as he pulled free of the dust, he looked back at his uncle and father.

"Ayyyy!" they shouted. "Raven Feather has made his first kill!"

The Feather raised himself up onto the back of his horse and waved his bow in triumph. He felt as if he were soaring on the back of an eagle.

The Elks spared that one solitary moment for celebration. Already others were hurrying back toward the herd. Deprived of its leader, the buffalo began circling. Three Toes charged a dust-cloaked bull and fired an arrow at it. The bull turned suddenly, though, and the arrow missed. Before the boy could notch a second arrow, a new lead bull emerged from the herd. The other animals followed as it swung back, and Three Toes was faced by the entire herd.

"Ayyyy!" Raven Feather shouted as he turned his pony toward his endangered cousin. Three Toes was skillfully weaving his way between the onrushing bulls, but his horse was tired, and it was only a matter of time before the animal's side was pierced by a horn.

"Feather!" Three Toes called.

"Nothing lives long!" Raven Feather screamed defiantly as he charged the herd. Before he could find an opening between the animals, though, Raven Heart sped past. Waving a blanket and singing like a demon, the Heart scattered buffalo as if they were ducks on a river. He pulled his horse alongside his nephew and tore Three Toes from his mount.

"Na khan!" Three Toes shouted as he pointed toward a large bull thundering down on them from behind.

Raven Heart frowned as he steadied his nephew and tried to turn back to face the new danger.

Raven Feather had seen it all. He was less than an arrow's flight away, and he drove his pony at the charging bull with fresh energy. The Feather felt new confidence as he reached into his quiver and drew out an arrow. He notched it and swung his horse alongside the bull.

"Give your life up to me, brother," he whispered as he pulled back the bowstring. The arrow flew swiftly, and it struck deep and hard. The bull fell, and Raven Feather galloped along past his startled uncle and cousin.

"Ayyyy!" they screamed. "There's a man of the people!"

Later that afternoon, as he sat exhausted in the hunters' camp atop the ridge overlooking the buffalo herd, Raven Feather didn't feel like a man at all. The day's hard riding had rubbed the insides of his legs raw, and he had more aches than teeth. Looking below, he could see the women cutting away hides and butchering meat. Overhead the hawks and buzzards flew, eager to make a feast of the leavings before the wolves and coyotes took their turn.

"This was a remembered day," Three Toes said as he brought his cousin a meaty rib to gnaw on. "You made your first kill."

"You'll meet with better fortune tomorrow," Raven Feather assured his cousin.

"I had good fortune today," Three Toes argued. "First my

uncle rescued me when the buffalo killed my horse. Then my cousin charged the bull that might have killed me."

"Raven Heart would have turned it," the Feather insisted. "You weren't in true peril."

"Yes, he was," Raven Heart argued as he joined them. "With both of us atop my horse, I couldn't reach my bow. Yours was a brave-heart deed, Na tsin' os ta. A double rescue. I can't remember seeing such a thing by anyone. By a boy, certainly never."

"Na khan, I was only following your example," the Feather noted.

"I don't think you'll ever again require an example," the Heart said, proudly touching his younger nephew's shoulder. "I'm proud of you both. But to you, Feather, I owe my life."

Raven Feather felt the warmth in his uncle's eyes, and he wanted to fall against Raven Heart's hard side as he used to. But the Feather sensed that something had changed. He wasn't as young as he'd been that morning. Even Three Toes noted the difference.

"It should have been me that first stepped onto man's road," he told Raven Feather. "You've always been taller, though. Now I understand why. Heammawihio has called on you to start your walk early."

Red Hawk, too, noticed the change in his eldest son.

"Naha'," he said to the Feather the following morning, "come, we'll make the morning prayers."

"I'll summon Raven Heart," the boy replied.

"No, you and I will walk alone this day. We've got words to share."

"Yes, Ne' hyo," Raven Feather answered obediently.

They climbed to the top of the ridge and silently stripped themselves. Red Hawk kindled a fire, and they smoked the pipe together as they waited for the sun to rise.

"You've been a good son to me," Red Hawk observed as he passed the pipe. "Always you've seen to the welfare of your mother and brothers. When we've needed food, you've gone into the thickets to trap rabbits."

"Yes, Ne' hyo," Raven Feather said as he touched his lips to the pipe.

"I've never asked difficult things of you."

"It's not been necessary."

"You've always hurried yourself toward man's road. Now it's growing close, and you must decide if you are ready."

"Raven Heart showed me how to pluck the hairs from my chin," the Feather told him. "Only two have appeared, but others will soon follow."

"Naha', I . . ."

"There's no deciding such things, Ne' hyo," Raven Feather said, sighing. "You and Na khan both have told me that a hundred times. I'm strong enough to pull a man's bow. I can't remain behind with the children."

"No, certainly not," Red Hawk agreed. "That isn't what must be decided."

"No?" the Feather asked. "Then what did you want to talk to me about?"

"A man's life is filled with many difficult trails, Naha'. I have always found the steepest mountains make the strongest climbers."

"Ne' hyo?"

"Burnt Willow Woman, your mother, is carrying a child," Red Hawk explained. "I've seen in a dream that it will be another son."

"I'm to have another brother then," Raven Feather said, laughing. So that was the secret! His father had never found it necessary to take him off alone before to announce such an event.

"I've watched you these past days," Red Hawk continued. "You and Raven Heart."

"Na khan?" the Feather asked. "I'm sorry, Ne' hyo, if I've neglected you. It only seemed to me that after winter's sadness, Raven Heart . . ."

"Yes," Red Hawk agreed. "Your uncle's heart was pierced, and I thought perhaps he would find some occasion to seek the solace of death. Winter Fawn Woman, too, worried, as did your mother. It warmed us all to see him smile. You brought the smile, Naha'."

"I did?"

"It's a hard thing to walk man's road without sons," Red Hawk noted. "A woman can bring warmth, and her soft hands and understanding heart chase winter's chill. But without sons, a man sees the end of his road, and he grows cold and dead inside."

"Ne' hyo?"

"Before riding to hunt Bull Buffalo I went off alone into the hills to seek a dream, Naha'. My father taught me that a man of the people must always place the needs of others ahead of his own, but my heart ached at the notion of what I might be asked to do."

"What?"

"Soon my lodge will fill with the cries of a fourth son, Naha'. Your mother and I will smile upon the child and be grateful for the gift Heammawihio has given us. As always, though, a man cannot be only the receiver of gifts. He, too, must give."

"Give what, Ne' hyo?"

"You, my son," Red Hawk said, gripping his son's hands. "Raven Heart is a good man, and he would never ask it of me, but I can see the hunger he has for a son. I can as easily cut off an arm as make such a giveaway, but my dreams have shown me the need I can see each day with my own eyes. When we return to the camp of the Omissis, Raven Heart will make a feast. When all have eaten, he will give away many horses to honor his new son."

"You want me to go and live in his lodge then?"

"Want?" Red Hawk said, gazing at the boy with tormented eyes.

"I understand, Ne' hyo," the Feather said.

"You have few days remaining before you'll go to the young men's lodge," Red Hawk noted. "You'll be missed, and I will think less of you if you don't visit your mother and chase your brothers. Be a good son to Raven Heart, though. Take Winter Fawn into your heart as well."

"I always have," Raven Feather replied.

"You've always honored me by standing tall among the people, Naha'. Be as good a son to Raven Heart."

"I will, Ne' hyo," the Feather pledged.

5

IT WAS NOT uncommon for a childless uncle to take a nephew into his lodge as a son. Among his age-mates, Raven Feather knew two other adopted sons. The feasting and giveaway Raven Heart made were unlike any other in memory, though.

"It's one thing to take a small boy into your lodge," the Heart observed. "To welcome a young man who has already counted coup on Bull Buffalo is another thing."

Raven Feather felt slightly embarrassed to find himself the subject of such goings-on. No one had ever made much fuss over him before, and to see old women smiling at him with their toothless grins and girls eyeing him from their fathers' lodges was almost more than he could bear.

"We should have waited until the people broke up and headed to their winter camps," the Feather told Raven Heart. "When can we return to the hunt? I'd rather face ten buffalo bulls than another old woman who believes she has a pretty granddaughter."

The celebrating did come to an end, eventually, and the

men resumed their hunting. Bull Buffalo was generous that year, and great herds roamed the plains near Red Shield River most of the summer. Raven Feather killed two other bulls before the Heart was satisfied enough meat had been taken to insure the people's prosperity.

"It's time to feast and celebrate," Raven Heart declared. "A man should speak thanks as well as invoke power."

The feasting had hardly begun, however, when a party of Bowstring warriors arrived with grave news.

"The Pawnees are coming into our country," a young man named Bad Ear announced.

"They follow Bull Buffalo," another named Badger Belt added.

"We should ride out and strike them hard," Yellow Horse argued. Several other young Elks howled their approval.

"Wait," Raven Heart urged. "Come and tell us what you know, Bad Ear. How many Pawnees are there? Where are they camped?"

"How many?" Bad Ear gasped. "All of them. Hundreds and hundreds. They'll take all the good things from our country and leave us to starve."

"We must fight them," Yellow Horse insisted.

"You'll do it alone, I suppose," Raven Heart muttered sarcastically. "Who will watch the women and children? You're too young to remember how we fought the Pawnees before. We fell upon them, led by Mahuts, the sacred Arrows. And what happened? The Arrows were lost to us! Let's not be hasty. If you want to make war, send pipes out to the bands. Tell our friends, the Lakotas and Arapahos. Meanwhile, we can make strong medicine and prepare a plan."

"Yes," the others agreed. "Let's make a good plan. Then we can run the Pawnees."

For the first time since the hunt was organized the council of forty-four gathered. Each band was represented by four chiefs in the council. There were also four men named to safeguard the welfare of all the people. The council was loud and long, but it had yet to make any decisions when word came that a band of Kiowas had fought the Pawnees a day's ride away.

"There can be no more talk," a chief named Alights on the Cloud argued. "The Pawnees are near. We must strike them before they attack us!"

As a lance carrier, Raven Heart prepared himself for battle. Many other Elks took down their shields and gathered their ponies. Raven Feather watched their somber preparations. Later, after Winter Fawn Woman served food, he walked with Raven Heart to look over the horses.

"Only last year all the tribes gathered to speak of peace," the Heart remarked. "How swiftly a dark wind can blow disharmony into our camp."

"The Pawnees are our old enemies," Raven Feather noted.

"And we must fight them," the Heart said, staring at the distant horizon. "The young ones rush into battle, unprepared. No one consults the medicine chiefs. They rely only on their courage. It's never enough, Naha'."

"You'll ride with the Elks?"

"I carry the lance. I have to go."

"Then I'm going with you."

"Later, when you're older."

"Now," Raven Feather insisted. "I'm your son, aren't I? I can't stay behind when others my age ride along."

"This won't be like stalking deer or shooting buffalo," Raven Heart warned. "The Pawnees are tricky. They have good guns that shoot far. And there are many of them."

"We'll be strong, too, Ne' hyo. Already there are parties of Kiowa watching the Pawnee camps. Bands of Lakota and Arapaho are arriving. Alights on the Cloud boasts we'll be three hundred when we strike the Pawnee camps."

"He's a brave man, Alights on the Cloud," Raven Heart noted. "Once, when we were both younger, a party of

Savane chased a Tsis tsis tas woman and her small brother. The Savane were many, and no one was certain how to fight them. Alights on the Cloud put on an iron shirt given him by his father. He then rode around the Savane, taunting them and urging them to fire their guns. The medicine of that shirt was strong, and it protected Alights on the Cloud. All the Savane shot their guns, but their bullets failed to strike down our brave heart. Once the guns were empty, we rode down on the Savane and cut them down. That was a remembered fight!"

"Does Alights on the Cloud still own the medicine shirt?" Raven Feather asked.

"Yes, and he'll wear it when he leads the young men into the Pawnee camp," the Heart answered. "We can only hope its medicine remains strong."

"Aren't you certain?"

"No," Raven Heart confessed. "My dreams warn of danger."

"Even with so many of us striking the enemy?"

"Numbers mean nothing," the Heart insisted. "If a man's medicine is strong, he can win great victories. If he holds no power, a thousand men won't make him strong."

"Your dream spoke of danger," Raven Feather said. "You won't die?"

"Many will," Raven Heart said. "It wasn't clear who, but I saw many scaffolds above Red Shield River. The mourning cries were loud."

"I'll watch over your horses, Ne' hyo," the Feather promised. "I'll go with you to make the medicine prayers."

"A man can ask no more than that of his son."

He could, Raven Feather knew. And if the battle turned against the Tsis tsis tas, and Raven Heart staked himself to the ground, then the Feather was prepared to stand there, too. It was what a man of the people was expected to do.

Early the following morning the soldier societies assembled outside the main camp. Elks, Foxes, Bowstrings, and Crazy Dogs formed war parties. Nearby bands of Lakotas and Arapahos met in council. Many went to the sweat lodges and purified themselves. Others made medicine charms or sought out medicine chiefs to invoke their powers.

Raven Feather followed his father to the Elk Warriors' camp. He joined in the prayers, even though he was not yet a member of the society. Red Hawk provided the boy with a painted war shirt, and Raven Heart tied elk-tooth charms behind the Feather's ears.

"If we find ourselves pressed by the Pawnees, hold on to the ponies," the Heart instructed. "Mounted, a man can always get away. Afoot, he's too easily trapped and cut down."

"Your dreams still warn of peril, don't they?" Raven Feather asked.

"The signs are all bad, but our hearts are brave, Naha'," Raven Heart said. "Courage can often make the difference."

There was a heavy fog hanging low over the valley when the Tsis tsis tas and their allies rode out to strike the Pawnee camps. It was impossible to see very far, so scouts were sent on ahead. Soon some returned with word that bands of Pawnees were killing buffalo nearby.

"We'll fall on them like hailstones," Yellow Horse boasted. "None of them will get away."

The first Pawnee camp the Elks entered was deserted. Bodies of slain Pawnees lay about the place; clearly another party had struck the place a short time before. No one had even knocked down the scalp poles erected outside the lodges.

"Kiowas," Raven Heart declared.

"How do you know, Ne' hyo?" the Feather asked.

"Look at the bodies, Naha'," Raven Heart told the boy. "See how they're marked? Kiowas."

Alights on the Cloud, White Horse, and Big Hawk now rode out ahead of the main body. A few Pawnees rode up, and the Tsis tsis tas leaders charged them. Alights on the Cloud counted coup on one Pawnee with the flat of his hand, a brave-heart deed. White Horse and Big Hawk struck down Pawnees with their lances. The Pawnees scattered, and the full force of the Tsis tsis tas war party fell upon a nearby Pawnee camp.

Here the Pawnees rallied. The camp was full of women and children, and their voices hurried their men to the fight. The Pawnees were soon mounted, and they turned the Tsis tsis tas charge back onto itself.

Suddenly Alights on the Cloud made a solitary charge on the enemy. Arrows flew everywhere, but the chief's medicine was strong. The iron shirt turned back the cascading Pawnee arrows, disheartening them.

For a moment individuals paired off, and there were many brave fights. For a time the Tsis tsis tas seemed to be winning. Then, suddenly, that changed.

Alights on the Cloud was the first important man killed. He relied on his iron shirt for protection, and it worked at first. Two Pawnees went down. A third, though, avoided the iron-shirted warrior's lance. This Pawnee's medicine was stronger. He seemed to be a magician of sorts, for he pulled out a bow and shot an arrow at Alights on the Cloud from an arm's length away. The arrow pierced Alights on the Cloud's eye and killed him instantly.

Now the Tsis tsis tas could see hundreds of Pawnees riding out from their camp. They swarmed over the hills like locusts, cutting down Big Hawk and White Horse. Other good men went down. Alights on the Cloud had a brother named Ear Ring, and when he learned the Pawnees had killed his brother, he attacked the whole Pawnee force single-handed. The fury of his charge sent the Pawnees retreating, and one of them was killed before the others surrounded the Ring and knocked him from his horse. The Pawnees clubbed Ear Ring and cut him to pieces.

"Ayyyy!" they cried, inviting the rest of the Tsis tsis tas to charge. One of them waved a scalp in the air.

Yellow Horse answered the Pawnee by cutting a nearby Pawnee corpse and waving a bloody trophy over his head. The young Elks formed up, and when the Pawnee again raised the scalp, they rushed out to retrieve it. Raven Heart tried to hold them back, but Yellow Horse had his blood up, and there was no stopping him. He died in a volley of Pawnee arrows, and two other good young men were unhorsed.

"Give me the horses now, Naha'," Raven Heart said, and Raven Feather handed over their ropes. With a shout, the Heart raised his Elk lance and charged out into the Pawnee horde. The Pawnees fell back long enough for Raven Heart to reach the surviving Elks. Quickly the lance carrier gave them his spare horses and covered their retreat.

Other bands of Pawnees were closing in, though, and what remained of the war party was forced onto a low hill. The Tsis tsis tas dismounted and formed a circle around their horses. Then, shouting defiantly, they waited for the Pawnees to charge.

One band of Pawnees rushed forward, but now it was the turn of the Tsis tsis tas to make a stand. Raven Feather stood between Red Hawk and Raven Heart. The three of them strung their bows and prepared to fire.

"Aim low," the Heart suggested. "You may miss the Pawnee, but killing his horse is almost as good. A Pawnee isn't much of a fighter on foot."

Raven Feather did as instructed when the Pawnees charged. His first arrow hit a spotted horse in the rump, and the animal screamed out in pain. A second arrow struck the pony's rider in the hip and knocked him from his mount.

The Pawnee charge finally reached the thin Tsis tsis tas line, but only three or four Pawnees were alive by then. Those who had survived were torn from their ponies and cut to pieces. Several young Elks ran out and started cutting up the wounded Pawnees. One young man, Crooked Nose, held up an enemy's heart and taunted the Pawnees unmercifully.

The Pawnee chiefs now took charge of the fight. They outnumbered their enemy four or five to one, and it was pointless to sacrifice brave men in small charges. Instead they surrounded the hill and readied a final assault.

"Nothing lives long," Raven Heart chanted as he drove is Elk stake into the earth and bound himself in place.

"When the Pawnees close in, mount your horse and try to break free," Red Hawk told the Feather. "There will be confusion, and a rider or two can make his escape."

"No," Raven Feather said, smiling at his two fathers. "I'm not a boy swimming in Horse Creek now. I'll stay and fight."

Raven Heart rested a hand on the Feather's slender shoulder, and Red Hawk embraced the boy.

"Brave up!" the Hawk shouted. "We three will fight. Who will join us?"

Others gazed at the determination painted on Raven Feather's face and smiled.

"We'll fight," Badger Belt vowed. "We'll stand here and die with the Elk's lance carrier."

"Die?" Bad Ear cried. "No, it's the enemy who will die!"

The Tsis tsis tas shouted defiantly as the Pawnees prepared to charge, and it unsettled their horses. Then, to make matters worse, fresh shouts rose from behind the Pawnees. They turned and stared in horror as a second swarm of Tsis tsis tas and Arapaho riders broke into their undefended camp. Crying and cursing, the Pawnees turned and kicked their ponies back toward the helpless ones. The fight drifted away from the hill, leaving the surviving Tsis tsis tas gazing out at a valley of butchered men and slain horses.

"Ne' hyo, the Pawnees forgot to kill us," Raven Feather

said as Red Hawk unbound his brother-in-law's leg and pulled the stake from the hillside.

"Yes, we're alive," Raven Heart agreed. "Many aren't, though. Too many good men have died here."

"Yes," Red Hawk agreed as he led his horse out to where Alights on the Cloud had died. Raven Heart followed. The Feather collected the other animals and brought them along later.

"They've taken the medicine shirt," Raven Heart said, frowning.

"Look how they've abused the bodies," Red Hawk grumbled. "He was a brave man, and they've torn off his arms."

Raven Heart gathered a band of Elks and posted them to watch the remaining Pawnees. He and others then began reassembling the bodies of their slain brothers. Each was wrapped in a buffalo hide and tied atop a horse.

Raven Feather tried not to look at the mutilated corpses. He knew the horrific faces would haunt his dreams. He saw Yellow Horse lying at the base of the hill.

"Fool," the Feather said, staring at the young man's empty eye sockets. Yellow Horse was too fond of taunts. To scream at a pony boy was one thing. To wave pieces of an enemy was to invite particular attention.

The Pawnees had cut away Yellow Horse's ears and nose. His tongue, too. His hands were bloody stumps, and he had been disemboweled.

"We'll never find all of him," Red Hawk remarked as he led Raven Feather away. "If his heart was equal to his mouth, he would have made a good fighter."

"He charged the enemy," the Feather pointed out. "He died fighting."

"It's a great thing to die defending a brother," Red Hawk observed. "Guarding a camp. Protecting the defenseless ones. A man wins honor counting coup. Killing's nothing. Yellow Horse was always ready to strike out at any enemy, but he didn't understand why. His heart was bad. I won't mourn him."

"There are plenty of others for us to mourn," Raven Feather pointed out.

"Many," the Hawk agreed. A short distance away a young Pawnee lay tangled with young Otter Pelt. The Pelt was only three years older than Raven Feather, and the two had raced ponies.

"They're hardly marked," the Feather said as he pulled Otter Pelt away from the dead Pawnee.

"Two boys who fought each other bravely," Raven Heart said, joining his relatives. "If not for the fashion of their hair, they might have been brothers."

Instead, Raven Feather thought, they had slain each other.

"Here's a Pawnee whose scalp hasn't been taken!" a Bowstring named Corn Dancer noted, pulling his knife.

"No, not that one," Raven Heart said, blocking the young man's path. "The Pawnees didn't mark Otter Pelt. We'll leave their young man for them."

It seemed odd, treating that solitary corpse with honor while elsewhere others were mercilessly butchering the remains of the enemy.

"I understand," Corn Dancer said, turning away.

It was strange, but Raven Heart did, too. He couldn't put the sense of it into words, but he did understand.

6

IT SEEMED TO Raven Feather that the death of Alights on the Cloud stole the heart from the Tsis tsis tas. Even after the three days of mourning, many relatives remained sad. Others, though, were angry. Young men rode around the camp, braving themselves for a revenge raid. Women who had seen the mutilations of their brothers and husbands screamed for revenge.

Again the council of forty-four met, but this time the medicine chiefs were consulted. The signs were all bad, and when two young Foxes carried a pipe about, none of the prominent warriors accepted it.

"Be patient," Raven Heart and others urged. "The scouts say the Pawnees have left our country. We must rest our horses and regain our strength. When winter passes, and the earth is once more reborn, carry the pipe to us. Then it will be time to speak of war."

The bands broke apart then, each heading out to find good grazing for their ponies. The Kiowas and Arapahos moved south and west into their favorite hunting grounds. Raven

Feather watched sadly as his cousin, Three Toes, rode south. The Omissis had decided to ride north toward the Oglala Lakota.

"We have many relatives among those people," Raven Heart told his son. "And they have good fighters. If the Pawnees come after us, we'll run them."

The Pawnees were nursing wounds, too, though, and summer passed with no more fighting. That autumn Raven Feather again hunted Bull Buffalo, and the Omissis had plenty to eat when the snows came.

By then Red Hawk had welcomed another son into the world, a small whining child born at first light. Red Hawk saw it all in his dreams, and he called the boy Morning Hawk and predicted he would grow tall, like his other children.

Raven Feather visited the wrinkled brother, but once he had satisfied himself the child was in good health, he returned to Raven Heart's lodge.

"It's good he was born before the cold came," the Heart observed.

"It's good he was born strong," Winter Fawn Woman argued.

"Even a strong child faces a hard road when born in winter," Raven Heart said. "The wind is always there, eager to steal a child's breath."

"I was born under the Big Wheel Moon," Raven Feather reminded them. "Red Hawk always said to grow strong a boy must face difficult challenges. I've heard you say it yourself, Ne' hyo."

"It's true," the Heart confessed. "But it's good to be born before the tests begin."

That winter, his twelfth, Raven Feather studied warrior's road. He learned how to make a good bowstring from a buffalo tendon, and he became adept at tracking game through the snow. He walked among the medicine chiefs, and they taught him the power of paint and the crafting of charms.

"What do your dreams tell you?" old Pronghorn asked the boy.

"Mostly I see hunts and fighting," Raven Feather told him. "Sometimes I find myself swimming in deep water, struggling for the distant shore."

"All life's a struggle," Pronghorn noted.

"But what does it all mean?" the Feather asked.

"Who can know for certain?" the medicine chief replied. "As you step onto man's road, more will make itself known to you. Come back and we'll talk again then."

Raven Feather scowled. He wanted to know it all now. His legs were stretching themselves longer and longer. Each day he found new hairs to pluck from his chin and cheeks. He was impatient to begin the long walk down man's road.

When the snows melted away and the people gathered to remake the world, Raven Heart looked upon his son with satisfaction.

"There's less boy to you each day," the Heart declared. "Your face has hardened, and your shoulders are broadening. Heammawihio is calling you toward man's road."

Raven Feather knew it was true. When he went to the river each morning with the other young men, he felt their envying eyes. He was taller and stronger than his age-mates, and he now wrestled and raced older boys. No one was as swift, and even the young Elks and Foxes who numbered fifteen summers found it difficult to pin Raven Feather to the ground.

"When we fight the Pawnees, he won't be going along to hold his father's ponies," Badger Belt observed. "No, the enemy will feel the sting of this young one's arrows."

Badger Belt wasn't the only one talking about striking back at the Pawnees. As soon as the New Life Lodge ceremony was over, young men set off carrying pipes.

"Our relatives have not been revenged!" women cried. "Where are the men who would punish the enemy?"

"They should stop this foolish talk," Raven Heart grumbled afterward. "Many Pawnees have already been killed. They won't come into our country like last year. How can we chase them east and make the summer buffalo hunt? The needs of the people must come first."

Raven Feather agreed. But outside, where the people voiced their anger at the old enemy, it seemed a different need was making itself known. The soldier societies gathered in the north to discuss war. They summoned Arapahos and Lakotas—Crows even. Kiowas arrived to join the discussion. Afterward, a small band of experienced warriors was sent out in search of the Pawnees.

"We'll fight them, Ne' hyo?" the Feather asked.

"Too many are hot for war," Raven Heart said. "What will it gain us? We have horses enough already. It's meat the children hunger for."

"Yes, Ne' hyo," Raven Feather whispered.

"It's the young men!" Raven Heart stormed. "Those like Corn Dancer, who have never known the sting of Pawnee arrows or felt the pain of hard blows."

"The women whip them up, Ne' hyo."

"They miss their dead sons and husbands. Do they think we'll all return from this fight? No, there will be more sad hearts. And for what?"

While the scouts stalked the Pawnees, the soldier societies met in council to consider a plan. Many of the war chiefs were young men chosen to replace brave hearts killed by the Pawnees. These young men were eager to prove themselves, and they urged their companions to make ready for a great battle.

The chiefs turned to Raven Heart and others for advice, but the Heart said little. He reminded his brothers of the obligation to see the helpless ones fed and protected.

"Why is your father afraid?" Badger Belt asked Raven Feather when they swam together in the river.

"Ne' hyo afraid?" the Feather asked. "When has he ever stood anywhere but in the first line of battle?"

"He argues against punishing the Pawnees," Badger Belt noted. "He speaks of the many Tsis tsis tas who will die."

"It's his obligation to look after the people," Raven Feather pointed out. "And as a lance carrier, if others run, he will be the one who stands and dies."

That same day the scouts returned. Criers went among the bands, urging the warriors to ride to the soldier camps. Once again Winter Fawn Woman bundled her husband's possessions. Raven Feather assembled his father's weapons. Then the boy made his own bow ready.

"You're not a warrior," Winter Fawn Woman scolded the Feather. "You can't walk out with the others. You must wait to be invited."

"Ne' hyo will never ask me along," Raven Feather argued.

"He will when it's time," she told him. "Grow taller first. The Tsis tsis tas have many enemies. Some will remain for you to fight."

Raven Feather set his father's weapons outside the lodge and left his mother to watch over them and the bundle she had prepared. He then set off to make the horses ready. When he reached the ponies, he discovered Little Hawk and Willow Boy already had several in hand.

"Should we cut out two for you, too, Nah nih?" Little Hawk asked.

"I haven't been invited," Raven Feather said. "But our fathers may have need of extra mounts. I'll bring two more along."

"It's good to be prepared," Willow Boy added, grinning.

The boys prepared the horses and brought them to the Elk camp. Raven Heart and Red Hawk took charge of them there.

"Wait here," Red Hawk said, holding Raven Feather in place while the other boys turned to walk back to the main camp. "Hold the remounts."

The Elks, Foxes, Bowstrings, and Crazy Dogs dressed themselves in their best shirts, painted their faces, and shouldered their shields. Some even painted their horses. Soon each soldier band in turn paraded around the camps, braving themselves for the coming fight.

"It's a hard thing, being left behind," a boy of thirteen named Withered Hand observed.

Raven Feather turned and nodded. Withered Hand had crawled too near a fire as a child, and his right hand had been badly burned. The Feather admired the determined way the Hand took on every assigned task. He'd learned to pull a bowstring with his left hand, and he was utterly fearless.

"You'll go," the Feather said, frowning. "You've already been invited to join the Elks."

"They told me not to paint my face," Withered Hand replied. "A man needs his medicine if he's going to war. No, I'll be left."

Once the Elks had paraded through the camps, they returned their horses and assembled beside their chiefs. Names were called out two at a time, and the war party was formed.

"We'll need boys to hold our horses," Red Hawk announced when he and Raven Heart were finally called.

Raven Feather turned toward the Hawk, but it was Raven Heart who addressed him instead.

"I have no heart for this fight," he told him. "It's my obligation to go, but I wish you to stay, Naha'."

"I can't," Raven Feather whispered, dropping his eyes in respect.

"He's always hurried himself," Red Hawk noted.

"Yes," the Heart agreed. "Heammawihio hurries him. What can I do?"

Scouts were dispatched eastward, to search out the

Pawnees. The soldier bands traveled along behind, with the main camps following. There were bad signs about—many buzzards circling ahead of the camps, and wolves skirting the horse herd. When camp was made that night, men sang warrior chants, and the great powers of the people, Mahuts and Is'siwun, the sacred Arrows and the Medicine Hat, were invoked.

Next day the scouts sent word of a large Pawnee village.

"They are dancing and growing fat on roasted buffalo," Wolf Face, one of the scouts, said. "We'll strike them hard!"

"There are Savane in the camp, too," Tall Bull added.

"If only Alights on the Cloud was with us," Corn Dancer lamented. "He ran all of them. We'll miss the power of his iron shirt."

While the warriors were without the iron shirt, they would have the Arrows and Medicine Hat. The sacred ceremonies were performed, and Long Chin accepted the obligation of wearing Is'siwun. Black Kettle tied the Medicine Arrows to his lance. But while the war party was formed correctly, a small band of young men moved up ahead, breaking the strong medicine.

"Fools!" their elders scolded. All the extensive preparations were wasted. When the war party moved toward the Pawnee camp, they discovered only the ashes of camp fires and the dung left by their pony herd.

"The Pawnees won't go far," Red Hawk observed.

"No," Raven Heart agreed. "They're close."

The scouts rode out ahead to seek out the enemy. Meanwhile Raven Feather and the other boys brought their fathers fresh horses.

"It's always a few who spoil the medicine," Withered Hand said as he rode alongside Raven Feather. Just ahead Three Toes galloped up. A light-skinned Arapaho named Hairy Knee was with him.

"The criers say we should keep a close watch on the

ponies," Three Toes announced. "They're worried the Pawnees may come and steal our animals."

"Let them try," Withered Hand cried. "We'll punish their foolishness."

But the Pawnees were busy elsewhere. War cries drifted out from a distant hillside, and the Tsis tsis tas strung their bows and sang brave-heart songs. A line of horsemen appeared, but they were other Tsis tsis tas.

"The Pawnee camp's just ahead!" one of them announced. "Let's run them!"

The warriors formed bands and galloped onward. The pony boys followed, choking on the dust thrown up by the war ponies. Finally, topping a hill, Raven Feather had his first good look at the fighting.

The Pawnees had situated their camp on the far side of a stream. They had thrown up a mound of dirt beside the water, and men were assembled there to defend the helpless ones. Other parties remained on horseback.

The young men who had been so hot for battle now hung back, waiting for the Pawnees to ride out and fight. The Pawnees were in a good position, though, and they remained safely on the far side of the stream. From time to time a brave Tsis tsis tas or Arapaho would gallop toward the camp, taunting the enemy. Each time he was met by a shower of arrows. Two good men were hurt that way, and a third was killed.

"Who will lead the brave hearts against the enemy?" Corn Dancer cried.

"Lead yourself," Badger Belt suggested.

The warriors tried to find a way across the stream so that they could strike the Pawnees from the flank or rear. The Pawnees guarded the only suitable ford, though. Finally a young Kiowa rode up with news that other riders were approaching.

"The Savane," Tall Bull guessed. "We saw them in the enemy camp."

The chiefs decided there was no long history of fighting these people, and a small party agreed to ride out and treat with them. These newcomers had good guns with long barrels, and they turned those weapons on the peacemakers. A young Kiowa was shot, and the others rode back to the main band.

"We must charge," the Kiowa chief, Satanta, cried. "Follow me!"

The Kiowas formed and ran after the Savane. Some Araphaos followed.

"We can't fight these Savane and the Pawnees both," Raven Heart complained.

"We'll run these and come back later to finish the Pawnees," Corn Dancer declared.

A line of Tsis tsis tas formed up and rode out to fight the Savane. Red Hawk and Raven Heart held back.

"Naha', bring us fresh horses," Raven Heart called.

"Ne' hyo, all the ponies are tired," Raven Feather replied.

"We've accomplished nothing," the Heart grumbled. "When will the young men stop breaking the power of our medicine?"

Raven Feather had no answer. Half the Tsis tsis tas party turned back to guard the camp against a Pawnee attack. The others rode out to help chase the Savane.

Raven Feather, as always, followed his father and a band of Elks. These men walked along, giving their ponies a chance to recover. Up ahead the booming of rifles warned of trouble. Angry screams mixed with war cries as desperate fighting ensued.

Many brave charges were made against the Savane riflemen. The Kiowas were foremost, and Satanta killed one Savane with a lance and counted coup on a second. Two Arapahos died bravely on a low hillside, fighting fiercely against the Savane. Corn Dancer made one charge, but his horse was shot, and he was thrown onto the earth.

It seemed for a moment that no one would rescue the

Dancer. He was not well liked. Many considered him foolish. Others thought he urged his companions into rash actions and then failed to join them.

Corn Dancer huddled behind his horse, pleading for help. He had shot away all his arrows, and his lance was no use at long distances. The Savane were finding the range with their rifles, and anytime soon one was certain to find flesh or bone.

"Nothing lives long," Withered Hand suddenly shouted, leaping on his horse. "Only the earth and the mountains."

"No!" Raven Feather called to his young friend.

The Hand was already charging, though. He ran his horse hard toward Corn Dancer, then swung low in an effort to pick him up. The Dancer leapt onto the pony but, in doing so, dislodged Withered Hand. The boy fell as the horse started away from the Savane.

If Corn Dancer noticed his rescuer's plight, he didn't show it. He galloped back to safety and continued on until he was well out of range of the enemy's rifles.

Withered Hand flung himself onto the ground as lead balls tore at the nearby earth. Raven Feather sighed, leapt upon his pony, and charged.

He wasn't alone. Twenty others joined the rescue charge. It was the Feather, though, who first reached his young friend.

"Hurry," he called to Withered Hand.

The Hand clasped Raven Feather's arm and pulled himself up onto the pony. Rifles popped behind them, and a ball passed through the sleeve of the Feather's shirt. His medicine was strong, though, and the two young rescuers retired to the safety of the main war party.

"It's pointless to continue," Red Hawk argued after he satisfied himself the boys were unhurt.

"Yes," Raven Heart agreed. "Enough have died already."

The Savane, too, seemed to lose interest in continuing. Each side retrieved its dead and went its separate way.

"You both did well," the Heart told Withered Hand and Raven Feather afterward. "One doesn't have to be tall or old to win honor. It's how he stands by his companions that mark him as a man."

The Feather managed a weary smile at his father.

"Men will remember this day," Withered Hand whispered.

"Songs will be sung," Three Toes added.

Raven Feather nodded. Songs and stories were not foremost in his thinking, though. It was the knowledge that he would never again be asked to stay behind that heartened him. He wouldn't be a boy much longer.

7

RAVEN FEATHER FOUND that his rescue of Withered Hand set him high in the esteem of his people. Raven Heart and Red Hawk celebrated the coup by giving away ponies, and when the buffalo hunt was organized, the Feather was invited to ride ahead with the scouts.

"It's always good to have young eyes with us," Swift Antelope said. "And if we find trouble, we'll all of us know that there's a rescuer among us."

The Tsis tsis tas had little trouble finding Bull Buffalo that year, and Raven Feather twice dropped large bulls. By the end of summer, enough meat was smoked and dried for each band's use. Women busied themselves making robes from the hides, while the grandmothers made lodge skins for the young women who would soon take husbands.

As the leaves began to yellow and fall, the Tsis tsis tas started the year's second buffalo hunt. Now, when the hides were thickest and the buffalo had fattened themselves on summer grass, it was time to insure the winter food supply. The best robes and floor coverings could be made from winter hides. Raven Feather followed his father once more to the hunters' camp. Prayers were spoken, and the scouts dispatched. Soon the Feather was charging Bull Buffalo once more.

It was later, when the Omissis had taken to their winter camp north of Platte River, that he faced a greater challenge. Ever since the gathering at Horse Creek, the Tsis tsis tas had maintained peace with their old enemy, the Crows. The two tribes had done no fighting, and Crows had even been invited along when Alights on the Cloud led the people against the Pawnees. Alights on the Cloud had made a present of good horses to the Crows' chief, but the Crows had failed to join the fight.

Perhaps for that reason or perhaps for some other, a band of young Suhtai had stolen some Crow ponies. There had been no fighting, nor even angry words. The Suhtai had crept upon the pony herd and drawn off five good animals.

"The Crows value their ponies more than their women," Red Hawk declared when word of the raid reached the Omissis. "Hear me and remember. Trouble will come of this."

The Crows, too, had hunting to finish, and a chill was on the wind when they finally ventured south to avenge themselves.

Raven Feather departed his father's lodge early one morning to check on his rabbit snares. Little Hawk and Willow Boy went along, as did Withered Hand. The Hand had become a good friend since the Savane fighting, and they had ridden to hunt Bull Buffalo together. Now they watched over the smaller boys and inspected the traps.

"Here's one," Willow Boy announced, scampering over to where a snare held a plump cottontail. "Ayyyy! Nah nih, it's a fat one!"

Little Hawk joined his brother. Together they freed the dead rabbit from the snare. Raven Feather started to join them, but Withered Hand waved him back.

"Listen," the Hand urged. "Hear it?"

Raven Feather stopped and listened. He waved Little Hawk and Willow Boy silent. Then he heard it. The snap of twigs under the hooves of horses.

"Take your rabbit and go home," Raven Feather told his brothers. "Warn Red Hawk. Alert the camp. There are riders approaching."

"We should take a look before stirring the camp," Withered Hand argued. "It may only be our own people coming."

"Maybe," the Feather said, frowning.

"You saw something else?"

"Not today," Raven Feather admitted. "But I had a dream."

That was strange in itself, the Feather realized. All his life he had heard of dreamers and the power that came with their visions of what would come to be. He had never experienced anything of the sort himself, though. His sleep was untroubled except by an occasional monster.

Suddenly he understood what the others had spoken about. Two nights earlier he had fallen into a deep sleep. Shortly thereafter he had found himself running through the clouds, led by a powerful white wolf.

"Come, Naha', taste the sky," the wolf had urged. "Follow me. Run the people's enemies."

Suddenly the wolf had vanished, and Raven Feather had found himself on that very hillside, staring through the mists at two young strangers approaching on horseback. Their hair was hanging down onto their shoulders in Crow fashion, and one carried a shield with a demon spirit painted on it.

In the dream, Raven Feather had faced those riders. Now he found he had fallen into the dream. The two riders emerged from the trees just ahead. Their faces were just as he had seen them.

"Crows," Withered Hand gasped.

"Yes," Raven Feather agreed. The two of them stood there, on foot, with only their hunting bows for weapons. The older of the Crows, a young man of twenty snows, laughed. He spoke to his younger companion, a boy of perhaps fifteen. They jabbered back and forth a moment before the older one pointed his lance at Withered Hand.

"Do you understand his words?" Raven Feather asked.

"He's speaking Crow, I think," the Hand said. "I don't understand Crow. Should we run?"

"The younger one's got a rifle," Raven Feather pointed out. "I'm not fast enough to outrun a bullet."

"Then we fight them," the Hand muttered.

"Maybe help will come," Raven Feather said. No one had arrived in his dream, though. He had awakened in a sweat just as the older Crow pierced his flesh with the lance.

"Where are your horses?" the older Crow suddenly asked, using Lakota words.

"Where are your fathers?" the second one added. "We didn't come to fight children."

"My arrows are as sharp as my father's," Raven Feather answered, using Lakota words.

"He talks big," the younger Crow noted.

"Come down off your horse and discover for yourself," Raven Feather challenged him. "I'll fight you."

The younger Crow held up his rifle, and Raven Feather frowned.

"Go," the older one told the Feather. "Run to your fathers and tell them Pretty Shield has come."

Withered Hand turned to leave, but Raven Feather planted himself firmly. He did not intend to let the Crows fall on the camp unhindered.

"Ah, fight me then," the older Crow shouted, quirting his pony. The animal charged forward, but Raven Feather darted behind a cottonwood, notched an arrow, and shot the rider in the right knee.

"Ahhhh!" the Crow howled as he turned away. The

second Crow fired his rifle, and the ball struck the cotton-wood an inch above Raven Feather's left ear. Splinters stung the boy's cheek and shoulder, but he stood his ground and fired a second arrow. This one struck the younger Crow's horse in the throat. The animal whined and reared up, throwing its rider into a thicket. Raven Feather dashed over and kicked the Crow's rifle away. The young man managed to roll back and regain his feet before the Feather could fire a third arrow.

"So, now we fight," the young Crow growled.

"Yes, we fight," Raven Feather answered.

The two boys circled each other three times. Each time the Crow tried to move closer to the rifle. Each time Raven Feather forced him back. The Crow began to grow nervous. Twice he glanced back, hoping help was coming. No one came. Finally the Crow charged toward the rifle. Raven Feather retreated a step, then leapt out, knocking the heavier boy off his feet. The two wrestled a moment, but the Crow had no strength in his hands. The fall had knocked the air from his lungs.

Raven Feather soon pinned his enemy and planted both knees on the young Crow's chest. The Crow gazed up with sad eyes, sighed, and whispered a war song.

"You didn't die in the dream," Raven Feather said, tearing a bear-claw charm from the Crow's neck and counting coup with the flat of his hand on the dumbstruck boy's shoulder. "Go and leave us alone."

Raven Feather scrambled away, took possession of the Crow's rifle, and motioned toward the other Crow, gallop-ing off northward.

The young Crow pointed to the rifle, but Raven Feather shook his head. Disheartened, the Crow managed to rise to his feet. He then stumbled off down the hill.

"You should have killed him," Withered Hand, who had witnessed the fight, complained. "He'll go and tell the others where we're camped."

"The other one will tell them anyway," Raven Feather said. "We'll have to move."

"You counted coup on him and captured his rifle. That's something, at least."

"Ne' hyo says killing brings a man little honor. He was young, that Crow. Perhaps he was only hunting, like we were. That's no reason to die."

"His face was painted," Withered Hand argued. "They came to raid our pony herd."

"Two of them?"

"Scouts," the Hand suggested. "We should follow them. Maybe there are others."

"We'll follow," Raven Feather agreed. "Not far, though. We have no ponies."

That need was quickly put behind them. Not an arrow's shot from the base of the hill the two Crows met up with a raiding party of twelve young men.

"I count thirty horses," Raven Feather whispered. "You were right, Hand. Horse raiders."

"Yes," Withered Hand said. "Can you see what they're doing?"

"Tending the wounded one," Raven Feather told him. "No one's guarding the ponies. Let's take some and ride back to camp. Warn the others."

"Steal horses from those Crows?" Withered Hand cried. "You're crazy, Feather. There are too many of them."

"I have the Crow's rifle."

"Do you know how it works?"

"No," the Feather confessed. He suddenly felt very foolish.

"I know," Withered Hand said, taking the rifle. "I'll watch over you. You take the ponies."

Raven Feather grinned. Satisfied his friend would protect his escape, the Feather crept from tree to tree and crawled through the tall grass to where the Crow ponies were grazing.

"Come, little horses," Raven Feather whispered. "You've ridden far. Run to my camp. It's close."

He stepped out behind a tall buckskin mare and grabbed its mane. As he had a hundred times, he climbed atop the animal's bare back and slapped it into motion. The mare bolted like lightning, chasing four others. Raven Feather shouted and slapped the mare, and all five horses galloped past the startled Crows and sped over the hill and onto the Tsis tsis tas camp.

Even as Raven Feather rode into camp, a party of men was forming to rescue him.

"He's taken their horses!" Withered Hand shouted as he ran along behind. "He's counted coup on one Crow and shot the other."

"And the rifle?" Corn Dancer called. "You took that, too?"

"He did," the Hand said, pointing to Raven Feather.

"Enough talk!" Raven Heart growled. "Where are the Crows?"

"Across the hill," the Feather told him. "Fourteen of them. We'll run them easily."

"That's for us to do," Corn Dancer insisted as he waved a group of young Elks along.

"Yes," the Heart agreed. "You've done enough, Naha'. Climb down and catch your breath. You've counted coup on the enemy now, and taken horses besides. We must celebrate."

Word of Raven Feather's battle with the Crows spread among the Omissis like a prairie fire. No boy or man in the camp had failed to hear one account or another by next morning. Corn Dancer, too, had stories to tell of running the Crows, but the Elks who had seen it said the Crows were already riding away when the Dancer first appeared on the hillside.

That next day there was much to do, so the celebrating was delayed. The chiefs thought it prudent to move the camp, and it was a considerable undertaking. Things were not put back in order for three days. By then Raven Feather had almost forgotten his coup.

The Elk Warriors had not. They met in council, and the following morning Raven Heart led the Feather to the river.

"An important occasion is coming, Naha'," the Heart explained. "Wash yourself. Pluck your chin and prepare for a sweat."

"Now?" Raven Feather asked. "There's a chill on the wind."

"Now," Raven Heart insisted.

The Feather didn't understand, but he knew better than to question his father. Raven Heart never did anything that wasn't necessary. Later that morning they entered the sweat lodge together. In addition to smoking the pipe and performing the purifying rituals, Raven Heart added sweet grass and sage to the fire, spreading a pleasant odor over them both.

"Ne' hyo, what's happening?" the Feather asked afterward.

"You'll have your answers later," his father promised. "Keep yourself ready."

Raven Feather nodded. When he returned to his father's lodge, Winter Fawn Woman was waiting with a beautiful blue war shirt. On the front was painted the head of a white wolf.

"How did you know?" the Feather asked.

"You spoke of it in your sleep," she explained. "Aren't I the daughter of a medicine chief? Don't I understand dreams?"

"I wish I did," he answered.

"There's time left for you to learn," she assured him. "You have good teachers. Listen to their words."

"Yes, Nah' koa."

The Elks held a second council that evening after the sun died in the west. Raven Heart set off to join his brothers.

Red Hawk followed. Even Withered Hand joined the Elk circle. Raven Feather felt small, alone.

It didn't last. A drum began beating loudly, and the Elk criers approached Raven Heart's lodge.

"There's a boy here known as Raven Feather," one announced. "The Elks invite him to join their circle. Will he come?"

"He will," the Feather answered solemnly.

Two young Elks then raced over, bound his wrists, and dragged him to their camp. Once there, he was placed among the younger men. The others shared brave-heart stories and ignored their young guest. For a time. Then Red Hawk rose.

"Long ago, before my hair began to whiten, I was a young man," the Hawk began. "My wife was heavy with child. I rode out into the hills and sought a vision with my wife's brother. I found no dream, but he did."

"I saw a raven flying high overhead," Raven Heart said, rising. "From its tail fell a solitary feather. I didn't know then the name I found would be for my own son. It was a boy's name, though. There are no boys here. He who was once Raven Feather is no more, and I give the name away to anyone who would have it."

"Rise," Red Hawk said, turning toward the nameless young man. "No one should walk the world unnamed. We've met and talked, smoked and invited dreams. Our wisest men have pondered the matter. They tell us the name had already come to you in a dream."

"Come to the fire, Naha'," Raven Heart said, waving his son nearer.

"From this time on, know this man as Wolf Running," Red Hawk announced.

"Ayyyy!" The Elks shouted. "It's a brave-heart name."

Withered Hand then appeared, leading four horses. Two were from Raven Heart's herd. The others belonged to the Hand.

"We, Red Hawk, Raven Heart, and myself, make this giveaway in honor of our brother, Wolf Running," Withered Hand said, leading the ponies around the Elk circle. He left one beside each of four young men whose fathers had fallen fighting the Pawnees.

"Now is the time to invite Wolf Running to join us all," Raven Heart announced. The Elk chiefs then took charge of the young man. He was painted, and the Elk medicine charms were passed into his possession.

Finally, Withered Hand recited the tale of Wolf Running's coup. Old Pronghorn rose from his honored place beside the fire and tied an eagle feather in Wolf Running's hair.

"There's a boy here no longer," the ancient one observed. "Here's a tall Elk Warrior, a brave heart who will keep the people safe."

"Ayyyy!" the Elks howled.

The Elks danced and sang most of that night, and Raven Heart sponsored a feast the next day. Wolf Running couldn't recall such eating and singing and dancing. It seemed as if the entire world was full of sunlight, even though the scent of snow was on the wind.

"So, Naha', you've set your feet upon man's road at last," Raven Heart declared as they walked together back to the lodge.

"Yes, Ne' hyo."

"It's a good name you've found. Wear it with honor."

"Always, Ne' hyo," Wolf Running vowed. "Always."

8

WINTER THAT YEAR, as always, was difficult. Snows fell heavily upon the Omissis camp, and many of the older people started the long walk up Hanging Road. Twice, while out hunting with Willow Boy and Little Hawk, Wolf Running spied a snow-colored wolf in the distance.

"I see you, Snow Wolf," Wolf Running whispered to the wind.

Each time he found an elk to shoot. The camp welcomed the fresh meat, and Winter Fawn Woman crafted good warm robes from the hides.

"Take them to your brothers," she suggested. "Winter's hard on little ones."

"Yes," Wolf agreed. He found a smaller garment of fox fur for Morning Hawk, too.

"It's good to know you haven't forgotten your relations," Red Hawk observed when Wolf Running presented his gifts.

"A man's sometimes fortunate," Wolf Running replied. "Who ever has enough mothers and fathers?"

"And brothers?" Little Hawk asked.

"Well," Wolf said, grinning, "sometimes you can wish for fewer of them."

By the time the Big Wheel Moon arrived, signaling the approaching end of winter, Wolf and the other young men were restless. The long nights confined to the camp troubled their young hearts. Wolf Running had now passed thirteen snows on the earth, and he was ready to join his age-mates riding the wind, hunting Bull Buffalo, and gazing toward the river when the girls set out to fetch water.

The Omissis had yet to break up their winter camp when the first bad news of the season arrived. A young Oglala Lakota, Two Clouds, brought word of Broken Hand Tom Fitzpatrick's death.

"It's said it was a Wihio fever," Two Clouds explained. "Already the Oglala medicine chiefs are dreaming of Wihio trouble. Broken Hand's word was good, and you could trust him. Now we have only scratches on a treaty paper. There's no trusting them."

"No," Raven Heart agreed. "Trouble's coming."

The first sign came in early summer. The buffalo herds were thin. Where once their numbers had spread from river to river, they now grazed in smaller bands. For the first time the soldier societies spoke harshly to the younger hunters.

"It's time we helped our uncle, Bull Buffalo," Pronghorn told the Elks. "When you ride out to hunt, strike only the bulls. Leave the cows and calves. Don't hunt too many of the younger bulls. Leave some to make good calves."

But although the Elks and the other soldier bands kept faith with the old man's admonition, others didn't. More than once the Elks crossed the trail of a Wihio wagon band. Not far away they would see the bodies of cows and calves rotting under the summer sun, shot down for no reason. No meat or hides were taken.

"Heammawihio must wonder if He did right, crafting the whites," Withered Hand told Wolf.

"They're crazy," Wolf agreed. "What use is shooting a calf? And leaving the good meat to rot?"

Such blind killing by the wagon people turned the Tsis tsis tas's heart against them. Although the chiefs reminded the people of their treaty pledge, many young men spoke loud and often of striking the wagons.

"No," Raven Heart told the Elks. "Even if the Wihio break their promises, we are bound by ours."

Soon the hunting was finished, and the bands broke up and went their separate ways. The Omissis moved north onto Platte River to camp among their old friends, the Oglala Lakota. Wolf Running had hoped to go south with the Hevataniu. Three Toes had joined the Foxes, and the two had spoken of leading their younger brothers on a raid against the Pawnee pony herds.

Up north, though, Wolf Running found another relative. Curly had grown, too.

"You're not yet tall," Wolf Running had observed when he greeted his cousin. "Older, though."

"You're tall," Curly replied. "But no smarter."

The two cousins quickly renewed their friendship. Withered Hand generally joined them hunting or raiding, but few Oglalas came along.

"Don't you have a brother-friend?" Wolf finally asked his cousin.

"They still wonder if my heart is Wihio," Curly explained. "My dreams tell me not to expect men to ride at my side. In time, though, many will gladly follow where I lead."

Wolf Running thought that likely. Curly was fearless, and he was as fine a horseman as anyone among all the Plains peoples. There was something unsettling about the young Oglala, though. He never wore paint or tied feathers in his hair, even though others spoke of coups he had counted fighting Oglala enemies.

"The Great Mystery insists that I be a modest man,"

Curly explained one day as they swam in the river. "I won't take scalps, and I'll wear no war shirt."

It seemed odd to hear a boy of thirteen snows speak with such an old voice, but Wolf accepted his cousin's words for the truth they carried. Anyone could see Curly's eyes possessed strong medicine. It would always be difficult to understand a man like that, but if you found an enemy near, Curly would be the man you would want at your side.

By late summer the Oglalas had moved their camp near the Wihio fort on Laramie River. Red Hawk and Raven Heart had split away from the main Omissis camp and headed north, into Crow country.

"It would be good to take some good Crow horses," the Hawk explained.

"Yes, theirs are the best," old Pronghorn agreed. "Be careful, though. Crows are hard fighters."

The small camp had hardly broken down its lodges and started the pony drags north when Split Chin, who agreed to scout ahead, rode in with word there were Wihio just ahead.

"Here?" Red Hawk exclaimed. "In this country? They promised to keep to Platte River."

Young men murmured and stirred angrily. Corn Dancer, who had come along uninvited, suggested burning the wagons and killing the whites.

"We won't break the treaty promise," Raven Heart insisted.

"They have broken it!" Split Chin argued.

"We'll ride out and tell them to go back," Raven Heart said. "They may be lost."

"Yes," Red Hawk agreed. "They have no eyes for reading trails, these Wihio. And no wise men to lead them."

Raven Heart and Red Hawk led the way toward the Wihio wagon band. Withered Hand and Wolf Running came along, as did Split Chin and two older men, Hairy Moccasin and Buffalo Calf. No one brought a lance or rifle, and none of them wore paint. Clearly it was a friendly band.

Wolf found the day amazingly pleasant for late summer. A fresh breeze blew down from the north, and the horses trotted along energetically.

"I'd like to punish these Wihio for ruining our horse raid," Withered Hand told Wolf Running as they trotted along a shallow creek.

"Yes, we would have taken some good horses," Wolf agreed.

"We might get some Wihio ponies instead," Split Chin suggested.

"Oh, they're always too slow," the Hand complained. "Wihio horses are good for pulling wagons, but they won't carry you anywhere when a Crow's chasing."

"They'd be good for pulling a pony drag," Split Chin observed.

"Maybe," Withered Hand admitted. "I'd rather take a Crow pony, though."

"Better a Crow horse than a Crow woman," the Chin said, laughing. "All of them are fat!"

"Not all," Wolf said, grinning.

"No, not all," Withered Hand agreed, laughing along with his friend.

They were suddenly silenced by a word from Red Hawk.

"There!" the Hawk announced, pointing just ahead to a bend in the creek. The Wihio wagons were formed in a circle, nine of them. Their horses were grazing inside, and three men with good rifles were posted as guards.

"What's that?" Wolf Running asked as he rode up alongside Raven Heart.

"A flag," the Heart said, pointing to a large white cloth with a black "x" scrawled across it.

"What does it mean?" Split Chin asked.

"I don't know," Raven Heart confessed. "Maybe these are some new people, a different tribe of Wihio. They may not know this country doesn't belong to them."

"Be careful," Red Hawk urged. "Many Wihio are crazy. Don't get yourself shot."

"He won't," Wolf said, riding up to join his father. "We'll go and treat with them together."

Raven Heart glanced back at Red Hawk, who laughed. The Heart appeared slightly annoyed.

"I, too, ride man's road, Ne' hyo," Wolf said. "It's better for us to go down there together."

Raven Heart nudged his horse into motion, and Wolf Running followed. As they rode, the Heart glanced back at the others.

"Red Hawk would have come," Raven Heart grumbled.

"And if trouble comes?" Wolf asked. "It's better the Hawk has charge of the others."

"Maybe," Raven Heart admitted. "If we need rescuing, though, we may be sorry it's not you."

"Withered Hand is there," Wolf said. "He'll come."

They rode slowly, cautiously, toward the Wihio wagon camp. Wolf Running expected one of the whites to step out and greet them, but instead one of the guards fired a shot into the prairie in front of their ponies.

"Ayyyy!" the other Tsis tsis tas shouted angrily. Red Hawk held them in check, though. Raven Heart raised his right hand, showing he was unarmed. He then turned to Wolf Running, who spoke and understood some Wihio words.

"Tell them we come to treat," the Heart instructed.

"Friends!" Wolf shouted, edging his horse ahead of Raven Heart's. "You're lost?"

"Not lost!" a tall Wihio answered. "We got sickness. Fever! Keep back unless you want to catch it, too."

Instantly Wolf Running turned away.

"Ne' hyo, they have fever in their camp," he told Raven Heart. The Heart, in turn, waved his companions back.

"Ask them what kind of sickness," Raven Heart told

Wolf. "We should know what medicine to make to protect us."

"What sickness?" Wolf Running called to the wagon camp. "Spotted fever? The big sweat?"

"No," the tall Wihio answered. "Coughing sickness. We've lost three little ones, and all the women are sick with it. We sent a rider to Fort Laramie, but he hasn't come back."

"I don't know this coughing sickness," Wolf said, sighing. "Is it a Wihio disease?"

"Don't know," the tall Wihio said, shrugging his shoulders. "We come by it on the Platte. That's why we pulled off the river. Buried too many of us there already."

Wolf frowned. He then explained the Wihio problem to the Heart.

"I've heard of this coughing sickness," Raven Heart said. "It killed many Kiowas in the southern country. Our people can't fight it. We have no medicine to turn its bad humors away."

"We must stay away from these Wihio then," Wolf declared.

"And we should avoid the fort, too," Raven Heart urged. "If they take it there, many more will die."

"What's to be done, Ne' hyo?" Wolf asked.

"It saddens me to say it, but we must leave these people to suffer the coughing sickness," Raven Heart said as they rode back to the others. "We must lead our camp north, away from them. Someone should ride down and tell the rest of the Omissis and the Oglala Lakotas. We must help our relatives avoid this sickness."

"It's for me to do, of course," Wolf said, reading his father's thoughts. "I have cousins in both camps, and they will trust my words for the truth they carry."

"I'm going, too," Withered Hand declared when he heard the plan.

"Where should we meet you, Ne' hyo?" Wolf asked.

"On the Crazy Woman's Creek, where the Lakotas sometimes make their winter camps," Raven Heart told him.

"Keep my brothers safe," Wolf said, nodding to Red Hawk. "The Hand and I will warn the rest."

The two young Omissis turned back toward Platte River. By the time they reached the Omissis and Oglala encampments near the Wihio fort, however, the coughing sickness was already there.

"There was a Wihio," Badger Belt explained bitterly. "He was sick, and we took him into our camp and tried to make a medicine cure."

"Pronghorn made the prayers himself, but he had no power to break the power of this strong sickness," Flying Squirrel, the old medicine chief's grandson, added. "Now my grandfather is sick."

"Many others, too," Badger Belt added. "It was a bad day for the Tsis tsis tas when the Wihio came among us."

"Sweet Medicine warned us long ago," the Squirrel said, dropping his chin. "Never treat with the whites! Stay away from them. But what good did it do? We're only men and certain to do the foolish thing."

The Omissis urged Withered Hand and Wolf Running to ride away, but they didn't.

"If the sickness is here, we'd only carry it with us to others," Wolf explained. "We'll both of us take a sweat and burn the sickness from us. Then we'll camp in the hills until it's safe to return to Raven Heart and the others."

They did just that. As the coughing sickness raged among the Omissis and Oglala camps on Platte River, and among the Wihio in the nearby soldier fort, Wolf and the Hand remained healthy. They watched sadly as men and women climbed Hanging Road. They sighed with sorrow when smaller bundles were taken out to be put upon scaffolds.

As for the Wihio wagon people who had caused all the trouble, they rode along Platte River a few days later. Some had died, but most were now well.

"We should punish those people," Withered Hand suggested. "Burn their wagons! Kill them!"

"They warned us away," Wolf argued. "They didn't invite the sickness into their camp. No, it's only another enemy the people must fight. Another sadness we'll overcome."

"I've heard my father make the morning prayers a hundred times," Withered Hand said, gazing eastward. "He always asked for struggles to make him strong. They come, invited or not, Wolf. And they never leave us stronger. Only dead."

"We're not all of us dead," Wolf Running argued.

"No, some are left. But for how long?"

"I don't know," Wolf confessed. "Who can? Only the Great Mystery knows our tomorrows."

"Your dreams sometimes speak to you, though."

"Yes, they do. But I haven't seen Snow Wolf in many days."

"Invite him to return and show you the way," Withered Hand urged. "Pronghorn is gone. Many of our strong medicine men, too. The white wolf has already led you from harm. Maybe he can show you how to safeguard all the Omissis."

"I'll ask him," Wolf Running said. "He may not reply."

"At least you will have asked, Brother. There's nothing else you can do."

9

SNOW WOLF DID visit Wolf Running's dreams, but the spirit beast said little. Instead the white creature raced among the hills and valleys north of Platte River, chasing horses and hunting Bull Buffalo. Only later, at the end of the dream, did Snow Wolf utter a warning. No words were spoken, but Wolf Running awoke with a chill. He'd seen a morning sky red as blood, and many Wihio soldiers had ridden along without heads.

"There's going to be fighting," Wolf told Withered Hand.

"Who will we fight then?" the Hand had asked.

"Wihio," Wolf Running answered. "Near Platte River."

Later, when the fear of spreading the coughing sickness had died away, Wolf and Withered Hand rejoined Raven Heart's band. The Heart and his companions had captured many good Crow ponies, and no one had been hurt.

"Many of our people have died of the coughing sickness," Wolf Running then told the others. "It's a sad place, Platte River."

"Is it safe to go there now?" Red Hawk asked.

"The sickness is gone," Wolf Running answered. "The dying is over."

"But not the grieving," Raven Heart muttered.

By the time Raven Heart's band returned to Platte River, hundreds of other Plains people were already there. The tribes had gathered near the soldier fort to receive the presents that were promised annually by the treaty. Most of the northern Tsis tsis tas had camped on Horse Creek. Many Lakotas were there, too. Crows and Arapahos camped farther west. Some Pawnee hung around the fort, close to the soldiers.

It was hot, and tempers were short. The soldier chiefs were delaying the giveaway, and many Tsis tsis tas had grown restless.

"Trouble will come of the delay," Raven Heart grumbled.

He was soon proved right.

A Wihio cow was at the heart of the matter. Some wagon people had let the animal wander, and a Lakota, seeing it had a broken leg, shot it with an arrow. The cow was butchered and eaten.

Now the wagon people had come to the soldiers, saying they wanted the cow-killer punished. They demanded payment for the dead cow.

"The Wihio are always greedy," Withered Hand told Wolf. "They didn't care about the cow when she had a broken leg. Now, hearing the people will receive presents, they want to take something away with them."

The Tsis tsis tas and Lakotas weren't the only ones who thought the wagon people in the wrong.

"It's not fair," Walker Logan told Wolf Running when the two met at Bordeaux's trading post. Walker was fourteen now and almost as tall as Wolf. His hair was as yellow as before, though, and even dressed in buckskins, he was clearly Wihio.

"Come, Wolf," Withered Hand urged, speaking only Tsis tsis tas words. "We should avoid this Wihio."

Walker frowned. Then he nodded.

"I understand," Walker said. "If I can help, though, ask. I owe you a life, after all."

Before, Wolf Running had only faintly recognized the young man. Now he remembered the river, the rescue—all of it.

"My father," Walker said, "told the soldiers they were making a mistake."

"So will the soldiers forget about the cow?" Wolf asked.

"Who listens to us?" Walker asked, shaking his head. "We've lived out here, gotten to know the tribes. But these soldiers come out here eager to make a name for themselves. Our words don't carry any weight."

"What will happen then?" Wolf asked.

"A young soldier chief, Lieutenant Grattan, says the Lakotas who cooked the cow need punishing," Walker explained.

"That young fool boasts he and thirty men could run all the Lakotas, and the Tsis tsis tas, too," Bordeaux said. "He's eager to get himself killed, and plenty others, too."

Wolf Running frowned. It was dangerous, having a bad heart lead the soldiers.

That morning the situation worsened. Grattan decided to ride out to the Lakota camps and confront the chiefs. He foolishly chose as his interpreter a half-Iowa, half-Wihio, Lucien. Lucien had married a Lakota woman, but he didn't speak the Lakota tongue any better than many others who made their home at the fort. And Lucien, sometimes called Wyuse by the Lakotas, was drunk.

Wolf was still at Bordeaux's store when the bluecoats came by, dragging their big cannons along. Bordeaux pleaded with Grattan to go back, that money had been offered to the cow's owner, and it was more than the animal was worth.

"I intend to teach these Indians a lesson," Grattan declared. He then invited Bordeaux to come and translate.

Lucien had gone off to treat with some Lakotas down at the river.

"I'm going nowhere with you and those guns," Bordeaux replied. "You'll only get yourself into trouble."

The big-talking soldier chief again boasted how he could run all the people. His ears were closed.

"There's sure to be trouble now," Bordeaux grumbled. He then asked the Oglalas and Tsis tsis tas who had come to trade with him to leave.

"That soldier's going to make trouble for me," Bordeaux explained. "It will be worse for me if he sees you hanging around."

Wolf Running and Withered Hand mounted their horses and prepared to leave. They didn't go far, though. The Lakotas were running their horses to the river, and a wall of dust choked the horizon. The rising sun colored it red.

Wolf instantly recalled the dream. He turned toward the Oglala camp, hoping to warn his relations. It was too late.

Lucien wasn't helping things. Already he had stirred up the Sicangu Lakotas. They were alarmed by the approaching soldiers, and some were collecting their weapons. Instead of speaking good words that would have calmed the Lakotas, Lucien began running his horse in front of them like a man did before a charge. Lucien vowed he would kill them all and eat their hearts!

The alarmed Lakotas sent their women and children to the back of the camp. Some men went, too. Runners were sent to the nearby camps, and small bands of Oglalas and Minneconjous stripped themselves for battle and hurried to the river. Wolf Running, who had only his bow and a few arrows, joined the Lakotas at the river. Withered Hand, as always, was at his side.

Conquering Bear, a great Lakota chief, saw the danger. He walked out to treat with Grattan. He spoke soothing words, inviting the soldier chiefs to come and sit at his fire. They would smoke and talk. Everything would be settled.

This Grattan heard none of it. Lucien didn't speak the right words. So the soldiers formed a line and surrounded the Bear. The big guns were brought up.

"Why?" Wolf Running asked.

Conquering Bear next offered the Wihio who had lost the cow a good mule. Later, five men pledged good ponies. Everything was done to satisfy the soldiers, but they only wanted a fight. They got one.

Grattan demanded the cow killer, a Minneconnjou named High Forehead, be turned over. The Forehead wouldn't go. His people had been shot at by wagon people, and everyone knew of the coughing sickness. The Lakotas didn't trust Grattan, either. No man brought wheeled guns to a camp to speak peace.

Nevertheless Conquering Bear urged High Forehead to go. The Forehead, in turn, said he was prepared to stand and die. His brothers were dead, killed by enemies. He wouldn't let the Wihio take him without a fight.

Grattan heard none of those strong words. Wolf listened as Lucien called the soldiers names and said Conquering Bear vowed to fight. The soldiers then shot the Bear's brother. The Bear, though angered by this, argued against fighting, saying the soldiers would be satisfied now that they had shot someone. The other chiefs fled.

Conquering Bear then faced the soldiers. He held out his arms, showing everyone he had no weapon. Grattan fired his cannons, and the soldiers shot off their rifles. The Bear fell, and some lodges had their tops torn off. Now the people's blood was up, and they charged the soldiers.

It wasn't much of a fight. Those of the soldiers who could run away did so. Their guns were empty, and hundreds of angry Lakotas were chasing them. Lucien managed to reach the nearby camp before he was caught. His own brother-in-law struck the first blow. Others then stripped him of his clothes and cut pieces from him. He lay there, mutilated and bleeding, while young men shouted insults.

Wolf Running saw that much. He'd spotted his cousin, Curly, and he stood but a few feet away when the young Oglala bared himself in front of the dying Iowa, a tremendous insult.

"Curly?" Wolf called. Curly immediately pulled on his breechclout and hurried away. The chiefs would think ill of a boy thinking so well of himself.

"Let's ride from this place," Withered Hand urged, grasping Wolf by the arm. "See how the Lakotas are scattering? Already their women are taking down the lodges. We should go back to our camp."

"No, we should see what can be done to cool the blood," Wolf argued.

"What can we do?" the Hand cried. "You carry a proud name, Wolf, but you're just a boy. No one will listen to us. Can't you hear anything? The Lakotas are killing the Wihio soldiers. Some say they're going to burn the fort! We're not needed here."

Wolf reluctantly agreed. He and the Hand got atop their horses and headed back toward Horse Creek. Along the way they saw an army of Lakotas swarming over Bordeaux's store, carrying away the treaty goods and dragging the bodies of soldiers from their nearby hiding places. Some of the bluecoats were still alive. Their pleas gained them nothing. The Lakotas had watched as good men had been cut down. Now they punished their enemy without mercy. Wihio soldiers were stripped and cut. One had his head cut off. The cannons were torn from their carriages and thrown into the river. The supply wagons were burned.

Grattan lay there, his empty eyes staring at the clouds.

"Do you think he's listening now?" one Lakota asked.

The soldier chief's body held fifty arrows.

Suddenly Wolf Running's attention was caught by the sight of two pale bodies being dragged naked to the river. Bordeaux was running after them, pleading for mercy.

"No!" Wolf shouted, whipping his pony toward a circle of Lakotas and driving them into the shallows.

"Are you crazy?" A Sicangu named Crane screamed.

"No." Wolf climbed off his horse and helped Andy and Walker Logan from the sandy ground. "These aren't soldiers."

"What's the difference?" Crane growled. "They're Wihio. They shot my uncle. I'll kill them!"

"I didn't shoot anybody," Walker said, speaking the words in fine Lakota fashion.

"They're traders' sons," Wolf pointed out. "Their father spoke up for High Forehead. They've brought us no harm."

"He's right," Bordeaux added. "They're no threat to you. Neither one of 'em's got a trace of beard, can't you see? Just boys."

Crane wasn't much older, but the wide, fearful eyes of the Logans chased away his anger. Bare and weaponless as they were, the Logans were too humorous to fight.

"I'd best find you boys some blankets," Bordeaux said, grinning.

"Hurry, Jim," Andy urged. "Won't be many left when everyone's finished yonder."

It was true. The Lakotas were emptying not only the warehouse filled with treaty goods but Bordeaux's own shelves as well. The old trader gazed at his ruin and frowned. Instead of pleading for his own safety, though, he interceded for the young Logans. Then, when some of the young war chiefs appeared, Bordeaux warned against attacking the fort.

"Look at me!" he shouted. "You've taken everything I own. I have nothing but my friendship to offer you. It's a bad thing that's happened. Conquering Bear is maybe dead. Other good men, too. Grattan and his soldiers as well. The bluecoat soldiers will be hot to fight you, but men like me will explain what happened. If you attack the fort, though, my words will be nothing. There are innocents there—

women and children. If they're harmed, the Wihio chiefs
will send armies against you."

"It's their own fault!" one of the Oglalas shouted.

"What can they do?" Charger, a Minneconjou, asked.
"Look out there. Their dead lay there, troubled by flies.
They aren't even strong enough to recover their chief's
body. We can ride down there and kill them all, destroy the
fort. We can free ourselves of these troublesome whites
forever."

"More would only come," Bordeaux argued.

"The trader's right," Little Thunder, a Sicangu chief,
noted. "We've killed Wihio before, but others always
follow. There's no killing all of them. Winter's coming
soon. We can't protect the helpless ones from the Wihio and
make the fall hunt. Forget your anger, brothers, and make
yourselves ready for the hard days that are coming."

Little Thunder's words were strong and convincing. Men
rode up, saying Conquering Bear wasn't dead after all.
Although shot many times, his medicine had shielded him
from a fatal wound.

"It's time we left," Withered Hand again urged. "The
people will need us as they break down their lodges and
leave Platte River."

"We'll go soon," Wolf Running agreed. "First I'll make
sure these Wihio are safe."

"You're crazy," the Hand complained.

"Maybe," Wolf conceded. "It's a white wolf that always
comes to my dreams, though. This is the second time I've
found myself saving this Wihio. Why? Who can say?"

"Only Heammawihio knows," Withered Hand whispered.

"Only He," Wolf Running agreed.

Wolf then dismounted his horse and walked among the
Lakotas, asking a few he recognized for some Wihio
garments. He brought some that appeared suitable to Bordeaux's store and gave them to the Logans.

"When you're dressed, I'll take you to your father," Wolf pledged.

"That would be even crazier than riding into those Lakotas," Walker said. "Any Cheyenne who rides near the fort will get himself shot."

"He's right," Andy added.

"You've done what you can for them," Bordeaux said, managing a tired grin for the young Cheyennes. "Best you head back to your camp now, son. These boys'll be fine where they are."

"Listen to him," Walker urged. "You've done enough."

"I have . . . an obligation," Wolf tried to explain.

"How so?" Walker asked. "You've gone and saved my hide twice, and Andy's, too, this time. I'd judge it enough."

"Sure is," Andy agreed.

"I saw this day in my dreams," Wolf said, sighing. "I don't understand everything, but I think we'll meet once more."

"Hope it's the next time I run into trouble," Walker said, offering his hand. "Got no silver piece to offer you this time."

"None's needed," Wolf said, turning to go.

The Grattan fight sent a shudder through the Plains tribes. In a few days only the Crows and Pawnees remained among the Wihio at Fort Laramie. All the other bands had scattered.

It wasn't the end of the fighting, though. Conquering Bear eventually did die of his wounds, and the Lakotas saw in his loss the end of any chance for maintaining the peace along Platte River.

The Wihio soldier chiefs, as Bordeaux had warned, spoke of punishing the Lakotas. That next summer they sent a colonel, Harney, up Platte River to punish the Indians. He was a hard man, some said, who intended to make only one big fight. The Wihio called it the Battle at Ash Hollow.

It was less a fight than murder.

The Wihio came upon the peaceful encampment of Little Thunder—the same chief who had argued against attacking the soldier fort. There, where their fathers and grandfathers had camped, the Sicangu Lakotas thought themselves safe from harm. Harney brought thirteen hundred soldiers with him—all grown men with good rifles. They had cannons, too. Once they surrounded Little Thunder's camp, they struck. The big guns opened fire, and the soldiers charged. The few men who managed to run out and grab weapons were quickly cut down. Some others managed to make a brave fight long enough for some women and children to escape. Most died or were taken prisoner by the bluecoats.

The first news the Tsis tsis tas received of this battle was when Lakotas stumbled into their nearby camps. Their bare feet bled from the ordeal, and little children wept as they recounted the terrible massacre of their families. Afterward, Raven Heart led a party of Elks to Ash Hollow. The bones of the dead still marked the spot.

"These weren't men," the Heart said, stepping down from his horse and touching a child's arm bone.

"This was not a brave-heart deed," Red Hawk agreed.

"Ayyyy!" Wolf screamed.

Afterward, there would be little effort to make peace with the Wihio. The talk now turned to fighting.

10

TWO WINTERS PASSED after the Wihio attack on Little
Thunder's camp. The Lakotas met with the soldier chief,
Harney, and restored a peace of sorts. The southern Tsis tsis
tas, too, managed to avoid a confrontation with the bluecoats, even though the Wihio violated the Horse Creek
treaty by building roads through the southern buffalo range.
In the north country, where the Omissis and Suhtai camped
along Platte River, it was difficult to avoid the Wihio
soldiers. They had many forts on the wagon road westward,
and they had built bridges across Platte River. Often small
numbers of bluecoats were camped near the bridges.

The Suhtai had made their spring camp near one such
bridge, and the Omissis, too, were nearby. Inevitably Tsis
tsis tas and bluecoats met each other. Each eyed the other
with suspicion, and the seeds for trouble were sown.

Wolf Running was now a young man of fifteen snows,
and he rode with the young Elks to hunt or raid ponies from
the Crows. He had stretched himself tall. Moreover, he

adopted the habit of riding pale ponies against the enemy. It marked him as a man to notice.

"Naha', you'll soon be leading the young men," Raven Heart observed. "Where you go, right or wrong, others are bound to follow. Keep your thinking clear. Remain at harmony with yourself and the world. Then you'll lead well."

Wolf had no desire to lead anyone. He had long since grown accustomed to seeing Stands Long Beside Him, as Withered Hand had come to be known, nearby. The two had rescued each other from Bull Buffalo, angry Crows, and vengeful Pawnees more times than either could easily recount. Now, however, younger men nudged their horses onto Wolf Running's trail. The weight of their admiration rested heavily on his shoulders, and Wolf worried he would prove incapable of safeguarding so many.

"I wish they'd just go away," Wolf remarked to Stands Long.

"And who would they follow?" Stands Long asked. "Corn Dancer? Little Bull? They'd gladly lead."

Wolf frowned. Those two would only lead good men to their deaths.

"You know it's up to you, Wolf," Stands Long insisted.

"Yes," Wolf admitted. It didn't make it any easier, knowing there wasn't any choice.

That year there were many Wihio wagon bands traveling the rutted road along Platte River, and the Omissis often crossed their paths. The recollection of spotted fevers and the coughing sickness kept the older men back, but some of the younger ones were eager to trade for Wihio tobacco or good guns, and they often treated with the wagon people.

Wolf Running did not. What he needed from the Wihio, he could trade for at Fort Laramie. The Logan brothers had set up a store there to provision the wagon parties, and they could be counted on to supply whatever Wolf needed.

"It's understood Wolf is their brother," Corn Dancer

sometimes told the younger men. "His heart is partly white. Maybe he'll cut his hair and give up his lance so that he can be a proper Wihio."

"He's done neither," Stands Long would answer, stepping close to the Dancer. "Wolf Running is always first to rescue the helpless ones. You, too, are first, Dancer. First to run away!"

It was true, and all the others knew it. Corn Dancer, for all his strong words, rarely finished a fight. And while he had two good hands and was taller and stronger, he wouldn't challenge Stands Long.

"Pain has taught me endurance," Stands Long explained once to Wolf Running. "When I start a thing, I stay with it until I'm finished."

Whether it was making an arrow or fighting an enemy, Stands Long would be there. Wolf knew he was fortunate to have such a good brother-friend.

The two young men were in the chalk hills north of the soldier fort when Raven Heart sent word for them to ride down and rejoin the main Omissis camp.

"Nah nih, there's been some trouble," Little Hawk, who was now thirteen, told him when he brought the message. Wolf sought no explanation. He had been expecting something. Snow Wolf was running in his dreams again.

Even before reaching Raven Heart's camp, Wolf knew horses were at the core of the trouble. He'd seen four white ponies in his dream, and when one of them vanished, the skies erupted with smoke and fire.

"Yes, it's horses," Raven Heart said when he gathered the Elks in council. The Heart had now given up the lance to Hairy Moccasin and accepted the obligations of a soldier chief. "The Wihio say we have four of their ponies."

"Do we, Ne' hyo?" Wolf asked.

"It appears that they're in the Suhtai camp," the Heart replied.

"These horses were running free," Corn Dancer explained. "The Wihio had lost them. Now they belong to our relations."

"Yes, it's true," Raven Heart said, frowning. "They're only four horses, though. It's clear from what the soldier chiefs say that we have the ones in question. They have iron shoes on their feet, and our people captured them near where the Wihio lost theirs."

"If a man loses a pony, he's lost it," Hairy Moccasin argued. "Already the Wihio wagons scar the lands. Their animals chew the grass and drive Bull Buffalo away. They spoil the water and bring sickness. Now they expect us to be their pony boys and find what they've lost!"

There was an unsettling murmur among the young men, and Raven Heart turned to them.

"It's always easy to fight," the Heart said. "Even to die. If these were Crows who came to us and asked for their ponies, we would laugh, knowing the Crows understand how foolish they appear to be. But these Wihio don't think right. They want to own everything. And if they choose to punish someone, it won't be you or me. No, they'll seek out another peaceful camp and cut down the defenseless ones. Who paid for that fool Grattan's killing? Little Thunder and his people. Who would the Wihio fight this time? Maybe our sisters or cousins. Maybe our wives and children. What do four ponies matter? Let's give them up."

"Raven Heart speaks sensibly," Red Hawk said, nodding to his brother-in-law. "Besides, the Wihio soldier chief has promised payment. We're a people rich with horses. We need things the Wihio might give us. We should urge the young Suhtai to turn over the horses."

It was decided then. Raven Heart spoke with the Suhtai leaders, and all agreed that the ponies would be returned. Three of the owners came in with their animals. The fourth, Coyote, insisted his was not one of the missing horses.

"I captured him far away from the Wihio wagon road,"

Coyote declared. "Why should I give up such a good horse? Take them another."

Coyote was an important man, and there was no persuading him. Raven Heart and Wolf Running accompanied the Suhtai horse owners when they brought in the three animals. Coyote came, too, eager to explain why he had decided to keep the other pony.

"Be careful, Ne' hyo," Wolf had whispered as they neared the bridge. "My dreams have told me there may be trouble."

"Then it's for us to make sure there isn't any," the Heart replied.

Wolf intended to turn his father's thoughts into Wihio words. He was afraid the problem that had brought on the Grattan fight might happen again, and he wanted to assure straight talk between the two sides. No sooner had the young Suhtai arrived with their ponies than a bluecoat demanded the fourth animal.

"There's a problem about that horse," Wolf Running said, dismounting so that he could look directly into the soldier chief's eyes. Raven Heart likewise climbed down. The Suhtai remained on their horses.

"What problem?" the soldier chief asked.

"We should sit together and discuss it," Wolf suggested. "My father has a pipe. We can . . ."

The soldier cut him off.

"We're not here to discuss anything," the bluecoat barked. "Hand over the horses."

Wolf translated for the others, but the soldiers didn't wait for him to finish. A handful armed with rifles circled the young Suhtai, and the soldier chief ordered the riders to dismount.

It was all happening too fast. Wolf had trouble turning the Wihio words into Tsis tsis tas, and besides, the Suhtai language was slightly different. The Wihio guns made everyone nervous.

"What of the reward?" one of the Suhtai, a young man named Bull Shield, asked.

The soldiers, who couldn't understand, turned their guns on the Shield.

"Please," Wolf Running cried. "Put away your guns. We're here to . . ."

"Take charge of the thieves!" the soldier chief shouted. "We'll show them once and for all how we deal with liars."

Wolf stared at the Wihio in disbelief. Thieves? No one had mentioned stealing. The ponies had run off. They were being returned, all but one of them. Couldn't the soldiers understand what was happening? Didn't they have eyes?

"Naha', something's wrong," Raven Heart said.

"Look," Wolf Running pleaded, holding out his arms as Conquering Bear had done. "We're unarmed! We can reach an agreement!"

The wind stirred, and Wolf noticed a wicked grin creep onto the soldier chief's face. His eyes! They were full of hunger, hunger for killing.

"Tell them to get off their horses!" the soldier chief demanded. "Now!"

Wolf turned to translate, but the young Suhtai had seen enough. Coyote turned his horse, and a bluecoat fired, striking him. Bull Shield bowed his head and began chanting. The soldiers fired at him, too. The back of the Shield's head exploded, and he fell, dead. The bluecoats then dragged a third young Suhtai, Fire Wolf, from his horse.

"This is wrong," Wolf Running argued. "This man's done nothing wrong," he added, pointing to Fire Wolf. "We brought you horses, and now you've killed a man, shot another, and taken this young man."

"Go before we take you, too," the soldier chief shouted.

Wolf Running turned to his father, but Raven Heart stood in stunned silence.

"Tell my family," Fire Wolf whispered. He then began singing his death chant.

"We must go," Stands Long called.

"We have to do something," Wolf Running insisted.

"What can we do?" Raven Heart asked. "They have no ears to hear the truth."

Wolf Running gazed hard at the soldiers who were now dragging Fire Wolf across the bridge. If they were hungry to fight the people, they would be satisfied soon enough. Treaties and good words were useless when dealing with treachery.

"We'll find other weapons," Wolf Running vowed.

The senseless killing at the Platte Bridge was beyond Wolf Running's comprehension. The Suhtai, when they heard of Bull Shield's death and the capture of Fire Wolf, became fearful. Most gathered up what possessions they could tie onto their horses and abandoned the painted lodges and other possessions that would have required pony drags.

"They remember what happened to Little Thunder's camp," Wolf Running told Stands Long.

It may have been wise, for a band of bluecoats soon arrived. They tore down the lodges and stole everything of value. If people had remained, they, too, might have been dragged off—or even killed.

Among the scattered northern bands of Suhtai and Tsis tsis tas, the Wihio outrage sparked cries for revenge. Fire Wolf's relations pleaded for his release, and when the Wihio soldier chief at Fort Laramie refused, they set off for Bear Butte in hopes of invoking medicine power in that sacred place.

Raven Heart spoke with some of these people, arguing against retaliation. He was eager to move his own camp, but he was worried some young Suhtai might stir up trouble by striking out at the first Wihio he came upon.

Raven Heart was right to worry.

An old trapper named Ganier who had ridden the plains

since the grandfathers' boyhood happened across the Suhtai. Ganier had married into the tribe, and most regarded him as a friend. He was ignorant of the trouble over the Wihio horses, and he approached Fire Wolf's angry relatives in friendship.

The Suhtai didn't recognize him as their old friend. Instead they saw a white face, and the hurt and rage heated their blood. Before anyone quite knew what had happened, several warriors fell upon the trapper, killing him and carrying away his scalp.

"A hard time's coming," Raven Heart told the Elks after receiving news of Ganier's death. "The Suhtai are crazy! They'll kill others, too."

Meanwhile, Lakota relatives urged the Heart to leave the northern country.

"Our people have suffered already," a Sicangu named Speckled Eagle argued when Raven Heart took his band into the hills north of Fort Laramie. "We're not strong here. The old men would turn you over to the bluecoats to keep their families safe."

"I could ride out and find our relatives," Wolf Running suggested. "They won't turn us away."

"And if the Wihio soldiers find us first?" Raven Heart asked. "Remember Harney's hundreds. They can't be far away. Even with all the Oglalas fighting with us, we would be unable to guard our camps. No, we have to insure the safety of the helpless ones. We'll go south and find the southern people."

It was a difficult journey. Crossing Platte River unseen was impossible for a large band, so the camp broke apart and made its way south in small groups. Many had to leave possessions behind. Good lodge poles, easily found in the northern country but scarce in the south, were lost crossing the rivers. When winter arrived, the people would suffer without them.

Wolf took charge of his brothers during the journey. Little

Hawk and Willow Boy were old enough to fend for themselves. Morning Hawk was still a child, and Burnt Willow Woman saw to his care. Red Hawk and Raven Heart, meanwhile, tried to maintain some control over the widely spread band. It just wasn't possible, though. Some of the Omissis people wouldn't be seen again until the people gathered to remake the world.

When they finally arrived at the first camps of the southern people on Red Shield River, there was a great stir. Wolf Running's little group found a Hevataniu camp. He was surprised to discover his uncle, Swift Antelope, there. His cousin, the young man called Three Toes and now known as Buffalo Horn, was there as well.

"We're glad to see you," the Horn exclaimed when he rode up. "Ayyyy! We'll race our horses! We'll hunt! It's sure to be a good summer."

"No, we bring sad news," Wolf replied. "Many bad things have come to pass. Our fathers will talk first. Then we younger men will have to make our plans."

Word spread quickly from camp to camp, and angry words flew around like stinging arrows. Wihio traders and trappers, used to coming to the Tsis tsis tas camps in summer to exchange powder and guns, and trade goods for buffalo robes, were warned to leave. Some Wihio stores were even raided, and bands of young men rode along the wagon roads, shouting warnings and even shooting arrows.

"We must gather the young men," Raven Heart declared. "They must put their anger aside. We've lost possessions and a few have been killed, but it's not too late to stop the bad feelings before hundreds die."

"Ne' hyo, everyone is hot for killing the Wihio," Wolf told his father. "You said yourself there's no treating with the bad-heart Wihio. It's a good thing to come into this southern country, where we're strong. Here we can make a fight."

"Fight?" Raven Heart cried. "We'll only find death here."

"I'll do as you advise, Ne' hyo," Wolf Running pledged, "and some will follow me. Most will ride off with Corn Dancer or some other man eager to lead them to war."

"Too many of our good young men will be killed."

"I know of the treaty promises, and I understand you don't want to break them," Wolf said, sighing. "It seems to me, though, that we should invite dreams and hold a council where everyone can say what's on his mind. Then we should all act together. Our chiefs should lead so that the young men are kept safe. If you and Red Hawk and the others turn away from warrior's road, who will remain to lead?"

"Others."

"Bad hearts, Ne' hyo. I pledged to watch over Little Hawk and Willow Boy. They're growing older. If a war party forms, we can expect them to go along to hold horses. You yourself told me I must stand tall among my age-mates. I have to lead. If the council decides to fight, I will ride out with the others."

"I'm a soldier chief myself," Raven Heart noted.

"You know how a fight is best accomplished. Lead us, Ne' hyo. Teach us."

"I always have," the Heart said, frowning.

"You always will," Wolf whispered.

11

RAVEN HEART CONTINUED to argue against attacks on the Wihio wagon camps. He was especially concerned about making trouble for the soldier forts on Platte River or the traders on the wagon roads bound for the southwest.

"Too many are angry, Ne' hyo," Wolf Running warned. "It's not possible to stay out of the way of every Wihio. Not with so many of them coming into our country."

"If they're all coming here, then we'll go somewhere else," Raven Heart declared.

The Elk criers soon went out among the neighboring bands, asking for fighters to strike the Pawnee camps to the east.

"Out enemies have grown fat and lazy," Wolf told one band of young men. "They're rich with good horses. We'll run them and bring back many ponies."

"It's a good notion," Stands Long agreed. "We'll be needing horses soon to present to some girls' fathers. A man has need of a wife."

"He should be more of a man than you first," Split Chin said, laughing.

"I'm enough of a man," Stands Long insisted. "Count the coup feathers in my hair! Has anyone done more?"

"It's not your courage that's lacking," Hairy Moccasin said. "A woman wants a husband who's taller than she is. Grow some. Then carve a courting flute."

"Grow some," Stands Long muttered as Wolf led the way to where they had tied their horses. "I'm as tall as he is."

"Don't let the Moccasin's words trouble you," Wolf Running told him. "Older men are always trying to hold the young ones back. His wife smiles at you, doesn't she? Girls aren't interested in fat old men. They want . . ."

"Want what?" Stands Long asked, laughing.

"I suppose I'm not the one to talk long about it," Wolf said, hiding his face.

"No," Stands Long agreed. "You might as well ask a buffalo cow what it's like to fly."

Even though Wolf wasn't an expert on courting maidens, he did manage to persuade thirty good men to join the raiding party. A handful of pony boys also pleaded to go along, but Raven Heart ordered them back.

"Soon you'll have a chance to hunt Bull Buffalo," the Heart said, gazing into the disappointed eyes of the boys. "What's needed here is patience and experience. The Pawnees are tricky, and if trouble comes, I don't want to give our old enemy a chance to kill anybody."

They set out as the first Green Grass Moon of summer filled the sky. Wolf Running and Stands Long rode at the head of the party, singing brave-heart songs and waving their new rifles in the air. Raven Heart followed a few steps behind, grinning at the young men. As they galloped westward, a party of Arapahos joined them. Later a few young Lakotas also attached themselves.

Raven Heart had a good plan in his head. He assigned the younger, less-experienced men to guard the spare ponies.

Those who had good guns were assigned the lead. Their task would be to hold off any Pawnees while the bowmen took charge of the Pawnee pony herd.

"We came to kill Pawnees," Corn Dancer complained.

"We came to take ponies," Raven Heart argued. "To win honor, too, but only to count coup on an enemy that's determined to fight us. If the Pawnees run, let them go."

Later, the Heart warned Wolf to watch Corn Dancer, Bent Arrow, and Little Fork.

"They neglect their obligations, those three," Raven Heart grumbled. "Twice they've left the ponies unwatched. If we find the enemy, they'll ride out ahead and break the medicine if no one holds them back."

"We'll hold them, Ne' hyo," Wolf promised. "Stands Long and I will do it."

As it happened, there was no need. Long before crossing into Pawnee country, the raiders splashed into Little Blue River. It was thick with wagons, and trouble soon appeared.

Most of the Wihio wagon people were new to the plains. The instant they saw the Tsis tsis tas riders, they shouted and fired off their rifles.

"We mean no harm!" Wolf shouted as he raced along in front of the others. "Don't shoot! Friends!"

A young Wihio, aged fifteen years or so, fired off his rifle, and Wolf's horse went down, struck in the throat. Two Wihio children screamed as they raced out from the cover of the tall river grass just ahead.

Wolf struggled to free his trapped left leg as an older Wihio approached, aiming his rifle. The Wihio raised the gun, cocked the hammer, and prepared to fire. Stands Long galloped over and fired his own rifle first. The Wihio dropped to his knees, then fell over backward onto the prairie.

The Tsis tsis tas screamed and waved their weapons. Wolf noticed them. Then, as he climbed out from beneath his pony, he saw the frightened eyes of the little Wihio children.

Couldn't they see he intended no harm? How could the Tsis tsis tas ever live peacefully with such a crazy tribe? Here a man was dead, and for what?

The young Wihio horse-killer escorted the children to the safety of the wagons while Stands Long galloped over to his shaken brother-friend.

"Help me strip my belongings from this dead pony," Wolf called. His leg ached, and his head was pounding with rage.

"Your father's bringing out another horse," Stands Long told him. "Maybe we should leave. The Wihio appear angry."

"They're not the only ones," Wolf said, pointing to the line of young Elks waving angry bows at the wagon people. Harsh words were spoken across the ground between the two groups. Only Wolf and a few others understood all of it, and fortunately they kept the insults to themselves.

"We should kill them all!" Corn Dancer screamed. "Who'll ride with me and kill these Wihio?"

"No one!" Raven Heart shouted. "Make up your own war party, Dancer. Then you can lead. These are entrusted to me, and I'll decide what to do."

That afternoon, after Wolf had removed his equipment from the dead horse and placed it on a fresh mount, Raven Heart led the way north toward Platte River. As night fell upon the land, the weary Elk chief spoke medicine prayers, and the leaders invited dreams. Once more Snow Wolf came to Wolf Running's dreams. The white creature turned away from a big camp of Pawnee lodges. Instead, Snow Wolf raced westward along the prairie, back toward the old buffalo range north of Horse Creek.

The dream offered little insight, but when Wolf shared it with his father that next morning, Raven Heart frowned.

"It's clear enough to me," the Heart said. "We should turn back."

"And leave the Pawnees undisturbed?" Wolf asked. "But our purpose was . . ."

"We've killed a man," Raven Heart pointed out. "The medicine that might have blinded the enemy is spoiled. We should return to our people and help make preparations for the earth renewal. There's hunting to do after that. Remember, Naha', the welfare of the people must always come first."

"Yes, Ne' hyo," Wolf agreed.

When the raiders met in council to discuss it, not everyone agreed to turn west.

"The Pawnees are close," Corn Dancer said. "We can still run them."

"Who would lead us?" Little Fork asked.

"I will," Corn Dancer boasted.

"You, Wolf?" Bent Arrow asked.

"I don't understand everything in my dreams, but I trust Ne' hyo," Wolf explained. "I follow him."

The Arapahos decided to continue, though. They argued that their medicine remained strong. Corn Dancer, Bent Arrow, and Little Fork chose to go with them. Everyone else vowed to follow Raven Heart westward.

Not long afterward, as Raven Heart and his small band made their camp on Platte River, a group of bluecoats rode up with an invitation to visit the nearby fort.

"Our captain is eager to meet you," a youngish Wihio told them. "He's asked you to come to Fort Kearny and speak with him. We can eat and smoke. Then maybe we can understand about your problems out here."

"Don't go," Wolf urged when Raven Heart turned toward the bluecoats. "Remember how it was at the bridge."

"Not all Wihio soldier chiefs own bad hearts," Raven Heart insisted. "How can they know our words if we don't speak them?"

"You'll need me to talk for you then," Wolf noted.

"And to hear for me, too," the Heart added.

"You're certain we should go, Ne' hyo?"

"The white wolf guided you in this direction," Raven Heart reminded his son. "It's right we go."

In all, ten Tsis tsis tas and a few Lakotas rode to the fort. It was a sizable place, with several log buildings and a party of wagon people camped nearby. The bluecoats led their guests inside a small room, but although there was a table there, no one brought any food or offered tobacco to fill the pipe Raven Heart had brought along.

"Cheyenne?" the Wihio chief growled from the far side of the table.

"Tsis tsis tas," Wolf answered. "Some Suhtai," he added, nodding to some of the others. "Lakotas," he said, pointing to Otter Skin.

"Not Cheyenne?" the captain asked.

"You call us that," Wolf said, frowning. The Wihio understood nothing. He didn't seem interested in his guests. He had questions to ask, and he asked them angrily.

"You've attacked wagon trains on Platte River," the soldier chief said, stating it as a truth rather than an inquiry.

Wolf shuddered, recalling the trouble they'd had. It wasn't on Platte River, though.

"We attacked nobody," Wolf answered. He then explained the question to the others.

"Kiowas," Good Bear suggested.

"Maybe Kiowas," Wolf said. "Maybe someone else. Pawnees even. They're tricky. If there's been trouble, though, we'll sit and talk with you about it. First we should smoke, though."

"No, we talk!" the Wihio shouted. "You say you haven't attacked any wagons. What are these?" he asked, waving to one of the other bluecoats. The young man who had carried the invitation set two arrows on the table. "Well?"

"These aren't ours," Wolf said, laughing. "Look at the feathers. They're old. They have Lakota markings."

"Lakota?" the captain asked, turning to his companions.

One of them was dressed in buckskins and had a thick reddish-colored beard.

"Sioux," the bearded man explained.

"You are Sioux?" the captain asked Wolf.

"Some," Wolf said, translating the question for the others. Otter Skin stepped over, studied the arrows, and admitted the markings were Lakota.

Wolf then heard footsteps on the wooden floorboards outside. He caught sight of six more soldiers, all armed with rifles. Stands Long saw them, too, and he slid out the door, taking some of the others along. Before Wolf could join them, the bearded man stepped over to block the door.

"Seize them!" the soldier chief ordered.

A fat Wihio jumped Otter Skin while the young Wihio, the message-bringer, grabbed Wolf Running. Wolf easily shook the frail young man off and moved to help his father and the others. The other six bluecoats then entered the room. In pairs they detained Raven Heart and Good Bear. Others wrestled Big Hairy Dog to the floor. Wolf leapt past Otter Skin and raced through the door. He ran as fast as he could toward his pony. Stands Long had the animal waiting. The young Tsis tsis tas then galloped away as bluecoats fired off rifles at them.

"What sort of chiefs do the bluecoats have?" Wolf grumbled when he reached the camp. "They invite us to go to their camp and then fall on us like snakes. Even the Pawnees don't treat a man like that!"

"We have to rescue them!" Stands Long cried.

"We will," Wolf vowed. "Let's rest our horses. Then we ride back and free our brothers."

As they waited, Stands Long went among the others, telling of the trouble. The Lakotas who had seen Otter Skin taken were particularly enraged. Where had those arrows come from? They couldn't be from the wagon people on Little Blue River. Only rifles were fired there.

"The arrows were old," Wolf noted.

"Maybe the soldiers had some left from the time they killed the helpless ones in Little Thunder's camp," Split Chin said.

The arrows weren't the important thing, though. The captives were. Wolf instructed twenty men to break down the camp and prepare to move south. The remaining handful mounted their ponies and followed Wolf back to the fort.

The bluecoats hadn't expected anyone to return. They held the three Tsis tsis tas in front of the building. Otter Skin was there, too. The young Lakota's hands were manacled, and he dragged a cannonball that was attached to one leg.

"Run!" Wolf shouted as he kicked his horse into a gallop and charged past a group of surprised bluecoats. "Run, Ne' hyo!"

Raven Heart turned and knocked down a bluecoat soldier that was aiming a rifle at Good Bear. Stands Long held horses for the captives. Good Bear and Big Hairy Dog ran to the ponies, climbed up, and raced away. Bluecoats were now firing off their rifles, and horses whinnied at the noise. Otter Skin broke away from his captors. Picking up the cannonball in his hands, he stumbled to where his cousin was waiting with a pony.

Raven Heart now ran toward Wolf Running. Wolf held his father's horse ready, and he waited anxiously for the Heart to reach it. The soldiers were now firing again, and bullets struck Raven Heart's back. Once, twice, three times he was hit. Wolf jumped down, grabbed his faltering father, and helped the bleeding man onto his horse. Stands Long raced back and forth to shield Wolf and his father from another volley. Finally, with Raven Heart mounted, the last of the Tsis tsis tas sped away.

Wolf was filled with a mixture of relief and fury. They had gotten away, but perhaps his father was bleeding out his life. The treacherous bluecoats were certain to follow, too. Already the dust from their ponies leapt toward the sky.

"Ne' hyo, is it bad?" Wolf called.

"Not so bad," Raven Heart answered. His coat was soaked with blood, and he threw it off, exposing the three wounds to view.

"We have to stop and make medicine," Wolf said, pulling up short.

"Not yet, Naha'," Raven Heart argued. "Later, when the others are safe."

So they galloped on past the camp. Most of the possessions were tied onto horses, and some men had already left. Others had bundled Raven Heart's belongings. Wolf left Stands Long to gather their blankets while he tended to his father.

"The wounds are serious," Wolf noted as he did his best to plug the holes.

"I can feel the Wihio poison working," Raven Heart said, laughing. "Who would have suspected this would be the way I met my end?"

"You're not dead," Wolf argued.

"Soon though, Naha'," Raven Heart whispered. "Look after your mother, Wolf. She's a good woman, and she has many good years left to give a man. I know her, though. She'll hurry her feet toward Hanging Road."

"Ne' hyo, I . . ."

"You, too, will rush yourself toward death," Raven Heart said, frowning. "Let the white wolf be your guide, Naha'. You draw good men to your side. Lead them well."

"You'll lead us all."

"Not for long," Raven Heart said, sighing. "Not for long."

The bluecoats sent out twenty riders, but Wolf managed to get his father and the few others who remained with him away. The Wihio did take thirteen ponies, but a party of Hevataniu led by Swift Antelope later recovered all of them. The Antelope even retrieved Raven Heart's discarded coat.

As for the Heart himself, he seemed to recover his strength. The medicine chiefs warned that the lead in his back was killing him, but the Elk chief refused to lie down and welcome his death. Instead Raven Heart gathered his band together and spoke out strongly against retribution.

"You wouldn't punish a snake for blindly striking out and biting your horse," the Heart noted. "These Wihio are the same way. They don't know anything. We must teach them the way a child is taught, slowly and with much patience."

"While they kill all of us?" Wolf cried.

"It's the only way, Naha'," Raven Heart insisted. "The only way. Take any other road, and we'll all of us perish."

"We will anyway," Wolf muttered. "Better we fight them."

"Let the wolf guide you, Naha'," Raven Heart pleaded. "Promise me that much."

"I promise to invite Snow Wolf into my dreams," Wolf answered. "But I won't turn away from war against the Wihio if they come to strike the people, to kill my family and burn my lodge. I'll fight them, Ne' hyo."

"I feel sad then," the Heart said, closing his eyes. "A hard time's coming, and I won't be here to guide you through it."

"It's for me to guide myself now," Wolf announced. "I'm a man."

"Yes," Raven Heart said, coughing. "Yes, Naha'."

Raven Heart opened his eyes once more. He turned to Winter Fawn Woman, who gripped his hands in her own.

"We had at least one son, didn't we?" the Heart whispered.

"A good one, Husband," she replied.

"It's time to begin the long walk, friends," Raven Heart whispered.

Then he shuddered, coughed twice, and died.

12

WOLF RUNNING ERECTED Raven Heart's burial scaffold on a high hill overlooking Red Shield River. There, where the Shield had remade the earth such a short time before, his spirit would begin the long climb up Hanging Road.

"The Omissis will long remember you, Ne' hyo," Wolf whispered to the sky overhead.

As was fitting for a dutiful son, Wolf tore his clothing and cut his hair. Many of the Elks, recalling their brave-heart chief, likewise observed the mourning rituals. Winter Fawn Woman nodded respectfully to them, but their grief was nothing compared to hers. One afternoon when Wolf Running was hunting deer, she rode out of the camp alone.

"Don't worry," Red Hawk advised. "It's not uncommon for a person to seek solitude."

"Ne' hyo warned she would have difficulty," Wolf replied. "She may . . ."

"Wolf, she's no child," the Hawk argued. "Doesn't she have a right to choose?"

"Perhaps she does," Wolf admitted. But he called his friends together, and they spread out through the hills to search for her anyway. Wolf discovered her two days later. Not far from Raven Heart's scaffold, he spotted her lying on a flat shelf of rock. She appeared to be sleeping, but when Wolf touched her shoulder, it was cold and stiff. The sadness had overwhelmed her, and her heart had ceased to beat.

"Ayyyy!" he shouted across the valley. "She, too, is gone!"

Wolf erected a second scaffold beside the first, and he found some satisfaction in the knowledge that two people who had walked the world in harmony would surely find contentment on the other side. As for himself, he felt like a man alone in a winter blizzard.

"You have to put the grief behind you, Nah nih," Little Hawk insisted a few days afterward as the Omissis broke down their lodges and prepared to gather on Smoky Hill River. It was time to remake the world.

"I'll go," Wolf told his brother. "As for the grief, it's a heavy load to move alone."

"We'll help you," Willow Boy said, bringing Wolf a horse. "But you have to promise to take us along when you go to scout Bull Buffalo."

Wolf Running studied his brothers' faces. Their eyes were so alive with expectation. As his once had been. They were losing the boyish softness, too. Little Hawk was plucking chin hairs now, and Willow Boy had marked his twelfth year on the plains. He, too, would soon be plucking hairs.

"We'll hunt," Wolf assured them. "First, though, we must remake the world."

"Naturally," Little Hawk agreed. "You'll come and stay with us when the bands assemble, though. Nah' koa worries about you, and it would be good to have our brother near again."

"I'm a boy no longer," Wolf told them. "I've been too long among the young men to return to Red Hawk's lodge."

The boys frowned, but Wolf lifted their chins.

"No one can step off man's road, See' was' sin mit. You'll soon place your own feet there," Wolf told them. "It's a steep climb sometimes, but having brothers along makes it easier."

The Omissis left Red Shield River that same afternoon. Wolf found the going difficult at first. But as the people continued riding, his grief lost its hold.

"The world continues," Stands Long remarked as he galloped up alongside. "You're not the first man to start his family up Hanging Road. You've done what you could for them. Now it's the living you should concern yourself with."

Wolf recognized the truth in his brother-friend's words and nodded his own agreement.

"Ne' hyo once told me only suffering can purge a man's bad feelings," Wolf said, sighing. "I'll hang from the pole in the New Life Lodge this year."

"It's a hard thing," Stands Long warned.

"The people have suffered, Stands Long. It's for young men like me to invite Heammawihio's generosity."

"Then I'll dance at your side," Stands Long vowed. "We're older now. It's time our chests bore torture scars."

"Ayyyy!" Wolf howled. "We'll do it together then!"

Many times Wolf Running had watched in awe and dread as young men had entered the New Life Lodge to fulfill their vows to hang from the pole. This torture was said to bring a man great power. It also benefited the people. Dancers as young as thirteen had been known to join the suffering, but that was unusual. Most waited until they had passed many summers hunting Bull Buffalo and growing tall in the eyes of their companions.

Wolf Running was tall, but there was no mistaking him for a full-grown man. He remained slender, and even grief had failed to chase the brightness from his eyes. Stands Long appeared even younger, though in fact he was a year older. When the two young friends announced their joint vow, some cheered them. Others scowled.

"It's a serious matter," Hairy Moccasin declared. "There's a great difference between scouting Bull Buffalo and suffering in the New Life Lodge. It's not a boy's game!"

Before being accepted as a dancer, each individual had to secure the services of an instructor, an older man who had previously completed the torture ritual. That wasn't easy, for an instructor gave up some of his personal power to each dancer he helped. Wolf Running approached several men, only to be refused. Finally Flying Squirrel agreed to act as instructor.

"My grandfather believed you possessed great medicine," the Squirrel said as he accepted three ponies as payment for his services. "You're attempting a hard thing. I myself danced when I was young. The suffering is worse. Older men manage it better."

"I could wait," Wolf admitted, "and no one would blame me for it. The people's need is now, though. I can't be older or stronger than I am."

Buffalo Calf was persuaded to sponsor Stands Long. Five Elk Warriors brought ponies to the Calf.

"It's important the two brother-friends share the torture," Split Chin explained. "Heammawihio will see their devotion and watch over all the people."

"Yes, it will be a good thing," the others agreed.

"Then I will accept the obligation," Buffalo Calf replied.

Early the following morning the sponsors of the New Life Lodge met with their instructors. All the ten bands had arrived, and the camps began their four moves. Wolf Running, who knew the ceremony well, took a sweat to purify himself for the dancing. Afterward, Flying Squirrel began the instruction.

On the fifth day of the ceremony, Wolf, Stands Long, and the four older men who had vowed to swing from the pole, faced the rising sun with the lodge-makers. They had already been taught the songs, and their instructors had painted their chests and faces. Now they held out their hands toward the east and began dancing.

The exertion of the dance posed the dancers' first trial. They would also forego food during the ceremony. Those next three days they danced often, especially in the evenings when the people gathered outside the New Life Lodge. Each day the instructors painted new shapes and symbols on the dancers' chests. Between dances the sufferers would chant medicine prayers.

Wolf Running was surprised to discover himself growing stronger through denial. True, his ribs were beginning to show, but he felt new power inside himself. Each night Snow Wolf walked in his dreams. The spirit creature seemed to smile approvingly.

"Be strong," Snow Wolf sang. "The suffering will pass."

The last night, when the instructors attached the rawhide strips to the center pole of the New Life Lodge, Wolf braved himself for the coming pain. As Flying Squirrel cut Wolf's chest and inserted the skewers under the skin, Wolf winced. Like his companions, though, he refused to cry out.

"Anything can be endured," the Squirrel whispered. "Always remember that your pain will bring you power. Your blood will remake the world. The people are glad they have brave hearts to suffer."

Flying Squirrel attached the rawhide strips to the bloody skewers and gave Wolf a reassuring tap on the arm.

"Dance now, Brother," Flying Squirrel instructed.

Wolf nodded and began.

It was a night he would always remember. He had known pain before and was sure to experience worse in the future. There would never be another time when so many admired men stood around, shouting encouragement. From time to time he could hear Red Hawk's deep voice. Burnt Willow Woman, who helped with the singing, directed her words toward him. Later, when others arrived, Wolf heard Willow Boy and Little Hawk.

"Brave up, Nah nih!" they shouted. "Be strong!"

Their words revived him. Whenever his legs began to buckle, someone would urge him on. Across the circle Stands Long danced. The two brother-friends moved back and forth from the pole, singing or blowing their eagle-bone whistles. Each time they neared the center pole, they nodded. Pain shared, after all, hurt far less. And when they swung back from the pole, straining the rawhides, blood flowed down their chests and dripped upon the remade earth.

The dancing and suffering continued a long time. Finally Painted Rock spit out his whistle and shouted toward the sky. With one final effort, he swung back and tore his way free of the pole. The onlookers howled with approval. Relatives then rushed out, took up his weary body, and carried him off to where they could offer him refreshment and celebrate his achievement.

Crow Charger and Two Rivers were next. Like Wolf and Stands Long, they were brother-friends. They had gone so far as to marry sisters, and their children ran and swam together like brothers or cousins. They blew on their whistles, and the shrill notes sent a shudder through the people. Then they broke away from the pole and were carried away.

Wolf gazed across at Stands Long. The two were of the same mind. They intended to make their breakaway together, as the older man had done. Wolf thought to do it now, leaving Owl Claw, an older and more famous warrior, to be last. The Claw seemed to understand. He spit out his whistle and made his try first, though.

"Ayyyy!" the people screamed as Owl Claw tore his way free. "Now only the young ones are left."

Wolf Running gazed out at his elders, feeling unworthy of the honor they were providing him. He hadn't intended on becoming the focus of the dance. Stands Long grinned from across the circle.

Yes, it's time, Wolf thought, closing his eyes. He could see Snow Wolf in his thoughts. All appeared right.

Wolf Running spit out his whistle and screamed. Stands Long did likewise. The two rushed toward the pole, then danced back away, straining at the ropes that held them. Wolf felt a fiery sensation as the skewers tore at his flesh. First one and then the other tore its way through the skin.

"Ayyyy!" Wolf Running howled.

"Ayyyy!" Stands Long echoed.

The two broke free at the same instant. Each fell to the earth, momentarily stunned by the pain and exertion. Instantly hands drew their tired bodies up from the earth and carried them away.

"The young ones have done it!" someone cried.

"Brave hearts are among us!" another added.

"Rest now," Burnt Willow Woman said as she placed a cooling cloth across Wolf's forehead. Flying Squirrel began painting the bloody scars with a numbing paste.

"You did well," Red Hawk said, clasping Wolf's hands.

From somewhere far off Raven Heart's voice whispered approvingly.

"Stands Long?" Wolf asked, rising with great effort.

"His family has taken charge of him," Willow Boy told his brother. "Nah nih, rest up. Nah' koa will see you're fattened up again. Then we'll hunt Bull Buffalo."

Wolf slept long and well. His ordeal had left him weak and feverish, but Burnt Willow Woman provided medicine, and Flying Squirrel brought charms over to chase the fatigue.

Red Hawk was gone most of those next few days, and Wolf Running assumed the Hawk was busy making preparations for the buffalo hunt.

"No, that's for others to do," Red Hawk announced later, when he returned.

"What kept you away then?" Wolf asked.

"I was talking with the shield-makers," Red Hawk explained. "It seemed to me the time was right for young brave hearts to be given proper protection."

Red Hawk then helped Wolf rise. Outside the lodge, perched on a tripod stand, was a shield. Its elk hide cover hit it from view, but Wolf Running knew it was for him. A second shield, likewise covered, stood beside the young man's lodge. Wolf knew Stands Long would also be honored.

The two brother-friends were called before the Elk council two nights later. As stories of their many rescues and brave charges were recounted, Wolf Running waited with great anticipation. Finally he was summoned by the Elk chiefs, Hairy Moccasin and Badger.

"All the people know of the bond between these two good young men," the Moccasin began. "Haven't they always stood tall when our needs were greatest? They've run their enemies and rescued their brothers from peril. Ayyyy! They're Elks."

"Ayyyy!" the others shouted.

"Now we've witnessed another great thing," Badger observed. "These two young men, who have only begun the long walk up man's road, have suffered for the benefit of the people. Their strong hearts carried them past every trial. Now, as we look upon difficult days coming, we must guard our best young men."

"Ayyyy!" the other Elks shouted again. "We must protect them!"

Now Red Hawk carried the first shield toward the fire. He drew back the cover, exposing a round shield, an arm's length in diameter. It was painted blue. A brown beaver stood in the center. Hailstones danced in the surrounding sea of blue.

Badger and Hairy Moccasin presented the shield to Stands Long. It was appropriate. Beaver had long been his spirit guide, and that tenacious creature shared many fine habits with Stands Long.

Wolf gasped when his own shield was revealed. He'd never seen its equal. A red-eyed wolf, white as snow, seemed to leap out of the center. The edges were black, but the color lightened from gray to white as it approached the center.

"It's a good thing our young men can find such protection," Badger announced. "The power of these shields will turn the enemy's arrows. As you carry them, remember the obligation they place on you. Stand tall among others. Lead the brave hearts. Protect the helpless. Run the people's enemies."

"Ayyyy!" The Elks cheered.

"I will," Wolf Running pledged.

"I will," Stands Long vowed.

Between the shield-giving and the start of the hunt, Wolf Running found time to walk by the river. Many young men went there to speak with maidens. Wolf was too shy to speak, but he had no trouble watching.

Stands Long, who usually held back when his brother-friend was near, now stepped forward.

"We'll both of us be wrinkled old men if we wait for you to speak up," Stands Long had complained the day before. "It costs nothing to talk to them. Their fathers won't sharpen a knife so long as you don't sit with them on a blanket or speak of running off."

"Yes," Split Chin chided the youngsters. "Make the proper arrangements first. You have horses to spare a father."

Wolf was in no hurry to take a wife, and he knew few girls that weren't relations. His long days spent hunting and fighting had kept him away from the camps, and those girls he actually saw were strangers.

"That's Summer Wind Maiden," Stands Long observed,

nodding toward a raven-haired beauty with long, slender legs.

"That's Pawnee-killer's daughter with her," Split Chin noted. "Little Fawn."

"She's pretty," Wolf confessed. When she glanced over, he hid his face in embarrassment.

"Look, who's that coming?" Split Chin asked.

"Oh, that's the busy-tongued girl," Stands Long said, sighing. "She'll make your ears burn with her many words."

Split Chin and Stands Long darted away, but when Wolf Running tried to follow, his foot slipped on a loose rock, and he tumbled backward into the path, upsetting the girl so that she spilled her water skins onto his face.

"Ahhhh!" Wolf cried, scrambling away as the frigid water chilled his bare skin. "It's freezing!"

The girl stood there, laughing.

"You look terrified," she said, shaking her head. "Never said a word as they cut your chest, and yet a little river water's upset you!"

"It wasn't just a little," Wolf argued. "And I'm not upset."

"No?" she asked, grinning.

"Surprised," he insisted.

"No more than I am," she grumbled. "Now I have to fill these all over again. My father will be angry."

"You can always say you were attacked," Wolf suggested.

"I wouldn't be far wrong, either," she replied. "You're certain it was an accident? I remember how you and your friends used to spy on us when we were bathing."

"When was that?"

"Five summers past," she answered. "On Platte River. Oh, you thought you were clever, hiding in the willows, but we saw."

"You did?" Wolf asked, shifting his feet nervously. "Your fathers never came to punish us."

"We never told," she said, laughing. "We had our revenge. Two days later, while you boys were swimming, we took your clothes and threw them in the river. You looked like plucked prairie chickens, running bare-skinned through the rocks in search of your breechclouts. It was funny."

"I always suspected our clothes didn't float away by themselves," Wolf muttered.

"And now you know," she told him. "Don't play any more of your tricks on me, Wolf Running. Not unless you want to run along the river naked like before. There's more of you for people to see now, after all."

"It's not proper, a girl talking that way," Wolf complained.

"A girl?" she asked. "You don't know who I am, do you?"

"Should I?"

"Well, our mothers used to carry us side by side on cradle boards when we were little," the young woman said. "You bit me when I was four. I still have a scar from the time you threw a rock at me the summer after that!"

"No," Wolf said, laughing. "You can't be that one. Not the girl with the red paint on her—"

"It's not paint," she interrupted. "I was born with the mark. Old Pronghorn considered it good fortune. And never you mind where it is!"

"You were called Spotted by the Sun."

"Once, when I was a child," she grumbled. "I've long since won a better name. Sun Walker."

"It suits you better," Wolf said, nodding.

"As yours suits you," she replied, picking up her emptied skins. "Now I have to refill these and get along to Ne' hyo's lodge."

"I didn't intend to delay you," Wolf apologized. "Maybe someday when I'm less clumsy, you'll agree to walk here with me. We can talk about our old adventures."

"Wouldn't you rather forget them?" she whispered.

"Maybe we could talk about something else."

"Perhaps," she agreed. "I'm here every day."

"I'll be off hunting Bull Buffalo soon," he told her. "But later, when the camp reassembles to smoke and dry the meat . . ."

"Yes, we'll talk then," she agreed.

After Sun Walker left, Stands Long stepped out from the shadows.

"Wolf, don't lose your ponies to the Pawnees," Stands Long said, grinning. "You might need some of them."

13

WHEN WOLF RUNNING left to scout Bull Buffalo that summer, he was surprised to find himself followed by a party of six young Elks. In addition, his brothers Little Hawk and Willow Boy had come along to tend the spare ponies.

"We're not scouts," Stands Long complained. "We're a war party!"

"You can't expect to ride out on your own anymore," a young man of sixteen summers named Bull Tail argued. "You both carry shields. It's only natural we should seek you out."

"I suppose he's right," Wolf said, sighing. "I do wish a few older men might have come along."

"Or a woman to wipe the younger ones," Stands Long said, laughing.

"That's not what you'd want a woman to do," Younger Dog said, galloping alongside Wolf Running. The Dog was barely fourteen, and he wasn't as tall as Willow Boy.

"Who invited you to come?" Wolf asked. "You should go with your father and hold his horse."

"My sister suggested I come," Younger Dog replied. "Sun Walker Maiden. I think she wanted me to keep you safe for her."

Stands Long laughed loudly, and the others turned their attention to the frail young Suhtai.

"If she worried over my safety, she shouldn't have sent another boy for me to watch," Wolf barked. "If we hadn't come so far from the others, I'd send you back anyway."

"It is a long way back," Younger Dog pointed out.

"Come along then, but stay back with my brothers and watch the ponies. I won't win your sister's favor by getting her brother killed."

"You don't know her very well," Younger Dog remarked. "I've been a torment to her. You'd probably gain her gratitude by having me trampled."

"No, I don't believe she would celebrate anybody's death," Wolf replied. "But I'm not so fond of you or her either that you'd be wise to run risks. I intend to run Bull Buffalo. If you get into trouble, look elsewhere for rescuers."

Wolf Running and his little band of scouts scoured the Smoky Hill country for Bull Buffalo, but they didn't even find fresh dung. Instead they continued northward. Not far from Platte River they struck a dung trail.

"Hair Rope, take Magpie south and bring the others along," Wolf said, waving two of the others back. "We'll continue on."

"Where should we meet you?" Hair Rope asked.

"Where's a good place?" Wolf asked the others.

"Big Island," Eagle Claw suggested. "There's protection from our enemies and good water."

"It's true," Hair Rope agreed.

"It's also close to the Wihio fort," Stands Long noted. "That's where we had all the trouble before."

Wolf Running gazed hatefully eastward. The bluecoats at that fort had killed Raven Heart. Instinctively he hungered for revenge. Just now he had the welfare of others and the success of the hunt to consider first, though. But if the bluecoats rode close, he . . .

"We'd better continue," Stands Long advised. "We should find the herd and keep it in sight until the main band can join us."

Wolf nodded. He then turned his horse and eased it into a gallop. The others followed.

They soon located the herd. It was a disappointment. There were only a hundred animals in all, and half were calves.

"Someone else has already struck these buffalo," Stands Long said, pointing out the few remaining bulls. "We can't shoot these. It's best we leave them."

"Grow strong, Bull Buffalo," Wolf Running called. He then turned back toward the east.

"Where do we go now?" Willow Boy asked, frowning.

"We have to find another herd," Wolf explained. "And we should keep our eyes open. It may be that the Pawnees are out here. See those buzzards circling? Let's have a look."

Wolf pointed to five birds turning wide circles in the sky a half day's ride to the east. Something dead lay out that way. As to what, Wolf was determined to find out.

The little scouting party made its way over one hill and down another. Each time they reached some height, Wolf scanned the distant horizon for Pawnees. He saw nothing most of that day. Finally, though, he saw a sea of bleaching bones. A great herd had been slaughtered there. The birds were still finding a few carcasses to pick at.

"We're too late again," Stands Long grumbled.

"Yes," Wolf agreed. "I wish I hadn't sent the others south. All we can hope to do is find a herd on Platte River."

"The Wihio will be thick there," Little Hawk said,

sighing. "The wagon people use the river road every summer."

"We'll try to avoid them," Wolf pledged. "The people must eat, though. If we have to fight soldiers or wagon people or both, I mean to find Bull Buffalo!"

Fortunately Wolf Running discovered a fresh herd before seeing soldiers or wagons. There were several hundred animals this time. He made camp on a low ridge overlooking Platte River. The next morning he split the scouts into two bands and rode out to strike the herd. He and Stands Long allowed Willow Boy and Little Hawk to make the first kills. Then they waved Younger Dog in. The Dog, small for fourteen, rode better than most. He charged a young bull, counted coup on the beast with the tip of his bow, and then made a killing shot with an arrow through the heart.

The herd ran on toward the river and along to the west. Wolf recalled the second band, and the young men began butchering the six dead bulls that they had killed.

They cooked some of the meat and smoked the rest. Then they swung west along the river toward Big Island. Taking care to keep the herd in sight, Wolf finally led his scouts across the river to the low island. They made a camp there and waited for the rest of the hunters to appear.

Three days and three nights Wolf and the others remained on Big Island, waiting. Finally the main band of hunters arrived. The medicine chiefs organized the hunting prayers, and the men rode out to strike Bull Buffalo. Wolf soon lost count of the many animals that were struck down. As before, the Tsis tsis tas took care to spare the dominant bulls, cows, and calves. Finally the women and children arrived with the pony drags. The Tsis tsis tas women swarmed over the fallen animals, skinning and butchering each one. Drying racks were set up in the nearby hills, and skins were stretched to make robes.

"It's a good day to be alive," Red Hawk remarked when he greeted his sons. Little Hawk and Willow Boy had killed their first bulls. Soon they, too, would set their feet upon man's road.

Wolf Running supposed that, camped on Platte River as they were, it was inevitable that some sort of trouble should find them. No sooner did the bands begin to break up and head back south than a mail wagon rumbled along the river road, bound for Fort Kearny. Wolf saw it, but when his young companions spoke of running it, he responded angrily.

"The Wihio on that wagon have good rifles," Wolf noted. "All you would find is death down there. It's never a good idea to approach Wihio when they're riding or traveling in wagons. They are much calmer when they're camped."

Not everyone listened to him. Corn Dancer and his young friends, Bent Arrow and Little Fork, also saw the mail wagon. Wolf watched in dismay as the three young men galloped toward the wagon, demanding tobacco.

"You have much!" Bent Arrow, whose father was white, called. "We only want a little."

"Fools," Stands Long grumbled as he prepared to ride down to their aid.

"No," Wolf said. "It's time they managed on their own. They never listen to good advice. Now they'll suffer."

It was hard, holding the others back, but it soon became apparent Corn Dancer and the others weren't in any danger. A Wihio fired off his rifle, but his aim was poor, and it was never easy shooting from a moving wagon. Bent Arrow and Little Fork made a charge, and they shot a few arrows into the wagon. Then, howling like crazy men, they galloped back to Corn Dancer.

"They're celebrating!" Stands Long declared. "Do they think they counted a coup?"

"I don't know," Wolf said, laughing. "At least they didn't get themselves hurt."

As Wolf Running soon discovered, though, Corn Dancer and his companions' attack wasn't without consequences.

The Wihio mail wagon raced straight to Fort Kearny. There it was met by the angry-eyed captain who had dealt with Raven Heart in such bad faith. While Wolf Running and his young companions were splashing across to their hunting camp on Big Island, the bluecoats were forming up on Platte River.

Everything was quiet that night. The hunters roasted strips of hump meat over a bed of coals, and overhead countless stars sparkled.

"We'll roll up our lodge skins," Wolf told the other young men who shared the lodge. "A cool wind will make sleeping good tonight."

"Ayyyy!" Willow Boy shouted. "It's a good thing."

"Tired?" Wolf asked his young brother.

"He's sore," Little Hawk explained.

"I need to make a better saddle for myself," Willow Boy muttered. "The old one's too small. It hurts me in all the wrong places."

Wolf couldn't help laughing.

That next morning they woke with the sun. Stands Long stepped out to kindle a cook fire, and Wolf roused the others.

"We're almost finished with this country," he declared. "Soon we'll turn back south and leave this scarred land."

"That's good," Younger Dog said, stretching his arms out to each side. "There are too many Wihio here."

Wolf started out to where Corn Dancer had erected his lodge. The Dancer liked to go his own way, but he often camped close to one group of hunters or another. Currently he had attached himself to Wolf Running. Before Wolf was able to get within a stone's throw of the second lodge, he noticed something in the trees beyond.

"Dancer!" Wolf yelled. "Quick!"

Wolf had already turned and begun to race back to his own camp when the first shots exploded the stillness of the morning. Bluecoats emerged from cover on all sides of the two hunting lodges. The Wihio fired wildly, and Wolf was grateful for that. If they had coordinated their attack better and held their fire until closer, none of the hunters would have escaped alive.

Enough fell anyway. Little Fork stepped out of his lodge, covered only by a blanket. Three bullets struck him, and he fell beside the door. Corn Dancer crawled out the far side and ran toward the ponies. Bluecoats were already taking charge of the animals, though. The Dancer turned and ran off into a stand of willows.

Bent Arrow called for help, but the Fork was dead, and Corn Dancer was no rescuer. The Arrow then crawled out of the lodge, calling to the Wihio in their own language.

"Please don't shoot!" he called. "I'm hurt. I've got no gun!"

Bent Arrow stepped out of the lodge with both hands raised. His side was bleeding, and he was naked. The Wihio soldiers laughed at the boy.

"You the breed wanted tobacco, huh?" a sergeant called.

"I'm a friend," Bent Arrow answered.

The bluecoats shot him anyway.

Wolf Running had collected his little party in a tangle of rock and brush. They had left behind everything but the clothes they were wearing and their weapons. Stands Long had managed to bring along the two shields, but they wouldn't offer much protection against the forty well-armed bluecoats closing in from all sides.

"Heammawihio, help us," Wolf said as he loaded his rifle and glanced out over the sights. The laughing bluecoat sergeant who had shot down Bent Arrow stepped out. Wolf fired at him, but the sergeant moved at the last minute. The shot sent the bluecoats dashing for cover, though.

"One of 'em's got a rifle, Lieutenant!" the sergeant shouted.

"What do we do, Nah nih?" Little Hawk asked fearfully.

"Brave up, See' was' sin mit," Wolf replied. "They haven't killed us yet."

"Not all of us," Younger Dog said, sighing.

There was more firing from the river, and the sound of horses splashing into the water attested to the fact that the Wihio had found still another of the hunting camps.

"They're getting closer," young Pony's Tail said, pointing at a soldier a hundred feet away. Rifle balls began to splinter rocks and branches close by.

"There's only one thing to do," Wolf said, studying the frightened eyes of his young companions. "Stands Long and I will draw their fire. When we do, Eagle Claw, you and the others run toward the river. Stay together. If you have to fight, you have a better chance if there are several of you."

"Why me?" Eagle Claw asked. He was clearly uncertain, but when Wolf eyed the others, he saw nobody was steadier.

"You're eldest," Wolf observed. "We're Elks, remember? We never shrink from the difficult things."

"Yes, we're Elks," Eagle Claw agreed. He grabbed his bow, notched an arrow, and motioned for the others to follow. Wolf Running and Stands Long then darted out into the open, using their shields for protection. A volley of rifle fire scorched the grass. One ball tore a hole in Wolf's shield, and a second nicked his left ear. Three struck Stands Long's shield, but none penetrated the tough hump hide.

"They're gettin' away yonder!" a bluecoat yelled. Rifles turned and fired sporadically. Eagle Claw went down. Younger dog stumbled, but Willow Boy helped him up. The two of them hobbled off toward the river together.

"Ayyyy!" Wolf howled, lifting his rifle like a club and charging the nearest bluecoat. He clubbed the man and continued on toward the river. Stands Long raced off toward Eagle Claw. For the first time in all their hard fights, the brother-friends were separated.

"Watch over him, Heammawihio," Wolf prayed as he leapt onto the back of a Wihio horse. He drove two others in front of him. When he reached the river, he found his brothers, Younger Dog, and Pony's Tail. He turned the three horses over to the boys.

"Nah nih, you're coming with us, aren't you?" Little Hawk asked.

"Later," Wolf told them. "Look after the Dog, Hawk. Pony's tail, watch over them."

The Tail wasn't much older than the others, but he nodded. Wolf then hung his shield over Little Hawk's shoulder and handed Willow Boy his rifle.

"Give me your bow," Wolf said, and Willow Boy instantly passed over the weapon.

"The rifle's good to keep the enemy back," Wolf explained. "For close fighting, the bow's better."

"You should take the shield, Nah nih," Little Hawk argued.

"I'll be back for it," Wolf pledged.

"And if not?" Willow Boy asked.

"My brothers will find a use for it. Now ride fast! Find Red Hawk. Tell the others what's happened here!"

"We will," Pony's Tail vowed. "We'll make the Wihio suffer!"

Wolf slapped the horses into a gallop. Pony's Tail led the way. Willow Boy, with the wounded Younger Dog holding on behind him, followed. Little Hawk trailed along, his hard eyes showing that he was prepared to make a final stand.

"It's not your day to die, little brothers," Wolf whispered after them. He then turned back into the dense brush.

He never was certain exactly how he found Stands Long. Or how Stands Long found him. Perhaps the brother-friends had ridden together so long that an invisible bond now drew them together. However it happened, the two did blunder into each other a short time later.

"Eagle Claw's dead," Stands Long said, nodding somberly. Clearly he was relieved to see a friendly face.

"Younger Dog's hurt," Wolf replied. "Pony's Tail and my brothers will get him away."

"You got them past the bluecoats?"

"I think so," Wolf said, shuddering. "Our people are certain to hear the shooting and ride out to have a look."

"Those that aren't already dead," Stands Long said, pointing toward a column of smoke rising from the far end of the island. "They've hit another camp."

"We should have been ready for this," Wolf said, pounding the ground with his hand. "These Wihio at the fort have bad hearts. They like shooting our people."

"No one could know for certain, Wolf."

"It doesn't make sense. To ride out here and start killing. They could have treated with us. They might have spoken. Instead they come here and start killing. What harm did Eagle Claw ever do to anybody? Bent Arrow and Little Fork chose poorly when they followed Corn Dancer, but they killed no one. Arrow surrendered, and they shot him anyway. His father is white!"

"This talk's doing us no good," Stands Long complained. "What do you want to do?"

"Kill Wihio," Wolf said, his eyes growing red with rage.

"You know we can't do much, just the two of us. It's better to wait and make plans. We can be effective that way."

"It's best," Wolf agreed.

"If we're quiet, we can clearly reach the river," Stands Long said. "Most of the bluecoats have gone down to the other end of the island. They've taken our ponies, but maybe one or two got away."

"Maybe," Wolf said, nodding to his brother-friend.

"There's something else we might do," Stands Long said. "We could take the bodies away."

"Without horses?"

"Not far," Stands Long explained, pointing to the framework of the young men's lodge that still remained beside the cook fire.

Wolf nodded. He then followed Stands Long to where Eagle Claw's body lay. The soldiers had found him, too. The corpse had been stripped of a silver bracelet and all its clothing, but the bluecoats hadn't cut it up like the Pawnees would have done. Stands Long took the body and lifted it onto one shoulder. Wolf Running then dashed toward the lodge poles. He knocked down the frame, grabbed two poles, and picked up a discarded blanket. He dragged the poles into the trees. It was possible to make a platform by resting the poles between the branches of two willows. Stands Long then wrapped the body in the blanket. Together the brother-friends lifted Eagle Claw up and rested him on the makeshift scaffold.

"Rest well, friend," Wolf whispered.

"Now you can begin the long walk," Stands Long added.

"We, too, have a long walk ahead of us," Wolf observed.

"Only if we can't find ponies."

First, though, they located the bodies of Little Fork and Bent Arrow. Those two hadn't been as fortunate as Eagle Claw. Soldiers had dragged the corpses into the empty lodge and set it afire. Now all that remained of the two young men were ugly black carcasses smoldering in the ruin of the lodge.

"We can do nothing for them," Stands Long said, sighing. "Let's go."

"Why burn them?" Wolf asked, rubbing his eyes.

"You can't expect to find answers where Wihio are concerned," Stands Long declared. "You've told me yourself that they're all of them crazy."

"I didn't believe it, though."

"Can you doubt it after today, Wolf? We'll meet and smoke and decide what to do. But whatever the older men say, I will ride out and punish them for this. I promise that."

"It's not a thing best done alone," Wolf noted. "We'll do it together."

14

WORD OF THE Wihio attacks on the Big Island hunting camps spread quickly. As wounded men staggered into their relatives' camps and those who found horses rode to others, the young Tsis tsis tas and Suhtai screamed for revenge.

Wolf Running and Stands Long Beside Him had managed to locate a small herd of ponies captured by the bluecoats. The Wihio soldiers weren't watching them carefully, and the two young men dashed in, climbed atop ponies, and broke past the startled guards.

Wolf led the way southward across Platte River. He and Stands Long had only gone a short distance when a large body of Tsis tsis tas horsemen met them.

"Our brave hearts are still alive!" Pony's Tail shouted, lifting his bow skyward and howling with relief.

"My brothers?" Wolf asked.

"Are well," Little Hawk said, emerging from the others. The boy passed Wolf's rifle and shield back to him.

"Willow Boy?" Wolf said, searching the remaining faces for his smaller brother.

"He remained to look after the Suhtai," Little Hawk explained.

"Younger Dog, you mean."

"Yes, Nah nih. He talks too much, but he's not badly hurt. A bullet through his leg. He'll soon be riding again."

"Now that you're reacquainted," Hairy Moccasin said, "what can you tell us? Are there more coming?"

"I don't know who was camped on the far end of the island," Wolf confessed. "We tended to Eagle Claw's body. He's dead. Little Fork and Bent Arrow were also killed. The Wihio burned them, and there was nothing to do."

"That makes six," Hairy Moccasin said, frowning. "Some more are missing. We'll go along Platte River and see if we can find them."

"And the bluecoats?" Stands Long asked warily.

"Ayyyy!" Split Chin howled. "We'll punish them."

"They'll be back at their fort," Wolf said. "With our ponies. All our other belongings, too."

"There's no attacking a fort," Hairy Moccasin declared. "But we may find foolish bluecoats out riding. We'll punish them."

Wolf Running sighed. He was weary. His limbs ached, and he wondered if he had the strength to fight. His heart pounded furiously, though. He couldn't erase the frightened faces of his brothers from his thoughts. He remembered the burned bodies. Even now Eagle Claw gazed with frozen eyes at the sky!

"What's your plan?" Wolf asked the Moccasin.

"We Elks will assemble on the north bank of Platte River," Hairy Moccasin explained. "The Bowstrings are remaining behind to watch the camps. The Foxes and Crazy Dogs are searching Big Island. They'll join us."

"We're many," Split Chin boasted. "We'll run the enemy!"

It was a fine idea, Wolf Running thought as he and the other Elks splashed across Platte River west of Big Island.

It made sense, bringing the different warrior societies together. It had only one flaw. As soon as the Elks reached the north bank, they were ready to ride out against the enemy.

"We agreed to wait," Hairy Moccasin insisted.

"You agreed," Split Chin said, angrily slapping his thigh. "Wait for the others if you want. Eagle Claw was my wife's cousin. I'll avenge him!"

Most of the younger Elks shouted their agreement.

"It's riding off in small parties that allowed the Wihio to strike us on Big Island," Hairy Moccasin pointed out. "We must make a camp and prepare medicine."

"Yes, we should," Wolf agreed. "It's good to have protection. But once the prayers are spoken and we paint ourselves, I'm going."

"Your father would—" the Moccasin began.

"Ne' hyo's dead," Wolf said, glaring at the Elk chief. "His good words won him a premature death. If we delay, the Wihio will think their treachery's gone unpunished. We must show them they will bleed when our young men are killed."

"Ayyyy!" the others howled.

"Wolf?" Stands Long whispered.

"We pledged ourselves to do it," Wolf explained. "Why wait for the others? We're enough now."

The Elks dismounted and let their ponies rest. The medicine chiefs built up a fire, and a pipe was brought out. After each man smoked, Flying Squirrel warned there were no positive signs of success.

"Yes, we may all die," Split Chin agreed. "We have to try, though. If we don't, the ghosts of our dead brothers will walk among us, asking why."

The Elks formed three war parties. Wolf Running and Stands Long followed Split Chin, who now carried one of the Elk lances. Twenty other good men came along. They rode westward, toward a small dust cloud. Late that afternoon they discovered four Wihio wagons making a camp at the Cottonwood Creek crossing.

"Wagon people," Stands Long grumbled. "I hoped we would find bluecoats."

"They're Wihio!" Split Chin exclaimed. "When did our enemies ever leave our defenseless ones alone? We'll punish these people, and the bluecoats will come out to fight us."

Wolf frowned. There were women and little ones in the wagon camp.

"We can take the mules, at least," Split Chin suggested.

Wolf nodded. He then swung out away from the others and sang a warrior song. Stands Long and Little Hawk joined him.

"It's for you to make the first charge," the Chin said, eyeing the two shield-carriers respectfully. "The rest of us will charge after you strike the first blow."

"Ayyyy!" Stands Long howled. "It's a good plan."

Wolf Running wished it was another day, a time when he might have gone down to the wagon people and smoked with them. He couldn't understand what a strange turn the world had taken. He was preparing himself for death, for killing!

"Remember our dead friends," Stands Long urged.

Wolf grew cold with the memory. He raised his rifle and screamed. Then he kicked his pony into a gallop.

The Wihio wagon people heard the shout and ran out toward the river. Two men hurried to find their rifles. They were still loading them when Wolf swept by, clubbing the first across the head. Stands Long killed the second one, dismounted, and took his rifle. Little Hawk jumped down and grabbed the first man's gun.

Split Chin and the others now descended on the Wihio camp. Several Elks broke through a makeshift barrier and looted the camp. Others ran the horses and mules. Split Chin himself sought out a tall Wihio, drew a knife, and cut the man down. The Wihio was still alive when the Chin took his scalp.

A woman ran frantically away from Corn Dancer and Pony's Tail. A boy, her son perhaps, tried to fight them off. Corn Dancer plunged a knife into the youngster's belly and tore the life out of him. The woman then dropped to her knees, sobbing. Pony's Tail dragged her toward a horse and tied her on. He then made off with his captive.

The other wagon people withdrew to the river. They stood there, defenseless, speaking prayers and awaiting their deaths.

"Enough!" Wolf shouted when Corn Dancer turned toward them. "It's time to leave."

"We should kill them all," the Dancer argued.

"If you had the heart to fight, you should have helped Bent Arrow," Wolf told him. "Go!"

Corn Dancer turned and rode off behind Pony's Tail. Wolf eyed the wagon people angrily.

"Go away," he told them. "Leave our country. Kill no more of our young men!"

He then turned and led the others away.

By nightfall they were back south of Platte River, safely finding rest in the main Omissis camp. By then Wolf Running had learned Corn Dancer had cut the throat of the captured woman, claiming she rode too slowly.

"Do you feel better now?" Red Hawk asked as he made a place for Wolf Running beside his fire. "Has the blood erased the pain?"

"No," Wolf confessed.

"No, Ne' hyo," Little Hawk said, dropping his eyes. "We only killed a few of them. We left the others."

"You killed enough," Red Hawk observed. "Killing darkens the heart. It drives a man from the sacred hoop and upsets the harmony of his life."

"Tomorrow we'll erect a sweat lodge," Wolf suggested.

"That would be a good thing," Red Hawk agreed. "It will restore your heart."

"I only wish the Wihio soldier chief could take a sweat," Stands Long said. "It's his bad heart that needs changing."

"He'll only be angrier," Red Hawk told them. "The eagle chief, Harney, will be back. This time it will be the Tsis tsis tas's turn to suffer. He'll strike in winter, when we're weak, as he did with Little Thunder's people."

"We'll strike first," Wolf vowed. "We'll convince the bluecoats to leave us alone."

"If you see that in your dreams, then I'll believe it," Red Hawk said, frowning. "Until then, words are only words. Fighting wagon boys is one thing. Soldiers are another matter."

Wolf built his sweat lodge. He, Stands Long, Little Hawk, and Willow Boy entered the lodge together. Flying Squirrel performed the ceremony, after which he passed to each of the young men a charm carved from buffalo horn and covered by an eagle's down feather.

"These will keep the needs of the people within your hearts," the Squirrel told them.

It was true. Wolf and the others stayed close to camp, watching for bluecoats, while others went on raiding. Wolf had new equipage to make for his war pony. He had also lost most of his clothing. Burnt Willow Woman provided a good buffalo robe, and Eagle Claw's mother brought him a pair of good moccasins.

"For seeing my son tended," she explained.

The following day a Suhtai warrior arrived with the gift of three ponies.

"A boy's life is worth more, but I'm not a rich man," the Suhtai explained.

"You're Long Dog then," Wolf said. "I know your daughter."

"My son, too," Long Dog said. "He says you saved his life."

"His wound wasn't so much," Wolf insisted. "And it was my brother who carried him to safety."

"Who provided the horse?" the Dog asked. "Remember, we Suhtai guard Is'siwun, the sacred Buffalo Hat. All of us know things. For instance, it's said one of the Elk shield-carriers suffered the loss of many horses at Big Island. A good man who rescues his brothers shouldn't have burdens."

"I accept the gift, Long Dog," Wolf said, smiling.

"Soon the winds will blow cold, and we'll make winter camps. My daughter would not refuse if you asked to sit and speak with her."

"And you?"

"I wouldn't be unhappy to see you, Wolf."

Wolf nodded gratefully. He then took the ponies along to the herd. They were all of them good animals. He kept one and gave the others to Stands Long and Willow Boy.

"And me?" Little Hawk cried.

"You have the Wihio horse you rode from Big Island," Wolf pointed out. "Besides, it was your brother who stayed to watch the Suhtai boy."

"It's true," Little Hawk admitted. "You didn't tend him, though. Stands Long didn't."

"We'll need the ponies," Wolf explained, avoiding Red Hawk's questioning eyes. "The Elks are riding to Platte River tomorrow. We're going along."

"No!" Burnt Willow Woman cried. "This raiding must end. Already women and children have been killed."

"Wihio women and children," Wolf said icily.

"Haven't you seen the little children dragged about our camp? Some are so thin you can count their bones. Little boys who haven't seen five summers. Girls, too. They cry for their dead mothers."

"Our own lodges shelter mourners, too," Wolf noted.

"You should take the little ones back," Burnt Willow Woman said, frowning. "It's too hard on a white skin to be one with the people. Look how your own cousin, Curly, has suffered."

"If these children suffer, it's their fault for being born Wihio," Wolf growled.

"Go! Leave this lodge!" Burnt Willow Woman shouted. "I gave birth to you, but you've become a stranger. Listen to your own words! Is a bear at fault for being born with claws? Should the Wihio shoot us because we're not white?"

"That's just what they do," Wolf said, shuddering.

"Yes, but they can't be blamed for it. They're all crazy. For a Tsis tsis tas to paint his heart so dark is for him to lose his way. Keep your eyes on the sacred path, Wolf Running. What you young men do now will bring only dark days for all of us."

"The dark days will come anyway," Wolf said, rising. "I can't sit blindly and watch the world burn all around me."

He stepped outside into the cool evening. Stands Long, as always, followed.

"It's time we rebuilt young men's lodge," Stands Long whispered. "It's not good, quarreling with your brothers' mother."

"I know," Wolf confessed.

"It's impossible to avoid it if you sleep in Red Hawk's lodge. It's women's nature to argue. It's bad enough there's one man there for them to annoy. Put as many as three there, and trouble's bound to grow from it."

Wolf found himself laughing.

"You're right, Stands Long," he admitted.

"Burnt Willow Woman was right, too," Stands Long added. "Too many innocents are suffering. You have to promise me that when we strike the Wihio, the defenseless ones will be left alone."

"I've never hurt one of them," Wolf said.

"Nor have I. If we ride, though, some will follow who are

eager to kill all the whites. It's a bad thing to harm little ones."

"We'll choose carefully," Wolf promised. "And we'll make certain no innocent is harmed."

They left just after sunrise the following morning. Wolf Running led the way. Stands Long and six other young men followed. Each had pledged not to harm any weaponless enemy. In the end, there were none of them to hurt.

West of the Wihio fort Wolf saw dust. He hoped it was the soldier chief, or even a small patrol. He wanted bluecoats to kill, but instead he saw a small carriage carrying three men. They were the same ones they had fought earlier at Cottonwood Creek, and Wolf shook his head at their misfortune.

The little war party curled around a hill and rode out onto the wagon road. The Wihio leader raised his hand in a peaceful greeting. Wolf raised his own in reply.

"Friends!" the Wihio called out. "We mean you no harm. We're going west, to Utah Territory. Understand?"

"I understand you're in our country," Wolf replied.

"Good, you speak English," the Wihio said, taking out a kerchief and mopping his forehead. "We can give you money to let us pass. Look, we've got lots of it."

The Wihio opened a small chest and held out handfuls of paper notes. Stands Long laughed. Wolf shook his head.

"Go back," Wolf warned. "No more Wihio wagons going into our country."

"We have to go on," the Wihio argued. "The first snows will come soon. Let us go. If you insist on blocking the road, we'll have to send for soldiers."

"Bluecoats?" Stands Long cried, comprehending only part of the warning.

"They'll kill you and all your people," the Wihio warned.

Wolf had heard enough. He rode up to the Wihio carriage and cut the horses loose. Little Hawk came along and ran them away.

"You go back," Wolf ordered.

One of the other Wihio then reached into his coat and drew out a pistol. Stands Long instantly fired his rifle, shattering the Wihio leader's hip. As he fell out of the carriage, the man with the pistol fired at Wolf Running. The bullet glanced off Wolf's shield.

"You only know how to lie!" Wolf shouted, raising his rifle and shooting the man with the gun through the head. The third Wihio jumped out and raced off toward the fort. Pony's Tail galloped after him, rode alongside, and cut the Wihio down with a war club. Pony's Tail then jumped down, cut away the Wihio's forelock, and held it high overhead.

"Ayyyy!" the Tail howled. "I've taken his scalp."

The Wihio leader remained alive. He glanced at his dead companion, then tried to spot the third man.

"Only death will come of this," the Wihio muttered.

"Yes," Wolf agreed, putting his rifle aside. "Yours first. Then mine."

"You do understand," the Wihio muttered.

"It's bound to happen," Wolf said, frowning.

Magpie rode up then. He stared at the bleeding Wihio and notched an arrow.

"Wolf?" he asked.

"It's pointless to leave him alive," Stands Long said, touching his brother-friend's shoulder. "You wouldn't leave a buck to bleed out its life in the woods."

"Do it," Wolf said, turning his eyes away. The arrow flew swiftly. When Wolf turned back, the Wihio was dead. The arrow had struck him in the chest and stopped his heart.

The younger men dragged the bodies out and stripped them. The Wihio leader had some silver coins and a beautiful gold watch. Pony's Tail helped himself to them.

Magpie took the pistol. He also found a box full of papers. Wolf suggested emptying the papers and using them to burn the carriage.

"And the paper money?" Stands Long asked. "It would buy us many good things."

"Where?" Wolf asked. "At Fort Kearny?"

"Your friends, the traders at Fort Laramie, would sell us powder and rifles," Stands Long suggested.

"Not for this money," Wolf said, sighing. "They would know it came from these dead men. It would be like with Fire Wolf. A long stay in a dark place. Then I, too, would be dead. Burn the paper money, too."

Stands Long took out his tinder pouch and put some wool beside the money. He then touched his knife to a flint slab. A spark fell into the wool, and the resulting flame caught the paper on fire. Soon the carriage was smoking.

"Let's go," Wolf urged his young companions. "The soldiers will come and investigate."

"Good. We'll fight them, too," Pony's Tail vowed.

"We're too few," Wolf argued. "It's time to leave. Come on."

Wolf Running turned south, away from the river. Stands Long hung back, driving the others along. They were well clear of the killing site when the soldiers appeared.

"Come up and fight us!" Pony's Tail shouted from the hillside.

"Show us how brave you are!" Magpie added.

Wolf watched the nervous bluecoats collect the naked bodies. They didn't bother with the burning carriage. Hurriedly they returned to the fort, leaving the taunting Elks on the hillside above them.

"Come on," Wolf called to the others. "It's time we left."

"We killed no innocents," Stands Long said.

"And we won no honor," Wolf said, swallowing hard. "What does it gain us, this killing?"

"Revenge," Magpie declared.

"Satisfaction," Pony's Tail added.

"Does it?" Wolf asked. "Or are we fighting the wrong enemy?"

15

THAT AUTUMN THE southern bands traveled to the trading fort William Bent had established on Arkansas River. The Wihio distributed the promised treaty goods there, and the eight southern bands were eager to receive what was due to them. The Omissis and Suhtai, the two northern groups, moved their camps above Platte River. They sent a delegation into Fort Laramie to see if the bluecoats would deliver the goods due them by the Horse Creek treaty.

"It's no good going there," Split Chin argued. "Remember how it was with the wagon man's miserable cow. With Fire Wolf, too. The bluecoats will chain up our men and hold them there."

"We need the food and blankets promised by the treaty-signers," Hairy Moccasin objected.

"And we need to find out what's on the minds of the Wihio chiefs," Red Hawk declared. "If they intend to fight us, we can prepare. If they want to speak of peace, we should be there to listen."

For days the older men debated whether to go to the fort or stay away. Finally Hairy Moccasin agreed to lead a group of Omissis to the fort.

"If there's trouble, come and rescue us," the Moccasin pleaded. "If everything's as it should be, I'll send a man back with the good words each day. If no one comes, though, you'll know the Wihio hearts have turned against us."

"Who will you take along?" Red Hawk asked.

Hairy Moccasin glanced around him. No volunteers offered their help.

"It's for me to do then," Red Hawk said, nodding somberly. "I don't speak the Wihio tongue well. We'll need someone to speak for us."

The older men turned to Wolf Running.

"I'll go," Wolf muttered. "Watch over my brothers, Stands Long."

"Your brothers can watch themselves," Stands Long insisted. "They're no longer children."

"Even Morning Hawk?" Wolf asked.

"We'll look after him," Little Hawk promised. "Nah' koa lets him sit with us and listen to stories. It's time we made him a boy's bow and taught him to shoot rabbits."

"Yes, it is," Wolf agreed.

"Then I'll go along," Stands Long told Hairy Moccasin. "We should take along some others, especially if we're to send riders back."

"It's for the young Elks to do," Pony's Tail said. "We'll do it."

The other young men agreed.

Once the leaders had been selected, a few lodges of women and children were also selected to come along.

"If we send only armed warriors, the soldiers will consider it an attack," Hairy Moccasin had argued. The Moccasin invited his own relations along, and several other families agreed to join them.

"It might be better for all of us to go," Corn Dancer grumbled once everything had been decided. "They wouldn't dare attack all our people."

"And if Harney's hundreds are there?" Wolf Running asked. "No, it's better to discover their plans before endangering the entire band."

Long Dog was one of the Suhtai selected to ride to the fort. Sun Walker Maiden came along, but each time Wolf tried to find her at nightfall, she was off helping her mother.

"Is she avoiding me?" Wolf Running asked Younger Dog.

"No," the boy said, laughing. "She's had her eyes on you most of the day."

"She never stops talking about you," the Dog's smallest brother, a boy of ten summers named Rabbit, added.

"Nah' koa's keeping her busy," a third brother, twelve-year-old Spring Fox, said. "I think she's worried we may lose our sister. She helps with the cooking and water gathering. A boy would easily be married off. Daughters are a different matter."

Wolf found himself laughing at the youngsters. He was reminded of the earlier days when he, Little Hawk, and Willow Boy all shared Red Hawk's lodge. So many boys could be a trial for anyone!

The first chill winds of the season blew the afternoon the Tsis tsis tas and Suhtai delegation approached Fort Laramie. Wolf Running and Stands Long rode ahead of the main band. Instead of approaching the soldier buildings directly, they sought out the Logan brothers' store.

"Lord, would you believe it?" Andy Logan exclaimed with the two young Omissis appeared at his door. "Walker! Walker, come see who's come to visit!"

"I'm busy stockin' shelves, Andy," Walker answered. "Who the devil's there now?"

"Best come see, little brother. You wouldn't expect 'em in a hundred years."

Walker Logan was mumbling under his breath when he

stepped out of a back room and gazed at Wolf and Stands Long.

"Cheyennes," Walker said, anxiously glancing around the store.

"You, too, have changed some," Wolf said, noticing Walker now boasted a fuzzy yellow-brown mustache.

"Wolf, we didn't figure you likely to travel hereabouts again," Walker said, staring out the door. When he spied a soldier approaching the store, he motioned Stands Long inside and closed the door.

"We came to treat with the agent," Wolf said. "We don't need to hide."

"Wolf, some of these soldiers have just come out here. They're like as not to shoot an Indian on sight. Especially Cheyenne. Don't you know you've got the whole country stirred up against you? All them attacks on wagon trains. Killin' women and kids! Agent Twiss won't be any too glad to see you himself."

"Then you have to talk to him," Wolf said, frowning. "We are coming in to talk. If there's danger, we'll turn away."

"That might be best," Andy advised.

"If we do go back," Wolf said, pausing to swallow hard, "there will be no second trip. Only war."

"Andy, maybe you best close up the windows," Walker said, taking off an apron and tossing it onto the counter. "See if you can find something for our friends here to eat. Guess I've got a trip to Mr. Twiss's house to make."

Wolf clasped the Wihio's hand, but Walker only laughed.

"How many times you saved my life, Wolf?" Walker asked. "Twice I know of for certain. I guess I can walk across the way for you."

While Walker was gone, his brother Andy closed the shutters and bolted the door. He then offered his guests bread and dried beef.

"Sorry we ain't got anything better, friends, but we can't

seem to keep a cook," Andy explained. "They run away and marry some soldier."

"You don't have a wife?" Stands Long asked. "A man as old as you?"

"We don't marry children, we Wihio devils," Andy said, laughing. "Truth is, I had my eye on the captain's sister, but he sent her back East when this latest trouble stirred itself up."

"You should come out and look over the Suhtai girls," Stands Long suggested. "They work hard, and some aren't too ugly. Wolf has picked one."

"Wolf?" Andy asked.

"I spoke with her once at the river. Stands Long would send me to her father with horses," Wolf said, shaking his head.

They might have discussed wives a little longer, but there was a knock on the door.

"Open up, Andy, and don't take too long," Walker urged.

Andy trotted over and swung back the bolt. Walker slid in through the door. The Laramie Indian agent, Thomas Twiss, followed.

"I didn't half believe it," Twiss said when Andy closed the door and secured the bolt. "I know you, don't I, young man?"

"Wolf Running, son of Raven Heart," Wolf said, touching the agent's outstretched hand.

"Raven Heart," Twiss said, nodding. "How's that fine fellow? Chasing buffalo, no doubt."

My father's chased no buffalo since the bluecoat soldiers shot him at Fort Kearny," Wolf said, glaring at the agent.

"Sorry," Twiss said. "I hadn't heard about that."

"The army didn't tell you it was killing Tsis tsis tas?" Wolf asked. "I would think our agent might be interested."

"I am," Twiss insisted. "I'm here, aren't I? I might have sent the soldiers instead."

"Come on now," Walker pleaded, motioning toward a

nearby table. "None of us is getting anywhere. If you're going to sit here complaining or calling each other names, we'll get nowhere."

"True enough," Twiss agreed. "I'm sorry about your father, Wolf Running. Raven Heart was a man who'll be missed. He spoke straight, and you knew he meant to stand by what he said. He spoke for peace. It's sure to be harder to come by if he's gone."

"He's not gone," Wolf said, sighing. "Only dead."

"So his son's standing in for him, eh? You did ride in to arrange a talk, didn't you?"

"To insure the safety of our chiefs," Wolf explained. "They have come as the treaty says to receive the giveaway. They also mean to talk about the soldier attacks on our people."

"But they're properly concerned about approaching the fort," Twiss said, sighing. "How far away are they?"

"A short ride," Wolf told him.

"Could they come in and make camp tonight, here, near the fort?"

"They could," Wolf said. "If they aren't attacked."

"Take me along when you ride out to tell them," Twiss suggested. "I'll lead the way. Even the stupidest lieutenant on the post knows better than to shoot at me!"

"It's a good plan," Walker said.

"Yes, a good plan," Wolf agreed. "We'll leave now."

"Not for just a bit," Twiss said, grinning. "Let me go ready my horse. By then the guard will come in for supper. Be only a couple of men out and about then, and they won't be paying any attention to a few riders."

"He knows what he's talkin' about, Wolf," Andy said. "He went out a while back to treat with the Oglalas."

"We can trust him then?" Wolf asked after Twiss slipped out the door.

"As much as you can trust any of us," Walker said, gripping Wolf's arm. "Be careful. There are hothead soldiers out here that make Lieutenant Grattan seem downright friendly by comparison."

"Yes," Wolf said, frowning. "We've seen such at Fort Kearny."

In a short while a handful of soldiers crossed the parade ground. Twiss mounted his horse shortly thereafter, and Wolf led Stands Long outside. The two Omissis joined the agent and escorted him to the main party. Twiss greeted Hairy Moccasin and the other principal men warmly. He then led them back toward the fort. Hairy Moccasin made his camp on the river a long stone's throw from the fort buildings.

The next day Twiss and two soldier chiefs came out to talk. The soldiers seemed nervous. Twiss was relaxed. He rolled out a blanket and sat across from Hairy Moccasin. The soldiers brought small chairs, which they erected behind the agent. Wolf frowned when he saw the soldiers were armed. It was a sign of disrespect to discuss peace while carrying weapons.

"Before we get started, friends," Twiss said, "the soldiers gave me a list of questions to ask. These are their principal grievances. If you want, we can discuss them now or later. Either way, I want you to explain your side of the story so that I can share it with the chiefs back in Washington."

Wolf translated for the chiefs. Hairy Moccasin suggested hearing the soldiers first. Wolf told Twiss as much, and the soldiers started.

"Let's begin with the problem at Upper Platte Bridge," the first soldier said.

"The shooting of our people?" Wolf asked. "The taking of Fire Wolf to the fort, where he died?"

"Wait," Twiss pleaded as Wolf glared angrily at the soldiers. "Be specific, Lieutenant. If you have a charge to make, state it."

"The Cheyennes stole four horses," the lieutenant declared.

"No one, until the day we came to the bridge, spoke of stealing," Wolf replied. "I know. I was there myself. We were asked to bring four horses that had wandered away. We found three. Those we brought in. Instead of giving up the promised reward, our young men were detained. One was killed. Another was shot. A third taken captive. As to horses, the soldiers took the ones we brought to turn over and then attacked the Suhtai camp on Platte River."

"We were searching for the other thieves," the lieutenant insisted.

"Now, what about the attacks on the wagon people?" Twiss asked.

Wolf translated the question, and Hairy Moccasin replied energetically. Wolf translated the reply for Twiss.

"Hairy Moccasin reminds you that our people have always had trouble with the wagon people coming along Platte River," Wolf explained. "They shoot off their guns, killing buffalo we need to fill our bellies in winter. They bring sickness to kill the children. They spoil the rivers and streams by throwing rotting meat in it.

"Now, whenever we ride near a wagon, people shoot at us. Many of our young men have died in this way. When the chiefs try to stop it, they are accused of attacking. If a wagon party loses a cow or a horse, we're accused of stealing it. Always the soldiers are eager to punish us if we defend ourselves.

"My own father," Wolf added on his own, "answered the soldier chief's invitation to come to Fort Kearny and talk. He was shown Lakota arrows, old and withered, and accused of attacking a wagon band. Then a young Lakota who rode with us was chained. What justice is this? If I have a bullet in my leg, should I kill the first man I see with a rifle?"

The soldiers muttered angrily, but Twiss motioned for silence.

"Do you know anything about the shooting of Raven Heart?" Twiss asked them.

"From what I've been told, the Cheyenne chief was running away," the first lieutenant replied.

"And the Sioux?" Twiss asked. "Did you have any real evidence that he attacked the wagons in question?"

"I see," the lieutenant said, rising angrily and kicking his chair out of the way. "You plan to take the word of heathens and murderers?"

"I intend to listen to anything they say," Twiss explained. "And to hear the army's arguments, too."

"We'll speak to you later, if you don't mind, sir," the second officer broke in. "I don't believe we're comfortable with those young bucks staring down at us."

"They're not the ones with the pistols," Twiss noted.

"If I was you, I'd be glad some white men with pistols were handy, Mr. Twiss. Lieutenant Grattan rode out to treat with these folks, and he got chopped up pretty bad."

"Grattan met with the Sioux," Twiss pointed out. "And I'm not any too certain he wasn't the cause of that fight."

The soldiers stormed off. Twiss, however, had more questions. He wanted to know about the mail wagon, the fight on Big Island, the other attacks on the wagon people. Hairy Moccasin replied to every inquiry. When he explained there were three white women and several children among the main Suhtai camps, Twiss brightened.

"If you would bring them in and turn them over, it would go far toward calming even the soldiers," Twiss explained. "They aren't hurt? They haven't been . . . bothered?"

Wolf didn't understand what the agent meant. The captives were in good health.

"Has anyone been with the women?" Twiss asked.

Wolf asked Long Dog, but he really didn't know. One of the women answered, "They've been with each other." Wolf translated for Twiss.

"There are a few Sioux and Cheyenne detained by the

army," Twiss said. "I'll make certain they're set free when you bring the captives in."

"That would be a good trade," Hairy Moccasin agreed.

"I can't bring back the dead," Twiss said, studying the solemn faces of the others. "I wish that were possible, but it's not. What we can do, all of us, is make sure the violence stops. We can have peace again if we all try."

Wolf translated, and the chiefs agreed that would be good.

"We have many things to ponder now," Hairy Moccasin said. "We'll send word to the others. Soon we'll talk again."

"Yes, soon," Twiss urged.

Actually, Twiss met with the Tsis tsis tas and Suhtai leaders twice more that autumn. As the Dirt in the Face Moon hung low in the evening sky, the council of forty-four sat down with the agent and completed an agreement for a setting aside of differences between the white government and the confederation known as the Cheyenne.

Wolf sat beside the chiefs, translating Twiss's words. The agent asked only four things. The Tsis tsis tas agreed to each. Attacks against the wagon people on Platte River would stop. All Wihio traveling through parts of the country pledged to the people would be allowed to come and go as friends. The Tsis tsis tas would not start any trouble with other tribes. Finally, no attack against the bluecoats was to be made.

It was a strong promise, and Wolf considered it a good thing that all the chiefs were present. Many young men would be hot for fighting the bluecoats and raiding the Wihio wagons when summer returned. It would take all the persuasive powers of the chiefs to stop trouble.

Agent Twiss, too, faced many obstacles.

"The army will make things difficult for all of us," he explained. "They would prefer to kill every Indian."

"Every one?" Wolf asked with wide eyes. It was beyond imagining.

"They won't be the ones to decide, my friends. If I have to sit down with the President myself, I'll see a good peace comes of our talks. This I promise."

Wolf translated, but the chiefs read Twiss's sincerity. It was etched on his face and reflected in his eyes.

"He's a good man," Walker assured Wolf as the Tsis tsis tas prepared to ride back to their winter camps. "You can trust him."

16

THE OMISSIS SITUATED their winter camp far to the south that troubled year. Most of the band formed a large camp circle along Turkey Creek, midway between Platte River and the Arkansas. It was a well-sheltered region, and camps there suffered far less than those in the mountains farther north.

Wolf Running busied himself those final days before the first snows hunting deer and elk. Often he would take one of his brothers along. Sometimes Long Dog's sons joined them from the nearby Suhtai encampments. Those were good days, full of adventure and learning. Both Wolf and Stands Long enjoyed instructing the youngsters. As Wolf showed the boys how best to stalk deer or make a killing shot on a windy day, he was carried back to earlier, better days.

"You were never as young as we are, Nah nih," Willow Boy complained when Wolf began a story of his own boyhood hunts. "Even when you were smaller, you had an old man's eyes."

"No," Wolf argued.

"They're right," Stands Long said. "You were born old, I think."

"Naturally," Wolf said, attempting to go along with their jest. "Everyone knows I sprang into the world full grown and ready to lead the buffalo hunt!"

Such lighthearted joking was common among the young Tsis tsis tas, but sometimes Wolf Running thought his brothers weren't far wrong. He did feel the weight of great responsibilities, and he couldn't recall a time when they weren't there. Maybe it was being tall that always marked him as a boy to notice. More probably it was walking the world in Raven Heart's shadow.

There was one advantage to standing tall in the eyes of others. Where another young man of fifteen snows might have been turned away when he appeared, courting flute in hand, outside Sun Walker Maiden's lodge, Long Dog welcomed Wolf Running warmly.

"Long Dog, I've come in hopes of walking with your daughter," Wolf announced the first time.

"Ah, I was wondering if you'd ever come," Long Dog said.

"A man has responsibilities," Wolf explained.

"Naturally," Long Dog said, grinning. "She may keep you waiting a time. For days, she's asked her brothers if today you'd finally come. I've watched her leap up and run out to the creek each time a horse splashed across the ford. She talks of nothing else. I'll call her, but she'll probably pretend to be annoyed. That's the way these women torment you."

"Maybe I'll go away and come back later," Wolf said loudly enough that anyone an arrow's shot away could hear.

"Don't let him run away, Ne' hyo," Sun Walker called. "I'm getting a blanket. A warm one."

"You have to let these women know who's in charge," Long Dog whispered. "Once they find they can order you around, there's no living with them."

"I'll try to remember," Wolf promised.

Sun Walker emerged from her father's lodge dressed in a beaded dress of yellow elk hide. She wore her hair long, with a shell comb decorating one side.

"Hello," Wolf said, trying to keep his hands from betraying his nervousness. "Maybe we can walk?"

"We can walk," she agreed. "We can also sit and talk. I brought a blanket to keep us warm."

He eyed the fine cloth blanket. The trader who sold it would have demanded many buffalo hides for it.

"My grandmother gave it to me," Sun Walker explained.

"I don't remember my grandparents," Wolf confessed. "Our family has never been long-lived."

"It may be different for you."

"Maybe," Wolf said, shifting his feet. He began sweating as she stepped closer. It was odd he should be so uneasy when she seemed to be doing it so naturally. Suddenly she stumbled on a rock and came flying at him. Surprised, Wolf barely had a chance to brace himself before she collided with his chest. They both fell over the cooking pots and rolled against the lodge. Kettles and pots clanged. A dog barked. Three brothers spilled out of the lodge, eager to investigate.

"It's only Wolf," Rabbit announced. "He's fainted."

"Are you certain our sister hasn't killed him?" Younger Dog asked. "She was angry enough this morning to do it."

"Oh, he's come now," Spring Dog observed. "Brought a flute, too."

Wolf managed to crawl out from under a kettle and sit up. He was totally humiliated. Sun Walker glared at her brothers, and they scrambled out of range. She then turned on Wolf.

"Clumsy!" she shouted.

"Clumsy?" he cried. "I wasn't the one who fell."

"So it's my doing, is it?"

"Yes," he told her. "I admit I wasn't very clever. I might

have caught you, but I was so surprised. You seemed so at ease."

"I did?" she asked, sitting up. "I felt like a fawn taking its first steps."

"You looked like one, too," Wolf said, laughing.

"You're having a good time, I see," she growled.

"Set the blanket down," he suggested. "Let's walk to the river. We're both of us anxious, and sitting here with your brothers listening to every word won't help."

Wolf heard sighs of disappointment inside the lodge. He nevertheless enjoyed the privacy of the river walk.

They moved back and forth along the river a dozen times or more. Sun Walker talked. Wolf listened. He always thought that a person should do what he can do best. Obviously Sun Walker agreed.

He learned a great deal about her that afternoon. She loved to ride, was a good cook, and could perform several medicine cures.

"I can mend torn clothes, make soft moccasins, and speak the old sacred Suhtai prayers," she told him. "They provide a man with strong medicine."

"Such a valuable wife would require many good ponies," Wolf observed. "I'm no longer rich in horses."

"You can get them by raiding the Pawnees," she suggested.

"The chiefs have pledged to make no raids on the other tribes," Wolf told her.

"That will never last," she argued. "The Pawnees always hunt Bull Buffalo in our country. They'll steal our horses and raid our camps. We'll have to strike back."

Wolf nodded. It was possible. When he spoke to Stands Long about it, his brother-friend frowned.

"Surely," Wolf said, "if someone else starts trouble, we won't be blamed."

"Who was blamed for the Grattan fight?" Stands Long

asked. "For the trouble at Platte River? For Big Island, even."

That long winter, as Wolf Running waited for the Big Wheel Moon that would mark the end of his sixteenth year upon the earth, he thought often of the future. He discussed it with Stands Long and his brothers. And he spoke of it with Sun Walker Maiden.

"As a man grows older," Red Hawk finally told him, "he discovers he can never be certain what lies over the next hill. It's not important. He prepares for today, leaving tomorrow alone. The world is a sacred hoop, remember? As long as a man remains at harmony with himself and his world, he should fear nothing."

"And if the Wihio come again?" Wolf asked. "If they bring their thunder guns and send all the soldiers against us?"

"We'll fight them," Red Hawk said. "Maybe we'll win. Maybe we won't. Nothing lives long, after all."

Wolf frowned. It was easier for an older man to think that way. A young man of sixteen summers was only tasting the first sweetness of living. That was hard to give up.

As winter began to fade into memory, Snow Wolf visited Wolf Running's dreams once more. The spirit creature burst out of a scarlet sunrise, howling with new fury. At first Snow Wolf appeared bewildered, lost. Then it spied a small child swimming in a shallow stream.

For several moments the dream was a fog. It was impossible to determine if the child was Tsis tsis tas, Pawnee, or even Wihio. It might have been a boy or a girl. Then the sound of many horses splashing into the water drew the little one's attention. He scrambled to the bank and beheld an army of bluecoats.

Only now did Wolf recognize the child. Younger, smaller certainly, but clearly the boy was none other than a younger image of himself.

"Ayyyy!" the child shouted, waving his weaponless arms

defiantly at the intruders. They continued on, trampling his frail body and leaving it shrouded by a cloud of dust thrown up by their passing ponies.

Wolf awoke shivering. His body ached. He felt each hoof that had pounded the breath out of his body.

"Nah nih?" Willow Boy asked, crawling over beside him. "What's wrong?"

"A dream," Wolf explained.

"You're bleeding," Willow Boy said, touching his brother's lip. Wolf now tasted the blood. He had bitten both his lip and tongue.

"What's happened?" a weary Stands Long asked, rising from his sleeping pallet. "Wolf?"

"I had a dream," Wolf explained.

"It was the white wolf then?" Stands Long asked. "You saw something?"

"Yes, I saw something," Wolf admitted. "But I understand none of it."

The others sat with him for a time. Willow Boy provided a warm buffalo robe, which Wolf Running used to fend off a chill.

"Can you tell us?" Stands Long asked.

"It's too confusing," Wolf said, shivering from a new, inner chill.

"Tomorrow you should seek out Flying Squirrel," Stands Long advised. "He'll help you make sense of it."

Wolf promised to do so, and the others returned to their beds. He did his best to find some peace that night, but he was unable to close his eyes. His ears rang with the sound of horse hooves, and he feared the dream would return.

Wolf was up long before the sun that next morning. He waited at a low hill overlooking Turkey Creek for the rising sun. As he had done countless times, Wolf kindled a small fire and made the morning prayers. Only afterward did he go to the river and wash himself. The water was biting cold, and he couldn't stay in it for long, but it sharpened his thinking. He wanted to be alert when he met with Flying Squirrel.

Wolf Running approached the medicine chief's lodge quietly, with reverence. He wore his best shirt and wrapped himself in a fine elk robe. He wore three coup feathers in his hair, and he brought the last two spare ponies he possessed.

Ten paces from the medicine-maker's lodge, Wolf paused. Flying Squirrel stepped out of his door and nodded.

"I've been expecting you," the Squirrel said. "Leave the ponies and come in."

"I'll find a boy to take charge of them," Wolf offered. "They're a gift."

"It's not appropriate," Flying Squirrel said. "Take them back or find a boy to hold them. You need no gift this time."

Wolf was baffled. He had been taught to bring a gift when consulting a medicine chief. Nevertheless, he trusted Flying Squirrel to know what was proper. He turned and led the horses back to the pony herd. He returned later, alone. Flying Squirrel stepped out to greet him again.

"Ah, that's better," the Squirrel said. "Come in. Let's talk."

Wolf stepped inside the lodge. The Squirrel's wife, Medicine Otter Woman, and their three children greeted him. They then stood up and silently made their way outside.

"How did you know I was coming?" Wolf asked after sitting beside a small fire alongside Flying Squirrel.

"How does a sparrow know to fly?" the medicine chief asked.

"Do you also know Snow Wolf visited my dreams?"

"No, but I felt you had something to ask. A voice seemed to whisper through my head, saying you were troubled. It's like that sometimes when a man instructs another how to suffer in the New Life Lodge. We'll soon be remaking the earth again. At this sacred time, a sufferer holds his greatest power."

"Is that why I dreamed?" Wolf asked.

"Some people dream all the time," Flying Squirrel told him. "But for your spirit brother to visit? That's another thing."

"Have you, too, seen the vision?"

"No, you must tell me, Wolf. Don't say only what you saw, either. Tell me what you felt, what you heard. Sometimes the meaning is hard to find. I must know everything."

"I'll share what I remember," Wolf said, sighing. "I'm confused by it."

"When we're finished, maybe you'll see it more clearly."

"I hope so," Wolf said, swallowing. He then recounted the odd vision. He included the pain he felt and the noise of horse hooves that still haunted his thinking.

"You're certain they were bluecoats on the ponies?" Flying Squirrel asked afterward.

"I saw that clearly," Wolf replied.

"Soldiers are coming," the Squirrel said, gazing sadly into the flames of the fire.

"What does it mean, though? The fact that I was a child."

"And weaponless," Flying Squirrel noted. "It means you're helpless to stop them."

"We're not helpless!" Wolf insisted.

"We can fight them when they come, of course. But we can't stop them from riding. It's what we've always feared, isn't it? The Wihio soldiers will strike our camps."

"Those fears are in the past," Wolf Running argued. "We made peace with the Wihio. All the chiefs agreed to end the fighting, and the Wihio agent, Twiss, promised we'd have no more trouble."

"Wihio promises are nothing," Flying Squirrel said bitterly. "How many promises have they broken? When they first came onto the plains, they said they wanted a single road. Now their roads cut our country everywhere. They wouldn't kill game, but they do. They wouldn't build forts, but they have. As I said, their promises are nothing!"

"What's to be done then?" Wolf asked.

"Nothing," Flying Squirrel answered. "What's sure to happen can't be stopped."

"We should ride out and meet with the soldiers," Wolf suggested. "Make another agreement."

"Nothing will change," Flying Squirrel insisted. "I know that much from my own dreams. Brother, don't you understand that's why I couldn't take your horses? I have no power to help you out of this dilemma."

Wolf frowned. Finally, he got to his feet and left the medicine chief's lodge. He had to find some way of changing things. If he was truly powerless, why had Snow Wolf come into his dreams?

The ten bands assembled on Beaver Creek that summer to remake the earth. Wolf's fears were compounded as the southern bands arrived.

"There are soldiers on Arkansas River," the southern people explained. "Some of the Wihio traders have told us to stay near Bent's Fort. The bluecoats intend to fight us. They can't protect us elsewhere."

"What about the agreement with Twiss?" Wolf asked.

"That man's no soldier," Swift Antelope pointed out. "He holds no sway over the soldier chiefs."

Wolf Running wondered if that was possible. Twiss had been so certain!

"Perhaps the people in the south haven't been told," Wolf suggested. "We made peace on Platte River. It's been winter, and riders from the north would have trouble reaching the soldiers down south."

"The Wihio sends his messages fast," Buffalo Horn pointed out. "There's no misunderstanding, Wolf. Only deceit."

"Twiss wouldn't lie," Wolf argued.

"Maybe he was being truthful, but is he in charge?" Stands Long asked. "Remember the soldiers who first met with us. They had only anger in their eyes. We heard no good words coming from them."

It was an impossible situation, Wolf thought. The people had promised so much. Now it appeared even that wasn't enough!

News of new soldier camps in the southern country and on Platte River continued to arrive as the earth-makers organized the New Life Lodge ceremony. That summer eighteen young men vowed to hang by the pole. Ten of them made the vow to safeguard the people from the expected bluecoat attack.

If he hadn't recently suffered in the New Life Lodge, Wolf would have joined the others. Instead he and Stands Long kept a close watch over the assembled camps. He worried the soldiers would strike before the ceremony was complete, before the power of the people was reborn.

No bluecoats arrived, though. The dancing and feasting revived the spirits of the people, and the soldier societies met to organize the buffalo hunt.

"Your fears were unfounded," Hairy Moccasin told Wolf when the young men prepared to ride out and scout Bull Buffalo.

"The dream was real enough," Wolf told the chief. "I saw what I saw. The bluecoats may come later, but they'll come. Good men should hang back and watch the defenseless ones."

"We'll be prepared," Hairy Moccasin assured the scouts. "But it's important you do nothing to begin a fight. Avoid the wagon roads. Don't harm any Wihio you see. And if soldiers come into our country, let them pass through as friends."

"And when they start shooting at us?" Stands Long asked.

"Ride away," Hairy Moccasin pleaded. "Don't give them a chance to kill you."

Not everyone agreed with the peace policy of the chiefs, though. Many younger men spoke loudly for fighting.

"Are we men?" Corn Dancer cried. "Should we stand still while the bluecoats come and cut our manhood from us? When do we fight? We're strong. Let's run them!"

"We can decide about this later," Red Hawk argued. "It's time to hunt. We'll watch for soldiers, but the important thing is to feed the people."

"Yes," others agreed. "We hunt first."

"We'll hunt," Corn Dancer agreed. "But when the blue-coats come, we'll fight."

The young men shouted and waved their bows. The chiefs stood little chance of controlling so many. If the Wihio soldier chiefs were determined to start a fight, there would be Tsis tsis tas to greet them.

17

BULL BUFFALO WAS generous that summer, and the hunting went well. Wolf Running and the other scouts had located two large herds on Red Shield River, and the main Tsis tsis tas and Suhtai camps had now moved to join them there. The killing and butchering occupied much of each day. Gradually the camps moved up Turkey Creek as the herds migrated northward.

The Green Grass Moon had begun to pass when Hairy Moccasin sent for Wolf Running.

"There are stories of soldiers coming down from Platte River," the Moccasin told him. "I want to send men north to see."

"I'll go," Wolf volunteered eagerly.

"Take only a few young men with you," Hairy Moccasin advised. "No more than you can control."

"Stands Long will come," Wolf said. "I'll invite my brothers, Willow Boy and Little Hawk."

"Ask Pony's Tail, too," the Moccasin suggested.

"He's hot for fighting," Wolf protested.

"He'll follow you," the Elk chief said. "His relations are good men. If Pony's Tail is scouting soldiers, they will be content to wait."

"You expect trouble?"

"I've heard of your dream, Wolf. There are other signs, too. I trust the Wihio agent Twiss, but if there's to be peace, why are so many soldiers coming into our country?"

"You know for certain that's true?"

"I have farseeing eyes, but they can't see past hills and rivers. Be my eyes, Wolf. Find out if the enemy's coming."

"Put away plenty of meat," Wolf said, sighing. "If there's fighting to be done, we may not be able to take many buffalo during the fall hunting."

"We'll prepare ourselves," Hairy Moccasin pledged. "Warn us in time to safeguard the helpless ones."

"I'll do it," Wolf vowed. "It's the obligation of a shield-carrier."

That next morning Wolf moved about the camp, speaking to those he wished to take along. Stands Long agreed immediately. Little Hawk and Willow Boy complained about giving up the hunt, but when they noticed their brother's somber eyes, they quickly put aside their own desires. Pony's Tail, as Hairy Moccasin had expected, accepted the invitation.

"If the Wihio soldiers are coming, we'll find them," Pony's Tail boasted. "Then we'll punish them."

"We're scouts," Wolf warned. "We'll bring word of the enemy. Before we start a fight, we'll need strong medicine and a proper plan."

Younger Dog heard of the scout and asked to go along.

"I'm as old as your brothers, and I ride a better horse," the Dog argued. "Besides, you're used to my talking."

"Your father might need you to hunt for the family," Wolf objected.

"No, we've killed enough buffalo," Younger Dog declared. "I have brothers to help Ne' hyo, and a sister and mother to strip the carcasses and smoke the meat."

Lastly, Split Chin joined the scouting party. Wolf welcomed him. The Chin was urging the chiefs to fight, but he was well known as a cautious fighter. If, on the other hand, there was need of courage, Split Chin was sure to provide it.

Wolf Running erected a sweat lodge, and Flying Squirrel again performed the ritual. All the scouts entered the lodge, and they purified themselves for the coming days together.

"Take only your weapons and a buffalo hide to sleep on," Wolf instructed after leaving the sweat lodge. "We'll take no extra horses. We'll shoot something to eat each day, so bring no food along. I want to be like a flea on a dog—difficult to notice."

As soon as they left the safety of the hunting camps, Wolf sought the cover of ravines and tree-topped hillsides. The country was far too flat to ride across unseen. He also took care to ride at an easy gait so that the ponies wouldn't throw up any dust.

"Are we scouts or ghosts?" Split Chin finally cried. "We do more hiding than looking."

"You're a lance-carrier and a more experienced fighter," Wolf acknowledged. "Maybe you should take charge. I was asked to look for an enemy, and this is the only way I know."

"It's important," Stands Long added, "to get away unseen so that we can warn the people. If we're chased into camp, what good would our warning be?"

"If we continue to drag our way across the country, we won't be far enough from the camps to be of any use," Split Chin complained.

"You may be right," Wolf admitted. "I don't know. Do you want to carry the weight of the choice, Chin?"

Split Chin looked into the concerned eyes of his young companion and laughed.

"No, you carry it," Split Chin told Wolf. "I can see you're

doing what you consider best. It's your dream that leads you. I trust the white wolf won't let the enemy elude us."

Wolf Running thought it unlikely, but he did worry about the dream. If there was nothing he could do to stop the bluecoats, what was he doing riding out to find them?

Three long days the scouts rode north. They saw small herds of buffalo and sometimes spied parties of Pawnee hunters. Twice they camped with Arapahos on Short Nose Creek. They found no bluecoats, though.

On the fourth day, as they turned north toward Platte River, Wolf spotted a line of curling dust to the north and east. He waved his companions into the cover of a stand of cottonwoods. Then he waited.

"Wihio," Little Hawk said, the excitement raising his voice to a whine.

"Riders," Stands Long warned. "Too early to tell who."

"It might be Pawnees," Wolf said. "Bluecoats would throw up more dust. They ride in columns of two, also. These people are in a single line, and they're spread out."

"If they're Pawnees, we can run them," Pony's Tail boasted.

"We've pledged to attack no one," Wolf insisted. "Hold yourselves ready, but leave your arrows in their quivers. We won't fight unless attacked."

"You'd turn away from Pawnees?" Pony's Tail gasped.

"We're here to use our eyes, not our bows," Wolf grumbled. "Keep quiet now."

The approaching riders emerged from a ravine and at last came into view. Their chests were bare, and they carried bows.

"More Arapahos?" Willow Boy asked.

"No, but friends just the same," Wolf said, exhaling in relief. "Oglala Lakotas."

Wolf Running was even more pleased to spot his cousin Curly among the visitors. He rode out of the cottonwoods, hand raised in greeting.

"Hau!" Curly called, nudging his pony into a trot. "Wolf! Where are all my relations? Don't you have buffalo roasting? We'll eat well, won't we?"

"Our camps are well south of here," Wolf said, clasping his cousin's hands. "We're only scouts."

"You haven't found a herd to kill?" Curly asked. "We've seen much sign."

"The hunters are hard at work," Wolf explained. "We're not looking for buffalo."

"You came to watch for the soldiers then," Curly said, sighing.

"You've seen them?" Split Chin asked.

"An army on Platte River," Curly told him. "Hundreds. They're planning a long hunt. There are wagons and wheeled guns."

"It's Harney, the eagle chief, then," Wolf guessed.

"I didn't see him," Curly replied. "We Lakotas won't soon be forgetting him, either."

"But it's a large force?" Wolf asked.

"Yes," Curly said. "We heard from some of the Platte traders that these Wihio are hot to fight the Cheyenne."

"Agent Twiss was supposed to stop them," Wolf muttered.

"Twiss appears to be a good man," Curly said, "but the soldier chiefs ignore him. The great Wihio chiefs are very angry with the killing of the wagon people. Our chiefs warned us to be careful when we left to visit. I think there will be trouble."

Wolf nodded. The other Lakotas continued southward, led by Little Hawk, Willow Boy, and Younger Dog. Curly agreed to lead Wolf, Stands Long, Pony's Tail, and Split Chin to the soldier camps.

"We were fortunate to cross trails," Wolf told his cousin as they rode north.

"Fortunate?" Curly asked, laughing. "I saw it in my dreams."

"I had a dream, too," Wolf said. He then told of Snow Wolf's visit.

"I, too, saw a fight," Curly added. "Many good men fell, and the cries of the mourning were fearful. Watch these Wihio, Wolf. They're tricky."

"Yes, I know," Wolf replied. "I must find out what they want, though."

The four Tsis tsis tas followed their Oglala guide north-ward two days. Curly then led them to a small stream south of Platte River. Hundreds of bluecoats were camped there. Wolf and Curly crept close enough that night to hear the soldiers talking. They heard nothing to quiet their fears.

"They're going to attack our hunting camps," Wolf told his companions when he and Curly returned. "We have to ride fast and warn the others."

"They know where our people are?" Split Chin asked.

"Pawnees told them," Wolf explained.

"I knew we should have run those Pawnees," Pony's Tail grumbled. "I knew it."

The scouts turned south that same night and rode until their ponies tired. They made a camp under the cover of a nest of willows and resumed the journey the next day. It required but a third day's hard riding to reach the hunting camps.

"The bluecoats are coming," Wolf told Hairy Moccasin. "The Lakotas have heard them boasting of how they'll punish us. I myself heard Wihio soldiers talking about killing."

"Where are they?" Hairy Moccasin asked. "How many?"

Wolf provided the required details. The bluecoats were headed toward Short Nose Creek. It wouldn't take them much longer. They had no women along to slow them down. Some soldiers walked, but most were mounted.

Hairy Moccasin then shared his own news. There were soldiers marching from the south as well.

"They plan to make a surround," Wolf said. "What can we do?"

"We can't avoid a fight," the Moccasin said. "Not with so many soldiers hurrying toward us. We have to hit them hard and drive them back."

"How?" Wolf asked.

"The answer lies with the young medicine chiefs," Hairy Moccasin explained. "They have powerful charms to give us. Their dreams promise a great victory."

"Flying Squirrel has had a dream?" Wolf asked.

"No, they are younger men," the Moccasin explained. "Ice and Dark."

Wolf shuddered. The two were well known for their promises, and the Crazy Dogs valued their advice. They had never delivered anybody from danger, though. Wolf glanced at Red Hawk, but the Hawk didn't betray his feelings.

"What do you want me to do?" Wolf asked.

"You've done enough," Hairy Moccasin replied. "Rest. Eat and grow strong. Others will take charge of the scouting now."

Wolf left confused. What had changed? When he'd left, the chiefs seemed eager to avoid a fight. Now everyone was preparing for battle.

"All the talking's over," Red Hawk told Wolf later. "Maybe it had been decided before you left. Dark and Ice spoke to the council of forty-four. They have convinced everyone of their power. They've had a great vision, after all."

"I, too, had a dream," Wolf observed.

"Hairy Moccasin's no fool," Red Hawk noted. "He sent you away so the people couldn't be reminded of your dream. Pony's Tail, whose father stands tall in the council, might have sided with you, so the Tail was included. Split Chin went along to keep you away."

"And I thought I had won a place of honor among the Elks," Wolf said, staring at the ground.

"You've done what you could," Red Hawk said, lifting the young man's chin. "You saw it in your dream. You were powerless to stop the fighting. Now we Elks must brave up. If there's to be a fight, we must run the enemy."

Wolf agreed. There was still much he didn't understand, though. As the arrow-makers busied themselves, and new bows were crafted for young men, Dark and Ice went among the men with rifles, giving them a powerful powder that would drive their bullets into the hearts of the Wihio. The medicine chiefs offered other charms, and each night they instructed a band of young men in the proper way to use their medicine and run the Wihio.

Wolf accepted their charms and kept his doubts to himself. The other warriors seemed alive with new confidence. As they sang and danced in their soldier society camps, many boasted of the enemies they would slay.

"Words never ran anybody," Stands Long complained as he joined Wolf Running in the young men's lodge.

"It's said they have great power," Wolf said, accepting a handful of arrows Stands Long had saved for his brother-friend. "They convinced the council."

"I wasn't worried the council would kill me," Stands Long explained. "It's the Wihio who require convincing."

That night Snow Wolf returned to Wolf Running's dreams. The spirit creature again burst out of a scarlet sunrise, and it approached the shadowy figure at the stream as before. This time Wolf saw himself older, taller, and there were others there with him. Willow Boy and Little Hawk stood on one side. Stands Long was on the other.

"Nothing lives long," Snow Wolf sang.

The bluecoats came splashing through the water, and the young Tsis tsis tas stepped out to stop them. They fired arrows and shot off their rifles, but the bluecoats continued unharmed. The dream filled with the cries of the helpless ones, and Wolf grew cold as he witnessed the killing of innocents.

"No!" he shouted as he jumped to his feet and frantically searched for his rifle.

"Wolf?" Stands Long asked, shaking his brother-friend awake. "Wolf, it's only a dream."

"Only a dream?" Wolf asked, dropping to his knees and fighting to steady himself. "Only?"

"What did you see?" Stands Long asked.

Little Hawk and Willow Boy were also awake now, and they hurried to their brother's side.

"Another dream?" Willow Boy asked. "Did you see us run the Wihio?"

"I saw a terrible battle," Wolf told them. "I saw many dead."

"But we ran them, didn't we?" Willow Boy asked.

"I saw mostly death," Wolf confessed.

"It was a warning," Stands Long suggested. "We must prepare for a hard fight. Tomorrow we'll practice our aim. We'll make medicine."

"But we already have the medicine Ice and Dark provided," Little Hawk pointed out. "Won't it be enough?"

"The white powder will guide our arrows," Willow Boy insisted.

"Perhaps," Wolf muttered. "But a little practice won't hurt you."

That next day Wolf Running and Stands Long Beside Him took small groups of young men off to practice their shooting. They urged the youngest to find older men and stand near them.

"Watch the men who have counted coups," Wolf advised. "Try to pick out an enemy who isn't bigger or stronger."

"Use your arrows before your knife," Stands Long added. "Watch for Wihio who come from behind or one side. They're tricky. They would rather shoot you down than fight you, so you must cut them down first."

Wolf and Stands Long finally drew the attention of the medicine-makers. Dark and Ice stepped over, smiling broadly.

"You were away when we explained to the others," Dark said. "We have prepared paint that will make our warriors invisible. We have powder to make your rifles shoot straight. Don't worry. Heammawihio will hand over our enemies and let us kill them."

"It would be a good thing," Wolf noted. "But there are so many of them. What will you do to stop their thunder guns? How will you stop their rifles from shooting back?"

"We'll explain it all to you," Ice promised. "If there's time. If not, trust our vision. Our medicine is strong."

Wolf wanted to believe. He needed to. Each night Snow Wolf brought the same images to his dreams, though, and he dreaded the coming fight.

One thing many of the older men found hard to understand. As scouts brought word there were soldiers on Short Nose Creek and later Turkey Creek itself, half a day's ride from the Tsis tsis tas camps, no one made any effort to move the women and children to a place of safety.

"They're safe where they are," Dark boasted. "We're going to run the Wihio. Then we'll want the others close so that we can continue the hunting."

"We'll have scalp dances to make," Corn Dancer said, joining the medicine chiefs. "It's best our sisters are nearby."

Wolf went directly to Red Hawk.

"I'm worried for my small brother's safety," Wolf said, eyeing little Morning Hawk. "A boy of five summers shouldn't be in a soldier camp."

"You want me to send him south?" Red Hawk asked.

"Or north," Wolf suggested. "He could go with Curly and the other Lakotas."

"They're not staying to join the fight?"

"Curly dreams, too," Wolf explained. "He hasn't seen encouraging signs."

"You haven't either."

"I know Little Hawk and Willow Boy must stay," Wolf noted. "But the little one might . . ."

"His mother would miss him," Red Hawk explained. "Do you really doubt the Dark and Ice medicine?"

"I don't know what to believe and what not to believe," Wolf replied. "I can see our preparations are far from complete. Who's made a plan? Which chiefs have taken charge of the young men? Each of us will fight our own battle, and that's no way to fight the Wihio. Even their wagon people fight as a group."

"You see things," Red Hawk observed. "But everything's been decided. If the Wihio run us, I won't be able to turn away and look to the welfare of Burnt Willow Woman and Morning Hawk. I would like to know someone else might protect them."

"I will," Wolf promised. "With my life."

"We must do our best," Red Hawk urged. "Don't give your brothers doubts to hold them back. It's for old men to safeguard the defenseless ones."

"Yes," Wolf agreed. And as he left the man he had once known as his father and still looked to for guidance, he realized his brothers had been right to say he was born old. He would always be concerned first with the welfare of the helpless.

18

THAT AFTERNOON THE men met in the soldier society councils, braving themselves for the coming fight. In addition to making the old warrior prayers, Dark and Ice provided buffalo-horn powder to turn away the Wihio bullets.

"Nah nih, how can we fail to win?" Little Hawk asked as he brought a pair of ponies out from the herd.

"Yes," Wolf Running said halfheartedly. "The medicine chiefs have provided strong protection."

"You're worried, though," the fourteen-year-old observed. "Why?"

"I can't explain," Wolf said, drawing his brother closer. "Sometimes you have a feeling, a sense that everything isn't as it should be. Dark and Ice may hold all the power they say. Still, I wish it was some older man who was urging us on."

"So what should I do?"

"Stay close to me," Wolf urged. "Hold yourself ready, but

don't wander far from where Stands Long and I are fighting."

"It's good for a young man to ride with shield-carriers," Little Hawk noted.

"Good, too, for brothers to fight side by side."

Wolf was also worried about Willow Boy. At thirteen, he should have been content to hold horses, but he was tall for his age.

"You stretched yourself tall," Red Hawk told Wolf. "Why are you surprised when your brothers do it?"

When Wolf Running finally located Willow Boy, the younger brother proudly showed the white circle Dark had painted on his chest.

"Don't worry, Nah nih," Willow Boy said. "I'm now invisible. The Wihio bullets won't find me."

"Come and help me paint the horses," Wolf suggested.

"Certainly," Willow Boy agreed. "When we have killed the bluecoats, we'll raid the Pawnee horse herds. Then we'll once again be rich in horses."

"Do you remember why we have so few animals now?" Wolf asked.

"The Wihio soldiers took them," Willow Boy replied. "We'll have our revenge on them soon."

Wolf started to speak a warning, but he stopped himself. There was no holding back the young ones.

"Your brother, Little Hawk, is coming with us," Wolf said instead. "He has no brother-friend to stand with him and help make the hard fight."

"He hasn't?"

"I was hoping that you might ride along and help him."

"You want me to ride out with you and Stands Long?"

"Brothers should stand together," Wolf said. "But if you would rather accompany Red Hawk . . ."

"I'll go with you," Willow Boy readily agreed. "Ne' hyo and the older men are sure to hold back. I'm eager to make my charge while the bulletproof medicine is strongest."

"We're glad to have another brave heart with us," Wolf said, clasping his brother's arms. "But wait for Stands Long and me to act. It's a brave thing, making a solitary charge, but sometimes it offends Heammawihio and breaks the medicine power."

"I remember the stories," Willow Boy replied. "I'll do what I'm told."

Wolf and his younger companions passed the rest of that afternoon painting their ponies and testing their weapons. Wolf personally inspected his brothers' bows.

"Your bowstring is too loose," he told Willow Boy.

"I have a spare," Stands Long said. "I always make new ones when we hunt Bull Buffalo."

"Fresh sinews are plentiful then," Willow Boy noted. "I'll remember that. When we resume our hunting, I'll make some, too."

Wolf was amazed at the calm that filled the soldier camps. Everyone went about their preparations as if the bluecoats were riding Platte River. They were close now. The war chiefs had picked out a place to fight, but they could only hope the Wihio had the patience to wait for them to ride out.

"We'll keep close watch tonight," Stands Long vowed when Wolf shared his concerns. "Remember, the Wihio are riding straight into the heart of our country. They're not showing any sign of fear. They welcome battle, too."

"I wish I could find a reason to be glad to fight," Wolf said, sighing.

"Yes, I remember Big Island, too," Stands Long replied. "Maybe the medicine will prove as strong as the chiefs say. Maybe the Wihio will run away."

"I hope so," Wolf muttered. "There are so many of them! It wouldn't be easy to kill each one."

That night, as Wolf Running slept with Stands Long and his brothers in the young men's lodge, he dreamed. At first he found himself drifting on the clouds, looking down at scenes of his childhood. Raven Heart still walked the earth, and Bull Buffalo was strong. He saw once more his rescues of Walker Logan. He tried to avert his eyes from the slaying of Grattan's soldiers, from the killing at Platte River, and the terrible morning on Big Island. Finally Snow Wolf appeared.

"What lies ahead?" Wolf Running heard his voice whisper as he walked with the spirit creature toward a nearby hill.

"Nothing lives long," Snow Wolf answered. "Only the earth and the mountains."

"We'll die then?" Wolf Running asked.

"Nothing lives long," Snow Wolf repeated, turning his great head away. "You can only be what you are."

Wolf Running awoke before seeing more. The air outside was chill, but he felt feverish. His forehead and chest were damp with perspiration. He dressed himself and walked outside.

"Tell me," he pleaded with the stars overhead. "Show me what's on the other side of that hill."

The wind stirred, and an eerie sensation chilled him to the bone. He thought he again heard the words of the Tsis tsis tas death song.

"Nothing lives long," Wolf whispered. "Well, if I'm to die, it will be as a brave heart."

He walked out to where his shield rested on its tripod. Sighing, Wolf removed the cover and gazed at the painted face of Snow Wolf, glowing white in the moonlight. He sat beside the shield, whispering medicine prayers Raven Heart had taught him. He added some of the ancient, half-forgotten ones recounted by the Suhtai. He thought about Sun Walker Maiden and the sweetness of her smile. He closed his eyes and imagined the good days they would have together.

He remembered Raven Heart.

"Ne' hyo, it's a hard thing, giving up life when it's

beginning to grow warm. Why can't the Wihio just leave us alone?"

Wolf gazed around him at the slumbering camp. How many young men, now resting nearby, would climb Hanging Road tomorrow?

It was more than a solitary heart could bear. Wolf leaned back against his shield stand and closed his eyes. He was still sleeping there at dawn when Willow Boy roused him.

"Nah nih, it's time to paint our faces," the boy said solemnly.

"Yes," Wolf agreed. "But first we'll make the morning prayers."

Willow Boy located Little Hawk while Wolf found Stands Long. Together the four of them walked past Turkey Creek and climbed onto the far bank. There they built a small fire. Wolf filled a pipe with tobacco and made the pipe ritual.

"Heammawihio, give us the struggle to make us strong," he whispered as the sun appeared above the eastern horizon.

Stands Long then sang one of the old Suhtai prayers, after which Wolf led his brothers in a more familiar medicine prayer. Finally Wolf stared somberly at his brothers.

"Give us the heart to do the difficult things," he prayed. "Shield us from the treachery of our enemies."

"The grass grows green, browns, and dies," Stands Long said. "Then spring comes, and it grows again. Keep us within the sacred hoop, Grandfather."

When they returned to the camp, Dark and Ice were busy waking the warriors. Individuals began walking around the camp. Some performed their personal ceremonies and began painting their faces. Others took down shields and readied themselves for fighting.

Wolf tied three coup feathers in his hair. He might have carried a coup stick with twenty others, but Raven Heart had always urged modesty. The shield marked him as a famous man anyway. And on that crucial morning Wolf mounted a white stallion.

"The other pony would be better," Stands Long complained.

"Yes," Wolf agreed. "A modest man would ride it. But today my brothers are with us. I intend to be the one to empty the Wihio rifles. They can do it later."

"Wolf, why were you sleeping beside the shield?" Stands Long asked.

"I hoped to find an answer to my dream."

"The white wolf came again?"

"But brought no answers," Wolf confessed. "It's going to be a hard fight, old friend. I know that much."

"We'll make it hard for the Wihio to kill us," Stands Long vowed. "Our grandsons will sing of the two brave hearts that ran the soldiers."

"We can only try," Wolf muttered.

"It's never enough, though, is it?" Stands Long asked.

"Maybe this time we'll have better fortune."

"Only Heammawihio knows that. We can only do what we can."

When Ice and Dark had completed their final preparations, they led the warriors from the camp. It was a considerable force, with the Crazy Dogs leading the way. Wolf nodded pridefully at his brothers. Painted for battle, with their bows strung and arrows ready, they no longer looked like boys in need of protecting.

"It's always hard to see the young ones joining the fight," Stands Long whispered as if reading his brother-friend's thoughts. "Still, it's good to have them with us."

There were other familiar faces among the war party, too. Curly and a small band of Oglalas, to Wolf Running's great surprise, rode down and joined the warriors.

"I thought you were riding north," Wolf called to his cousin.

"We couldn't elude the Pawnee scouts," Curly explained. "We'll go after they're all dead."

Buffalo Horn rode with the Hevataniu. Wolf raised his rifle in a salute, and the Horn hollered a greeting. A bit later, Pony's Tail and Younger Dog galloped alongside, howling encouragement.

"Can we follow you?" Pony's Tail cried.

"Why not?" Wolf said. "You've fought beside us before."

They rode northward from the main camp until they came upon a lake. Its surface was calm and clear. The reflection of the sun overhead sparkled magically on the water. Beyond the lake, the plains spread out far and wide.

"Here's the sacred place," Dark announced. "We can now begin the final preparations."

The medicine chiefs dismounted. They then motioned for the warriors to come down off their ponies. One by one the men approached the lake. Dark, Ice, and the other medicine chiefs then washed each man's hands in the water.

"When you ride against the Wihio, raise your hands," Ice explained afterward. "The power of this medicine will knock down the bluecoats' bullets. You can then charge and cut down the enemy with your arrows."

"Ayyyy!" the warriors shouted. "We'll run them then."

"Run them?" Corn Dancer cried. "We'll kill them!"

The medicine chiefs spoke additional prayers, invoking the Great Mystery's power and protection. Then the men remounted their horses. The war chiefs then took charge of things. Ice and Dark moved back.

Wolf led his little band to where Hairy Moccasin stood, eyeing the other Elks.

"Brave up," the Moccasin urged. "Remember, you're Elks!"

"We're Elks!" the others shouted.

Split Chin, who carried one of the lances, rode forward and offered encouraging words.

"Brothers, it's for us to chase these crazy people from our

sacred country," he said, gazing into the eyes of old friends and young boys alike. "Whatever happens, I'll stand and fight. Don't run away and be shamed. Stay and strike the enemy hard. Make this a remembered fight!"

"Ayyyy!" the Elks howled. "He's a brave heart."

It was now time to throw the scouts out ahead of the main body. Wolf didn't wait to be asked to lead. Instead he rode out on his white stallion alongside Hairy Moccasin.

"So, you'll find the enemy for us," the Moccasin said, grinning. "Or perhaps the Pawnees will see you first, riding that horse. I can offer you a pony if he's all you have to ride."

"I have a spare pony," Wolf answered. "This animal is like the Wihio, though. He runs into his enemy's camp!"

The others howled their approval, and Hairy Moccasin waved Wolf Running onward. Stands Long, Pony's Tail, and Younger Dog galloped along. Willow Boy and Little Hawk trailed behind.

Ice and Dark had assured the warriors the bluecoats were nearby. Instead, Wolf and the other scouts had to ride most of the morning to locate the enemy. While others rested in the shade of a narrow line of cottonwoods along Turkey Creek, Wolf Running, his brothers, and their young friends were counting the enemy.

"It's another Wihio trick," Little Hawk grumbled as they rode. "Here we come, eager to fight, and the Wihio sits in his camp, chewing salty pig."

"They may not be as lazy as you think," Wolf warned. "They've come a considerable distance, and they ride slow, heavy horses. They've got wagons, too. It takes them a long time to get started, but they're not easily turned back."

"They're like beavers," Stands Long observed. "Determined."

"Only not so swift in water," Little Hawk said, laughing.

"No," Wolf agreed as he recalled rescuing young Walker Logan. "They don't know the sacred path, but their guns shoot a long way. It's easy to be killed by them. When you're dead, it doesn't matter if your enemy struck you down at close quarters with his lance or shot you accidentally while aiming at a prairie chicken."

Wolf Running and his little band of scouts weren't the only ones riding out ahead. The Crazy Dogs and Bowstrings, too, had men searching for the Wihio. There were Foxes out as well. It required a keen eye to note the difference between the other scouts and the enemy.

Wolf was fooled for an instant when he saw them. There were only two, and they were naked except for breechclouts. They had feathers in their hair, too. Only when he closed the distance did Wolf note the distinctive way they wore their hair in a single strip from crown to forehead.

"Pawnees," Stands Long muttered hatefully.

Wolf nodded. He turned to Little Hawk.

"See' was' sin mit," Wolf instructed, "ride back and warn Hairy Moccasin. We've found Pawnee scouts."

"Nah nih?" the Hawk cried, disappointed.

"You have the fastest horse," Wolf explained. "Ride!"

Little Hawk frowned and turned away. He then galloped back to warn the other Elks.

Wolf, meanwhile, rode out toward the Pawnees.

"Nothing lives long," he called as he loaded his rifle.

The Pawnees, too, readied their rifles. They then climbed down from their ponies to take aim.

"Now?" Stands Long whispered.

"Yes," Wolf shouted. He kicked the white stallion into a gallop and hugged its neck. He then raced back and forth before the Pawnees, hurling insults and daring them to fire. He remained cautiously out of close range, but his taunts were more than the two Pawnees could stand. First one and then the other fired. One bullet flew past harmlessly. The second nicked Wolf's shield.

"Ayyyy!" Stands Long screamed as he raced out from the

Pawnees' flank, driving off their ponies and running them closer to Wolf Running. Wolf, smiling, charged the two.

The Pawnees frantically tried to reload their rifles. There wasn't time. Wolf pulled up in front of the first, fired his rifle into the surprised Pawnee's chest, and struck the second one down with a hard blow across the forehead.

The other scouts then fell on the two Pawnees. The first man was already dying. The second was muttering a death chant. Pony's Tail scalped the first. Willow Boy cut away the second Pawnee's forelock.

"You should never have ridden into our country," Willow Boy scolded the terrified enemy. Pony's Tail then began cutting on the Pawnees. The first one quickly died. The second man's screams didn't cease for a considerable time.

"That's enough," Wolf finally announced. "We have to find the bluecoats."

Pony's Tail stood, notched an arrow, and fired it through the Pawnee's chest. The Tail and Willow Boy took the Pawnees' rifles and shouted in triumph.

"Brave up!" Wolf urged his companions as they mounted their ponies. "It's easy enough to kill men who've fired their rifles. The Wihio won't be so careless."

Wolf first spied the Wihio soldiers at Rock Creek. The horsemen were mounted in three long columns of two men each. They had cannons with them, but they were having difficulty getting the big guns across the muddy stream. Well behind the horse soldiers, dust rose from what must certainly have been the foot soldiers and wagons.

"Should we charge them?" Willow Boy asked.

"We could delay the crossing," Pony's Tail noted.

"Why?" Wolf asked. "They could shoot us easily enough. Don't we want them to come on? It would be good to fight the horse soldiers while their big guns are useless and the foot soldiers are being left behind. No, we'll let them see us and then retreat."

Wolf galloped down toward the creek and halted just out

of rifle range. The bluecoats' Pawnee scouts rode out after him, and Wolf turned back toward the others. Pony's Tail waved the fresh scalp, and Stands Long, who knew something of the Pawnee language, warned the enemy scouts to stay back.

"Don't worry," Stands Long added as Wolf led the way south toward the main band of Tsis tsis tas. "Who ever knew a Pawnee who took good advice?"

"It would be good if they didn't follow too closely, though," Wolf argued.

"We'll keep them back with our rifles," Stands Long boasted, "if they ride too close. If not, we'll lead them to the others."

"And to death," Younger Dog vowed.

"Yes, it's waiting for all of us," Wolf noted. "Let's not hurry it, though. There's time to die when everything's ready. If we're patient, we may all live to see tomorrow."

19

WOLF RUNNING LED his little scouting party slowly southward. He didn't hurry. And whenever the trailing Pawnees fell behind, he held up so they could close the distance.

"They're afraid to come on alone," Stands Long observed. "They don't want to get ahead of the bluecoats."

"They're in no hurry to die," Pony's Tail said, laughing.

"We could turn and strike these other Pawnees down, too," Willow Boy suggested.

"We didn't come out here to run Pawnees," Wolf reminded his companions. "We intend to fight the Wihio. We have to turn them back before they reach the defenseless ones."

"Besides," Younger Dog noted, "our medicine is intended to turn bullets. It won't protect us from Pawnee knives."

The others agreed, and Wolf nudged the white stallion into a trot. One Pawnee galloped ahead of the others, and for a time it seemed he might charge the scouts. He finally drew up short, though, and waited for the others to catch up.

"Courage is one thing," Stands Long said, nodding respectfully at the Pawnee. "Dying's another."

When they reached the narrow strip of sandy ground that lay between the creek and a rocky ridge, Wolf grinned. It was a perfect place to trap the bluecoats. He gazed up into the rocks for some sign that the chiefs had brought the fighters up there, but he saw only sage and buffalo grass.

"Yes, I know," Stands Long agreed. "It's a good place to fall upon the enemy. Ice and Dark saw the fight up ahead, in the open. The people will be waiting there."

"In the cottonwoods?" Wolf asked.

"It's a shaded place," Stands Long pointed out. "Good for waiting."

"And that's all they've done all morning, stand around and talk," Wolf grumbled.

"Perhaps they're waiting for our news," Willow Boy suggested.

"Didn't I send Little Hawk back with word of the Wihio?" Wolf asked.

"For all the brave talk, no one's eager to start a fight," Pony's Tail grumbled. "That's why I'm glad I came with you, Wolf. You'll ride out and strike the enemy. You don't wait until he begins to burn your lodge."

Wolf turned to study the Wihio approach. The Pawnees fell back. The three columns slowed. Then the right and left lines stopped. The center continued alone. Later, the left and then the right fell in behind.

Wolf smiled. The bluecoats were riding in single columns of twos now. They had left the foot soldiers and the cannons far behind. It would be a simple thing to trap them if only some men had been left on the ridge!

Wolf continued on ahead. He followed the curve of the creek and rode out onto a broad plain. Ahead horses grazed aimlessly as their riders rested in the shade of the cottonwoods.

"I see they're prepared," Stands Long complained bitterly.

Wolf then rode out toward the other warriors. He made signs, warning the enemy was in sight. He then turned his horse in a broad circle, the old Plains way of telling a friend the enemy was coming.

Finally the other warriors returned to life. A few men rode out to greet the scouts. Chiefs began to form up their men. Wolf led his own little band to where Hairy Moccasin was chastising the Elks. Little Hawk rode over and took station on Wolf's left side.

"I told them," the Hawk whispered. "They did nothing."

"There's time left," Wolf replied. "Now's the time to strike the blow."

As Wolf stroked his stallion and waited for the dust raised by three hundred war ponies to settle, he saw the bluecoats approach. It was a stirring sight! The column broke apart in fours. It looked like some odd Wihio dance as men moved here and there. Suddenly, almost before Wolf realized, the bluecoats had formed four straight lines of horsemen. There were seventy or more in each line.

"Good," a Crazy Dog shouted. "There are enough for each of us to kill one."

Wolf wasn't thinking of killing just then. He gazed around at familiar faces. Stands Long stared hatefully at the bluecoats. Little Hawk and Willow Boy had lost their eagerness. The boys looked a little unsettled by the Wihio's calm. Hairy Moccasin, too, appeared concerned.

"What are they doing?" he asked Wolf. "We expected them to ride along with their wagons. They come out like brave hearts to fight us!"

The Tsis tsis tas and Suhtai were growing concerned. It was hot, and many were sweating. Those who had chosen to wear their war shirts or elk robes began pulling them off. The ponies pawed the ground anxiously.

The bluecoats, on the other hand, were a picture of order.

The midday sun reflected brightly off their brass belt buckles, and their dark blue shirts and feather-topped felt hats formed a solitary line across the clearing.

"Brave up!" Hairy Moccasin urged as he rode out in front of the Elks. Split Chin, raising his sacred lance overhead, joined the chief. Likewise, the leaders of the Foxes, Red Shields, Bowstrings, and Crazy Dogs moved ahead of their men.

The bluecoat chiefs shouted orders, and their little horns blasted defiantly. In reply the Tsis tsis tas and Suhtai, along with their Lakota and Arapaho friends and relations, sang out old warrior songs.

"Brave up, brothers," Wolf called. "It's time to fight."

The Bowstrings threw up their hands in order to drive off the Wihio bullets. Others, too, performed the magical motions.

"Nothing can harm us," Corn Dancer sang as he readied his rifle. "We're protected."

From the far left of the Wihio line one of the Pawnees rode out alone. He raced his pony toward the Tsis tsis tas line, halted, and fired his rifle. The shot missed, and two young Foxes rode out to drive off the Pawnee.

"There he goes," Stands Long observed as the Pawnee turned his horse and returned to the safety of the bluecoat line.

"Even a Pawnee wouldn't stand with an empty rifle and let himself be cut down," Willow Boy said, laughing.

"Those aren't all Pawnees," Wolf argued as the Wihio soldier line stirred. Wolf studied the formidable line, waiting for them to draw up, dismount, and move ahead with their rifles. Once on foot it would be easy to circle around and drive off the pony-holders. Then the bands would begin their suicide charges. Finally, the rest would run in and cut down the surviving Wihio.

Everything went terribly wrong, though. First of all, the Wihio didn't dismount. They left their rifles in their saddle scabbards. Instead they drew out the long steel knives the whites called sabers.

"What's this?" Hairy Moccasin shouted. "Where are the guns?"

Others, too, mumbled nervously. Dark and Ice had made strong medicine, but it was only good for turning bullets away. It would have no effect on the sabers.

"Hemmawihio, protect the people!" Hairy Moccasin called.

Among the soldier bands, some men broke away and retired southward. Most stood their ground, though. The Wihio blew their horns and trotted forward. Hairy Moccasin motioned one band of Elks to the right, and Red Hawk led fifty men off in an effort to get behind the bluecoats. Some Crazy Dogs tried a similar maneuver on the left side. Bluecoats broke away to block both parties.

"They're coming," Hairy Moccasin warned as the bluecoats started their charge. "Give them some arrows to chew!"

The younger warriors notched arrows while those men with rifles took aim. As soon as the bluecoats got within range, Hairy Moccasin howled, and a cascade of deadly arrows flew out with a "whoosh!" A bluecoat in the second rank fell, and two horses went down. The startled Wihio fell back a moment.

"I hit nothing!" Corn Dancer screamed, discarding his rifle. "What about the powder? It wasn't possible I missed!"

All along the line Tsis tsis tas and Suhtai alike questioned the power of their medicine. Some men muttered and threw down the charms handed them by Ice and Dark.

"Deceivers!" Split Chin shouted. "Traitors! You've left us here to meet the enemy with no power to stop him."

Wolf tried to ignore the turmoil. He had never trusted the new medicine. He relied on the old charms made for him by Pronghorn and Flying Squirrel.

"Trust in your bow and in a hunter's eye," Wolf told his young companions. "We must drive them off."

"All of them?" Willow Boy asked with wide eyes full of disbelief. "There are too many."

The Wihio had reformed their ranks. Now, with horns blowing again, they raised their sabers and stood high in their stirrups. On they came again. The Tsis tsis tas met them with a halfhearted volley of arrows. The soldiers raced onward, colliding finally with the thinning Tsis tsis tas line.

Any order that had withstood the sight of the raised sabers quickly dissolved. Some warriors raced off in small groups. Others fled individually. Men dropped bows or shot off arrows without taking aim. Bewildered pony boys found themselves facing wild-eyed, saber-wielding Wihio demons. Some left their animals and flung themselves behind rocks and trees, hoping to escape the enemy's attention.

Wolf frowned. It was disgraceful. There was no dishonor in being driven from the field by a superior force, but the Wihio owned no numerical advantage. Their far-firing guns remained attached to their saddles. These bluecoats were fighting with sabers! Hand to hand, a Tsis tsis tas was the equal of anyone.

"Ayyyy!" Wolf cried as he made his first charge. A youngish bluecoat gazed with surprise as Wolf galloped alongside. The Wihio slashed out with his saber, but Wolf nimbly avoided it. "I'm first!" Wolf shouted as he slapped the young white across the chest and knocked him from his pony. The unfortunate bluecoat fell on the blade of his saber, opening up the back of his left thigh.

"Ayyyy!" Pony's Tail screamed as he fired an arrow into the stricken Wihio. The Tail needed three to finish the bluecoat.

"You were first," Pony's Tail said, turning to Wolf Running. "Do you want the scalp?"

"Leave it to the pony boys," Wolf suggested.

"No, it's a good scalp," Pony's Tail complained as he

jumped down and tore off the young bluecoat's hat. He then cut a considerable portion of the young man's reddish-yellow hair away before stripping the corpse of pistol belt, shirt, rifle, and hat.

Wolf left after he was satisfied Pony's Tail was once again mounted.

"Wolf!" Stands Long called from the river.

Wolf turned and spotted Stands Long guarding the muddy river crossing. Some of the pony boys were trying to free themselves from the sinking sand that plagued that stretch of the river.

"Nah nih, the horses!" Willow Boy shouted.

Wolf turned and spotted a dozen stray ponies. Instantly he swung behind them and shouted. The horses immediately started for the river.

The battle continued as small groups of warriors fought on. The bluecoats, too, had broken up their line into smaller bands. Many of the Wihio fought in pairs. Wolf Running and Stands Long fought one such group. A tall, bearded young soldier chief and a somewhat younger companion charged the crossing. Wolf emptied his rifle at the first, but the ball only nicked the bluecoat's elbow.

Stands Long charged toward the second man and blocked a saber blow with his rifle. He kicked the bluecoat hard in the side. The Wihio lost his balance and tumbled off his horse. Stands Long captured the Wihio's pony and offered it to a pair of escaping pony boys.

"Go to the camp," Stands Long told them. "Do what you can for the defenseless ones."

Wolf, meanwhile, waited for the first Wihio. The bluecoat chief pulled up short, slipped his saber into a scabbard, and pulled out a pistol. Grinning, the hairy face aimed at Wolf's head.

Wolf instinctively hugged his horse's neck and held out the shield to deflect the bullets. The bluecoat fired five times from short range. The first missed. The second and third lodged in the thick hump hide of the shield. The fourth tore through the shield and nicked Wolf's left forearm. The fifth tore into his side, deflected off a rib, and went on out his back.

"Ayyyy!" Wolf shouted. He threw caution to the wind, tied his empty rifle behind him, and drew a good iron knife from a sheath on his hip. With a savage war cry, Wolf kicked his horse into a gallop and flew at the bluecoat chief. The Wihio gazed at his empty pistol and then threw it away. He managed to get his rifle halfway out when Wolf leapt off the white stallion and slammed against the surprised Wihio.

"Lord, no!" the bluecoat exclaimed as Wolf plunged the knife into the hairy face's soft belly. It sank to the hilt, and Wolf then jerked it up into the enemy's vitals, cutting the life from the man.

The Wihio's blood was everywhere, and Wolf rolled off his horse and fell to the ground, sickened by the smell of death.

For an instant Wolf was lost in a maze of death and confusion. He glanced around, trying to locate the white stallion. Surely he could find that horse even in a fog!

"I got you now, chief!" a low growl of a voice called.

Wolf turned in time to see a little bluecoat with three yellow stripes on one sleeve. The soldier had a pistol, and he moved his horse closer to make sure of the kill. The hairy face suddenly moaned, though, and the three-striper turned in amazement. Wolf, too, couldn't believe it. The soldier chief was still alive!

"Ayyyy!" Wolf shouted, running toward the Wihio with the pistol. Before the young Elk reached his enemy, the Wihio slapped his horse clear. He turned back to fire the pistol, but an arrow flew past Wolf's ear and pierced the Wihio's hip.

"What?" the three-striper cried, staring at the wound. Wolf glanced back in time to see Willow Boy's grinning face as he grabbed the white stallion and held the animal for his brother.

"And I came to keep *you* safe, See' was' sin mit," Wolf remarked.

"We better go now," Willow Boy urged. "Our medicine is broken, and there are only a few of us left here."

"The others are dead?" Wolf cried.

"No, just gone," Willow Boy explained. "Let's go now."

Wolf climbed atop the white and tried to catch his breath. He glanced down at his bloody arm and frowned. His side was throbbing.

"You're hurt," Willow Boy observed.

"Not badly," Wolf insisted. "Where are the others?"

"Gone back to the camp," Willow Boy said, waving past the river.

"Not everyone," Wolf said, trying to calm himself. "Stands Long. Little Hawk. Younger Dog."

"The Dog followed a band of Suhtai," Willow Boy explained. "Our brother rode north along the creek toward Red Hawk."

"Red Hawk?" Wolf asked.

"He led the flankers," Willow Boy explained. "They were having a hard fight up there."

Wolf sighed. There were twenty fights going on all around them. Men were still struggling to get through the sinking sand on both banks of the creek. The bluecoats, who were unfamiliar with the country, had the worst of it, but some of the younger Tsis tsis tas were also struggling.

"Take out your bow, See' was' sin mit," Wolf said, tying his shield behind him and drawing out his own bow. "We'll use them to help the pony boys."

Wolf then showed him how. He found the rocky crossing and waded out into the stream. He then moved along to where the boys were trapped, held out his bow, and allowed the youngsters to pull themselves up behind him. He then rode across to the far side and found them a riderless pony.

"Ride back and protect the helpless ones," Wolf urged again and again.

"As you have, Brother?" one boy asked.

"Yes," Wolf said, grinning. "It's a brave thing, rescuing. But a hard habit to break."

"We're fortunate it's so," the youngster declared.

Wolf managed to pull six young men from the bog before a line of bluecoats charged the river. There was no way to stop so many. Wolf waved Willow Boy along, and the two of them moved off to the north toward where they expected to find Stands Long and Little Hawk.

"Who would have imagined it?" Willow Boy asked as they topped a small hill. "The bluecoats ran us!"

"We've been beaten before," Wolf observed. "This time we'll pay a heavy price, though. The camps are nearby. The Wihio will fall on the women and children. We have to find a way to turn them back."

"First we have to bind your wounds," Willow Boy insisted.

"It's mostly the hairy face's blood," Wolf argued.

"No, it's your own," Willow Boy said, cutting strips of rawhide. "Come closer so I can bind your arm."

Willow Boy did his best. Actually, the boy did a very satisfactory job on the arm and wrapped Wolf's side tightly so that the bleeding there stopped, and the pain abated.

"Who taught you that?" Wolf asked.

"I passed some time with the medicine chiefs," Willow Boy explained. "They may not have farseeing eyes like you do, Nah nih, but they know something about healing."

"I wish my eyes could have foreseen this battle," Wolf muttered.

"They saw it," Willow Boy observed. "Why else would you have asked me to ride along? I asked Little Hawk. He didn't send you. In fact, he said you asked him, too."

"I was worried," Wolf admitted. "It's a brother's place to watch over you."

"And Little Hawk?"

"We'll ride out and find him," Wolf vowed.

Once Willow Boy tied off the bindings, Wolf nudged the white into a trot. The weary horse complained at the effort, but it made its way north nevertheless. A pair of discarded buckskin mares grazed beside the river, and Willow Boy threw a rope over each.

"It's time we switched ponies," Willow Boy said. "Can you manage it?"

"I'm not dead," Wolf replied. "Just hurt a little."

They climbed onto the bare backs of the buckskins. Willow Boy hid the other animals behind a stand of cottonwoods. They continued north a short distance before spying Stands Long and a dozen other young Elks holding back a small party of Wihio from a small hill.

"Ayyyy!" Wolf shouted as he waved to his brother-friend. "It's good to see someone's still fighting. Maybe it's time to go, though."

"Not yet," Stands Long replied solemnly. "We're fighting here for a reason."

Instinctively Wolf glanced around, searching for Little Hawk.

"Nah nih?" the boy called from the high buffalo grass a stone's throw away.

"You're not hurt?" Wolf called.

"Not me," Little Hawk said, waving Wolf closer.

Wolf dismounted and left the buckskin with Willow Boy. His legs wobbled, and his head began to ache. He sensed something was terribly wrong. He never expected what he found, though.

Little Hawk knelt beside his father. Red Hawk rested on an elk robe, his tired eyes fighting off the approaching fingers of death.

"He fought off ten of them," Little Hawk boasted. "Alone, he turned back the bluecoats twice. They had good guns, though. The bulletproof medicine lacked the power to turn them all."

Red Hawk's legs and chest were torn apart. Wolf easily

counted seven bullet holes, and there may have been more. Both lungs were punctured, and Red Hawk's heart was laboring.

"Ne' hyo, we did what we could," Wolf said, gripping his father's limp hands.

"It's good to hear you call me Father once more," Red Hawk said, smiling faintly. "You know what's to be done. Watch over your brothers, especially Morning Hawk. He's small."

"We were all once small," Wolf noted. "Your sons grow fast, though."

"Tall, too," Red Hawk whispered. "Your dream warned you. Trust Snow Wolf to guide you. Protect . . ."

"The defenseless ones," Wolf completed the thought. "Nothing lives long."

"Nothing . . ." Red Hawk mumbled.

"Only the earth and the mountains," Willow Boy said, sitting beside his father. "Why, Nah nih?"

"Who can say?" Wolf said, shivering as life departed his father's eyes. "Only Heammawihio knows such things."

"Only Heammawihio," Little Hawk agreed. "And he's turned away from the people."

20

WHEN WOLF RUNNING and his brothers returned with their father's body to the great Tsis tsis tas and Suhtai encampment, they found a world of confusion. Many of the southern people had already left. Some dragged their lodge poles along, but more than three hundred abandoned their lodges and set out on horseback, without the food, clothing, or cooking implements necessary for sustaining life on the plains.

"What's happening?" Wolf cried. "Are the bluecoats coming?"

No one knew. The chiefs hadn't dispatched scouts to watch the Wihio soldier camps, and no soldier society protected the remains of the camp. Everyone was rushing about in panic, trying to get his family away to safety.

"What should we do?" Little Hawk asked. "Ne' hyo is dead. Nah' koa is all alone with our brother."

"We have the burial ritual to perform," Wolf insisted. "There will be time to consider the future when Red Hawk has started the long walk."

Others argued it was more important to leave.

"Come with us," Buffalo Horn urged. "We're going south, where the Kiowas are camped. We'll be strong there."

"We were strong here," Wolf argued.

"We followed the wrong medicine chiefs here," Buffalo Horn complained. "No longer. The Hevataniu will renew themselves. We'll be strong again. To do so, we'll need good fighters. There's a place for you, Wolf. There are so many with no one to protect them."

"You have to protect the defenseless ones," Wolf answered. "My obligation is to the man who was once my father. I promised to look after his family, and I intend to do it."

"I understand," the Horn said, nodding gravely.

Curly and his Lakota companions also invited Wolf Running to go with them.

"Our people are hunting north of Platte River," Curly explained. "You and your brothers are welcome there. Many men lost wives when the Wihio attacked Little Thunder. Maybe Burnt Willow Woman can find another man to look after her."

"That's for me to do," Wolf said. "I intend to ride north, but I won't be looking for the security of a friendly camp. Now I must bury Red Hawk. Later I'll be making war against the Wihio. Platte River is thick with the wagon people. I'll make the bluecoats sorry they rode into our country and killed this good man."

Wolf was appalled at the way the people took flight.

"They run like quail chased by foxes," Willow Boy observed.

The Suhtai and most of the Omissis people departed the camp, too, but they escaped westward, toward the favored buffalo country. Most expected to head north later, after the bluecoats grew tired of killing Tsis tsis tas. Wolf watched his old friends leave. He didn't beg anyone to stay for the burial feast or the giveaway of his father's possessions. Most people left better things behind than Wolf could offer them.

"I have to help my father look after my family," Younger Dog explained when he brought Sun Walker Maiden out to the makeshift camp Wolf had made in the hills overlooking the deserted camp.

"I understand," Wolf told the boy. "Each man has his own obligations."

"It's a hard thing, burying two fathers," Sun Walker said. "When you've finished, I know the old prayers. If you want, I could help you free yourself from the ghosts."

"I would be grateful," Wolf told her. "I hope we'll have time to walk a river again before winter arrives."

"That would be pleasant," she agreed.

Pony's Tail brought some food, but he, too, was leaving. Others offered ponies, and many presented good elk and buffalo robes they were unable to carry away.

"It's a sad day," Stands Long observed as he helped Wolf and his brothers carve the scaffold poles.

"Maybe you, too, should leave," Wolf whispered. "Your family needs protecting."

"My brothers are all older," Stands Long argued. "I've been a long time walking man's road. We'll soon be taking wives, and then we'll have separate obligations. For now, I'm also your brother, Wolf."

They placed Red Hawk and two other men killed by the Wihio on a tall bluff overlooking Turkey Creek. Wolf set his father's weapons at his side and wrapped the bloody corpse in a painted elk robe. Little Hawk and Willow Boy killed three ponies and tied their tails to the scaffold pole.

"Ne' hyo loved to ride," Little Hawk said. "Now he'll have swift ponies to carry him on the other side."

It troubled Wolf that no medicine chief remained behind to speak the ancient prayers or invoke Heammawihio's favor. Willow Boy had learned some of the prayers, though, and Wolf decided his own words, and those of his brothers, would help their father on his journey.

Burnt Willow Woman took her husband's death stoically. She cut her hair and tore her clothing, but she didn't turn away from the work that needed doing. She had a small son, after all, and she valued Morning Hawk's needs above her pain.

They waited the required three days on Turkey Creek, praying and suffering. Below, the Wihio soldiers finally came upon the camp. They helped themselves to what they wanted and burned everything else. Three Pawnees noticed the burial scaffolds and climbed the bluff. Perhaps they were eager to loot the scaffolds, or maybe they just wanted to see which old enemy had climbed Hanging Road.

"It's a lot of trouble to take," Wolf noted as he crept closer to the trio. Stands Long, as always, was with him. The two notched arrows and shot two of the Pawnees at close range. Wolf pounced on the third, clubbed him senseless, took his scalp, and kicked the still-breathing enemy over the edge of the bluff.

"I've never known you to take a scalp," Stands Long said, frowning at the bloody bundle Wolf held in his hand.

"Raven Heart told me once that a modest man needs no trophies," Wolf explained. He carried the scalp to Red Hawk's scaffold and placed it with the pony tails. If the Pawnees walked the other side, they would know to respect Red Hawk.

The death of the Pawnees caused a stir among the bluecoats, and they kept a close watch over their camps. They didn't remain among the blazing lodges. Instead they had built a fort of sorts out of mud, farther north. There they kept their cattle and horses. The cannons guarded the place, as did hundreds of foot soldiers.

"So, what do we do now?" Little Hawk asked when the mourning rituals were completed.

"Leave," Wolf said.

"Where do we go?" the Hawk asked. "North? South? We have cousins in both places."

"I'm going west," Wolf said, frowning. "Among the Wihio soldier camps. Many of our people are camped to the north, on Red Shield River. Nah' koa can camp there safely. You could take her there."

"And what do you intend to do?" Willow Boy asked.

"Punish the Wihio," Wolf told them. "Make them remember our people. They may kill all of us, but it won't be painless."

"You pledged to protect our mother," Willow Boy reminded Wolf Running. "Don't you think we're aching, too? Why don't we see her safely northward? Then there will be time for fighting."

Wolf frowned. He wanted to punish someone then, in that very place.

"They're right," Stands Long told him. "Wolf, we'll escort your mother. She can stay with your father's relations in the Oglala camps. Or maybe one of the Suhtai people will ask her to stay with them."

"Everyone has a heavy burden already," Wolf noted. "Who can we ask to take her?"

"We'll provide for her, Nah nih," Little Hawk said, turning to Willow Boy and then back to Wolf. "We'll help our small brother onto man's road, too, when it's time."

"Yes, we will," Wolf agreed.

They completed their preparations that next day. Then, as darkness cloaked their movements, Wolf led the way down the bluff and past the bluecoat camps on Turkey Creek. They rode along, carrying only what they could pack on four spare ponies. The lodge had been burned, but they had iron kettles, a frying pan, plenty of good hides, and several warm robes.

Four days Wolf and his family rode north around the Wihio before they joined a large Omissis camp south of Platte River and west of Fort Kearny. The people remained fearful, and many urged a move either north or east. Some even argued a new camp should be built at Big Island.

"It's easily protected," Hairy Moccasin pointed out.

"There are too many ghosts there," Wolf complained. "The Wihio killed us there before. They can bring their cannons up to Platte River and shoot them at us. We're defenseless against those big guns, and the river would prevent our escape. No, we're safest in open country, where we can scatter if there's need."

Hairy Moccasin glared at Wolf. It wasn't appropriate for so young a man to argue with a chief. Everyone remembered Wolf's rescue of the pony boys, though. They knew he had remained behind to tend the dead when many had bolted. The story of how he and Stands Long had killed the Pawnees had excited the young men and pleased their elders.

"Have you had a dream?" Pony's Tail asked. "Has Snow Wolf suggested anything?"

"I haven't dreamed," Wolf replied. "I can't invite a spirit creature into my heart when it's in such disharmony."

"We're all upset," Hairy Moccasin said, softening his tone.

"We must build a sweat lodge so that the young men can find their way back to the sacred hoop," Flying Squirrel advised.

"It's a good notion," Wolf agreed. "I'll help."

Many others stepped forward to volunteer, and it was done quickly. That very next day the first party of men entered the sweat lodge. Wolf waited respectfully as older men went before him. He entered with Stands Long, Pony's Tail, Little Hawk, and Willow Boy. Three other young Omissis also came along. As the water splashed against glowing rocks, steam began to fill the little hut. All the anger and pain boiled up inside Wolf Running, and he shuddered as it began to flow out of him.

Flying Squirrel had long since passed on the ritual, and

Wolf himself spoke the words and performed the pipe ceremony. He also guided his companions through the renewal.
Each put the past behind and tried to find the harmony of the
sacred path.

Afterward Wolf swam in a shallow pond with his
brothers.

"You've changed," Little Hawk told Wolf. "The pain's
left your face. Is it gone from your heart?"

"I'll never be as whole as before, when good men guided
my steps," Wolf told them. "I have dark memories that
continue to bother me. I'm not hot for killing like I used to
be, though. I understand what's most important."

"What's that?" Willow Boy asked.

"My brothers," Wolf explained. "My family. My people.
I'll pray and suffer in hope of finding a vision, a direction.
Snow Wolf has been a good guide. I have to trust him to find
my way."

"You won't fight the bluecoats?" Little Hawk asked.

"I'll invite a vision, See' was' sin mit," Wolf replied. "I
don't know what it may show. I hope it will lead us all to a
better day. But if it's necessary for me to die, then I will."

"I'm not afraid of dying," Willow Boy declared. "Only
suffering. Seeing those I love killed."

"It's harder sometimes to go on than to give up," Wolf
observed. "But we're a long way from dead, See' was' sin
mit. We have battles left to fight and buffalo left to hunt."

That night Wolf found the first true rest he'd known since
the fight at Turkey Creek. He rose early the next morning
and walked out past the edge of camp to make the morning
prayers. He'd scarcely begun when Little Hawk and Willow
Boy appeared.

"We thought that you might enjoy some company," the
Hawk explained.

Wolf welcomed them. As they performed the pipe ritual
and welcomed the beginning of another day, Wolf felt the
emptiness inside him flow away. In its place grew a new

belonging. When the brothers had completed the prayers, they returned to the pond and joined several other young men in the water.

"When will you seek your vision?" Little Hawk asked after the brothers had raced from one side of the pond to the other and back again.

"Tonight I'll ride into the hills," Wolf told him. "I remember how the grandfathers used to do it. They would stay out under the stars, eating nothing. Each night they'd cut the flesh of their arms and bleed. As they sang and danced, they prayed for a vision. Finally, they would collapse. If Heammawihio was satisfied with their suffering, he would give the dream."

"Have you ever done it before?" Willow Boy asked.

"No," Wolf confessed. "Others have."

"You'll need a watcher," Little Hawk observed. "I'm your brother. It's for me to go."

"You should stay and hunt with the others," Wolf argued. "You, too," he added, turning to Willow Boy. "Stands Long and I have shared many struggles. He can go."

"If the Pawnees find you, he'd be a better man to have along," Little Hawk said, sighing.

"It's not because he's older," Wolf assured the boys. "It's because he has brothers to feed his family. I'm placing the heavy burden on you two. See our small brother and his mother have enough to eat. Burnt Willow Woman is sewing hides into a lodge skin, but she'll need more than what she has."

"You'll share the dream, won't you?" Willow Boy asked.

"Of course," Wolf promised. "I'm not seeking the dream for myself. It's for our people. Snow Wolf may show us all a path to walk."

The sun was hanging high overhead when Wolf and Stands Long departed the Omissis camp. Wolf again rode the white stallion. He didn't bring his shield, though, or any weapon. Stands Long had a rifle, a bow, and two quivers filled with good arrows.

"The Oglalas say the Pawnees are thick in these hills," Stands Long explained. "It's good to be prepared."

"And even better to have a brother-friend to watch for danger," Wolf replied.

They didn't venture far from the camp. Wolf found an appropriate place—a small clearing on the side of a ridge overlooking Platte River. He built up a small fire, rolled out hides to rest on, and performed the pipe ritual. Stands Long joined him for the smoking. Afterward Wolf drank some water and began his fast. He waited for nightfall before starting the dancing.

He began with a warrior song. Then he began dancing. Each time he circled the little fire, he drew out his knife and cut the flesh of his arms and chest. The blood flowing down his arms and chest drove him to further exertions. He pounded his feet on the rocky ground and screamed old Suhtai medicine chants. He went on the whole night. Only at daybreak did he pause to rest.

All that next long day he sat silently before the fire. His belly ached for food. When night returned, he repeated the dancing and singing and suffering.

Wolf could feel the fever coming the following morning. He gazed at the sun and realized his eyes were seeing distorted images. He was growing weak, and his legs wouldn't hold his weight. He went on praying and meditating that entire day. As darkness settled in, Wolf stared into the flames of the fire. He could see Snow Wolf there.

"Wolf?" Stands Long called.

"I'm going on a walk now," Wolf announced. But instead of standing, he lay back on the buffalo hides and closed his eyes.

The dream came swiftly. Wolf had never doubted it would come, but he was surprised at how vivid the images were. He saw Platte River and the bluffs that lined sections of the river. He saw Eagle Claw's bones resting on their scaffold on Big Island. He heard the ghostly voices of Bent Arrow and Little Fork. It seemed as if an entire army of the dead rode along the river there, shouting encouragement.

Finally Snow Wolf appeared.

Wolf Running shivered from a sudden chill. He saw himself in the dream. He was naked, and he appeared younger, thinner. His hair was short. He stepped toward the edge of a bluff and gazed out at the river.

"Show me the way, Snow Wolf," the young man pleaded.

Down below, the river churned its way eastward, eating away at the land as always.

"Nothing lasts long," Snow Wolf sang. "Not earth. Not mountain. Not the creatures of the earth or sky. Everything changes."

"And Tsis tsis tas?" Wolf heard himself ask.

"Hard times are coming," Snow Wolf explained.

Wolf Running now envisioned two trails. The first was steep, treacherous. It wound through high mountains, and there were many places where it was easy to slip and fall. At the end was a solitary lodge protected by an outcropping of rock. Inside an old man sat singing old warrior songs.

The second path led through a valley marked with the bones of Bull Buffalo. Wagon ruts scarred the land, and Wihio forts were everywhere. Fires blazed, and an odor of blood and death filled the air. A young man raced along the river, shooting stone-tipped arrows and shouting warrior songs. His flesh was bronze and hard, and many jagged scars attested to a warrior's life.

This path led to no lodge. Instead Wolf saw a burial scaffold. He couldn't see the face of the body on top, but he could tell from the single hand that protruded from an elk robe that the man resting there hadn't been very old. Pony tails decorated one end of the scaffold. A shield stood at the other end—an impressive thing torn by several bullets. In its center was the fiery-eyed face of a white wolf.

Wolf Running awoke. The morning sun blazed overhead, and he was wearier than he imagined possible. He couldn't believe the night had already passed, and when Stands Long explained he had slept through one day and well into a second, shivering with cold and burning with fever, Wolf could hardly believe it.

"You found the dream, though," Stands Long observed. "What did you see?"

"A choice," Wolf explained. "I can grow old walking a quiet, solitary life."

"Or?"

"I will die young."

"A warrior's death," Stands Long said, nodding solemnly. "You said you had a choice, but you don't."

"I know," Wolf said, sighing. "It was decided long ago. I didn't ask for the dream to determine my own future, though. It's the fate of the people that's got to be decided."

"There's no choice there, either," Stands Long insisted. "We're Tsis tsis tas. Turning away from warrior's road would make us something else."

"Maybe you're right."

"You know I am. So, what will we tell the others?"

"Everything," Wolf said. "They won't see a choice either, though."

21

WOLF RUNNING AND Stands Long Beside Him returned to the Omissis camp that next day. Some of the young men ran out to greet him. Everyone expected Wolf to speak of a great vision. He didn't.

Instead, Wolf sat beside a small fire and told his brothers of the choice Snow Wolf had offered them.

"Choice?" Little Hawk asked. "You might as well ask me to choose between having my feet or my head cut off."

"We can't be Tsis tsis tas and turn away from warrior's road," Willow Boy added.

"There can be only one path then," Wolf said, nodding to his brothers.

That next morning, after making the morning prayers, Wolf and Stands Long rode out to Platte River. There they spied a long column of dust on the rutted wagon road.

"Are the soldiers coming here, too?" Stands Long asked.

"Not soldiers," Wolf said, studying the dust. "Not wagons, either."

"What then?"

"Cattle," Wolf observed. "Horses. Very few men to watch over them. It wouldn't be hard to steal everything."

"We need ponies," Stands Long admitted, "but cows?"

"Their hides wouldn't be as good for making lodge skins, but it would be easier to kill them. Their meat would fill the children's bellies."

"Cow meat has no taste," Stands Long grumbled.

"It's not so bad," Wolf argued. "Besides, why would the Wihio bring so many cows out here? They must be the soldier's winter rations. If we can't kill the bluecoats, at least we can make them hungry."

The brother-friends shared a laugh. Then they picked their way down the ridge and hurried back to the camp. Wolf was eager to share his news and organize a raiding party.

Others, too, had seen the dust from the Wihio cattle herd. Already many Omissis families were breaking down the makeshift shelters that had replaced the burned lodges.

"Wolf!" Little Hawk called. "I'm glad you've returned. There are soldiers on Platte River. We have to leave this place."

"Soldiers?" Wolf asked. "Where?"

Little Hawk explained how Corn Dancer and three other scouts had spied the soldiers on Platte River.

"The Dancer must be blind," Wolf said, laughing. "There aren't any soldiers closer than Fort Kearny. It's a cattle herd. Horses, too. We should ride out and take them. We'd have enough food for the women and children to eat. Plenty of hides, too."

"And horses!" Stands Long added.

Hairy Moccasin heard Wolf's words and walked over with some of the other older men.

"No bluecoats?" the Moccasin asked.

"I saw only men dressed in buckskins," Wolf told him. "Maybe twenty of them. We can easily run off the animals."

"And the men?" Hairy Moccasin asked.

"If they fight us, we'll kill them," Stands Long boasted. "If they run, let them go. They're nothing."

"They'll tell the bluecoats at Fort Kearny," Hairy Moccasin warned.

"Good," Little Hawk said, grinning. "Then we'll have bluecoats to kill."

"We have to protect the camp," Wolf said, gazing around him at the frightened faces of the women and children. "It's time we moved away from here anyway. There are too many Wihio and too few friends here."

"Yes," Hairy Moccasin agreed. "We'll do it."

"Who's to lead the raiders?" Corn Dancer asked. "I'm the one who saw them first."

"You only planned to run," Wolf pointed out. "Stands Long and I will lead the way."

"It would be better if an older man led," Hairy Moccasin objected. "Split Chin knows what to do."

"I would follow the Chin," Wolf agreed.

Others murmured their agreement, and the thing was decided. Wolf helped his brothers pack up the family's belongings.

"Who will stay with Nah' koa?" Willow Boy asked, turning toward Burnt Willow Woman.

"My older sons are warriors!" she barked at them. "I expect all three to strike the enemy. Just leave us two ponies to carry the possessions. Morning Hawk and I will be fine."

"It would be best . . ." Wolf began.

"I have many friends," she said, cutting him off. "Have you forgotten the times I've tended my sons while their father rode out to fight the Pawnees? Don't be foolish. Go and walk man's road!"

Wolf felt uneasy, leaving her to manage on her own, but he didn't argue. Most of the other women had more than one child to tend, and other young men left their mothers behind and joined Split Chin's raiding party.

As the main band prepared its retreat to Red Shield River,

Wolf and the other raiders assembled to make medicine and paint their faces. It was still early, but already the sun was blazing overhead. The warriors stripped to their breech-clouts and readied their ponies.

Wolf slung his bow over one shoulder.

"Where's the rifle?" Stands Long asked.

"I left it with Burnt Willow Woman," Wolf explained. "In my dream I had only a bow."

"I hope you saw it clearly," Stands Long said. "Your rifle was a good one. It could kill a man from a great distance. The bow may be better at close range, but if we have trouble . . ."

"We won't," Wolf told his brother-friend. "A man will fight hard for his wife or his house. But for cows?"

Nevertheless Wolf warned his brothers to stay close.

"These Wihio should run, but sometimes they'll fire off their guns anyway," Wolf explained. "I've buried too many relatives. No horse or cow is worth a brother's life."

"We have to feed the helpless ones, though," Willow Boy argued. "If we bleed, it's for them."

"Yes, for them," Wolf agreed.

Split Chin instructed the twenty-five men of his war party in the traditional way of fighting. He cautioned the younger men to hold back and wait for the more experienced fighters to strike the enemy.

"There's no need for suicide charges," the Chin added. "We only want to run the animals. I've traded with some of these herders. Many know us. They won't fight unless pressed hard. Leave them their lives so long as they don't hurt anybody."

"If they do," Corn Dancer vowed, "we'll kill them!"

Wolf winced. He had never placed much value in Corn Dancer's boasting. Now the Dancer's very face was becoming a plague.

"Go and ride with the others," Wolf growled when Corn Dancer and two young men rode up beside him.

"We thought to ride with you and the other children," Corn Dancer explained.

"You get people killed," Wolf grumbled. "You hurry others onto Hanging Road, but you yourself survive. Keep away from me."

"What's this, old friend?" Corn Dancer asked.

"I'm not your friend," Wolf pointed out. "You don't have any old ones, either. You get them killed long before that."

Corn Dancer opened his mouth to argue, but he grew strangely quiet instead. Wolf glanced over his shoulder and saw that Stands Long had notched an arrow.

"It would disturb the harmony of the world for me to kill a Tsis tsis tas," Stands Long said. "If you continue, I might have to do it. Go!"

Corn Dancer and his young companions galloped off.

"It's time now," Wolf told his companions. Split Chin waved his lance, and the riders set off, singing warrior songs and braving themselves for the coming attack. They quickly covered the short distance to the river. Then, after Split Chin had scouted the cattle, he divided the raiders into three groups. Each had its own task. Wolf would take the first group and draw off as many guards as was possible. Split Chin would hit the front and side of the herd. The remaining Tsis tsis tas would cut out the mules and horses.

Wolf was disappointed to discover his band faced most of the fighting while others would run the ponies and mules.

"We should insist on sharing in the captured animals," Willow Boy complained.

"None will be taken if we worry about the others," Wolf argued. "We're fighting so the little ones won't be hungry. Aren't we Elks? We always accept the heaviest obligations, don't we?"

The others howled their agreement. Wolf then led them past Split Chin and on toward the rutted river road. Everything was as expected there. The herders seemed unaware of the looming danger.

"Ayyyy!" Wolf howled as he notched an arrow. "Nothing lives long!"

"Nothing!" Stands Long added as he fired his own arrow into the back of a nearby herder. Wolf shot a second man through the thigh. Instantly the remaining herders tried to form a weak line to defend the herd. That wasn't possible. There were as many herders as raiders, but in the dust Wolf supposed the handful of Tsis tsis tas must have seemed more like a hundred.

"Let's run them!" Wolf urged as the Wihio jumped off their horses and took shelter in a wooden wagon.

"Get the horses!" Little Hawk cried as he and Willow Boy chased a pair of good stallions toward the creek.

Wolf turned to Stands Long.

"The others are taking charge of the cattle," Wolf noted. "We should strike hard a final time and leave."

"Yes," Stands Long agreed. The two brother-friends then charged the wagon, taking care to avoid the rifle shots exploding from the front and back. Instead they darted in from both sides, cut the horses loose, and galloped away.

The firing began to die away after that. The herders formed a circle near the river. They were tired, dusty, and afoot. Wolf almost felt sorry for them.

His own challenge was just beginning. He and the other Tsis tsis tas had to turn the cattle south, away from water. That was difficult anytime, but the gunfire and howling had started the cows running. It was a close thing, getting them turned south.

For days after the raid, the Omissis warriors did their best to run the cattle away from Platte River. There were almost nine hundred animals, though. Small groups broke away and scattered themselves up ravines and along streams. Once the raiders rejoined the main camp, the slaughtering began.

Hairy Moccasin organized hunting parties, but it wasn't the same as riding out to strike Bull Buffalo. The cattle wouldn't turn and fight. Most milled about, waiting to die. The medicine chiefs knew no proper prayers, and it was like plucking pears off a bush.

Mostly the killing was left to the younger men. Boys as young as ten galloped up to the cattle and fired their arrows. Women then marched out to the carcasses and began butchering. A smell of blood and death plagued the tepid air. It soon became necessary to move the camp daily. Birds descended from the sky to pick at the bones. Wolves howled hungrily in the distance, waiting for nightfall to cover their approach.

"We'll soon be able to make lodges again," Stands Long said as he and Wolf made their way through the Omissis camps. "These cows don't have thick hides, and you wouldn't want to carry a shield made from them. There's not so much hair to scrape, though, and the hides make good leggings and shirts."

"Moccasins," too, Wolf noted. "Killing them's not hunting, though."

"No, but I take satisfaction in knowing the animals would have fed a big Wihio army. Now the enemy is hungry. Maybe he'll freeze when winter comes. I wouldn't be sorry if the bluecoats felt some of the torment our people have suffered."

Half a moon passed before the bulk of the cattle had been slaughtered. By then a lot of meat had been dried and put aside for winter. New lodge poles were cut, and once again conical lodges rose from the Omissis camps.

"We've survived," Wolf told his brothers the day they led their mother to her new lodge. True, it was scarcely more than a big square tent, but it served to keep off the nightly chills. When winter came, it would suffice.

"What do we do now, Nah nih?" Willow Boy asked. "It's too early to make our winter camp. With the cattle herd killed, we don't need to strike Bull Buffalo."

"That's true," Wolf agreed. "I thought we might return to

Platte River and search out our Oglala friends. Maybe we can annoy the Wihio wagon camps. We might even find bluecoats to run."

"Ayyyy!" Little Hawk howled. "That would be a good thing!"

Older men warned against it. Hairy Moccasin ordered a council fire lit, and he invited all the Omissis warriors to meet with him.

"Already some of our young men have been taken captive on Platte River," the Moccasin pointed out. "Soldiers have taken the promised presents at Bent's Fort. The southern people are suffering. We won't receive our goods, either. The bluecoat chiefs will see to it."

"If the supplies are at Fort Laramie, we can take them like we did before, after Grattan's death," Corn Dancer suggested.

"We could always treat with Twiss," Wolf argued.

"We did that before," Hairy Moccasin growled angrily. "What good came of it? We were attacked!"

"That wasn't the agent's doing," Wolf objected.

"You can't trust the Wihio," Split Chin insisted.

The men went on quarreling all of that night and most of the following day. Wolf had heard enough. He led his brothers aside.

"It's time to go north," he told them. "Nah' koa will be welcome to winter with the Oglalas."

"We need ponies," Little Hawk grumbled. "Our mounts are breaking down, and it's a long distance to go."

"We should have shared in the animals taken from the herders," Willow Boy argued.

"Yes," Wolf agreed. "It's already done, though. On our way north we can watch the wagon camps. Maybe we'll raid one or two and take some ponies. Perhaps the Pawnees will come out and let us take some of theirs."

"It's a good idea," Stands Long noted, "but we're too small a party to leave on our own."

"Hairy Moccasin's content to stay where we are," Wolf pointed out. "He has a son and a nephew taken prisoner by the bluecoats. He'll do nothing to trouble the Wihio now."

"Shouldn't a father do what he can to keep his son safe?" Stands Long asked.

"I don't fault the Moccasin," Wolf said. "I'm only saying we can't continue to follow him."

"I'll ask around," Willow Boy volunteered. "Maybe some others will come with us."

"Ask," Wolf urged. "When summer is this long and hot, winter inevitably strikes hard."

"It will trouble the bluecoats more than us," Stands Long argued. "They're unaccustomed to the damp and the cold."

"Our lodges are in disarray," Wolf said, frowning. "There are few warm robes. We'll be suffering, too."

Willow Boy made his way among the Omissis lodges, asking each man what his family planned to do. When word spread that Wolf Running planned to ride north and join his Oglala relations, many Omissis asked to come along. Some were older men worn down by the hard fighting and the fearful flight that followed the battle. A few were younger and considerably more welcome.

Wolf was especially glad to see Pony's Tail and his family. Other young Elks also began breaking down their lodges. Wolf was less delighted by the sight of Corn Dancer.

"I expected you to lead your own band," Wolf told the Dancer. "If you come, hold your tongue. I won't have disharmony in my camp."

"You'll have it with or without me," Corn Dancer insisted. "I'll remain quiet, though."

When he was satisfied everything was prepared, Wolf smoked with Hairy Moccasin and explained his plans.

"It's a hard road you're choosing," the Moccasin warned. "Walk it carefully. Stay away from Lodgepole Creek. The Wihio burned a small camp of ours there."

Wolf hadn't heard that. He frowned.

"There's trouble everywhere," Hairy Moccasin went on to say. "Bluecoats camp at Bent's Fort, on Red Shield River, and at their mud fort on Turkey Creek. Their wagon bands cut roads across the buffalo hunting country. They kill us with their bullets and their sicknesses."

"That's why I intend to go north," Wolf explained. "We have strong friends there."

"The Wihio have killed Lakotas, too," Hairy Moccasin argued. "They'll kill more of them."

"Why?" Wolf asked.

"Because we're here," the Moccasin growled. "We're in the way. We've moved out of the old country, farther and farther south and west. There's nowhere left to go."

"If you believe that, ride with us," Wolf urged.

"My son, Pale Calf, is in the hands of the Wihio," Hairy Moccasin explained. "My nephew, Bull Charge, is with him. They may be dead already. Who can say? I only know I can't fight the Wihio and hurry their dying."

"If I act, I may endanger them," Wolf confessed.

"You're young. It's too much to ask a young man to stand by while his people are cut down. That takes old age and great patience. I've never known either before, but I'm learning. I won't ask you to put aside your weapons. No, just ride east or west of us first so the enemy will see it wasn't me."

"I understand," Wolf said, gazing at his weary feet.

"Go and punish the Wihio then," Hairy Moccasin urged. "Strike hard and swift."

"I will," Wolf promised. "And I'll watch over the helpless ones."

"I didn't bother asking that," Hairy Moccasin said, clasping the younger man's hands. "Everyone knows Wolf Running as a man of the people."

22

WOLF RUNNING LED his small band of Omissis north-ward. The whole party consisted of only ten lodges—forty people. Many of those were women and children. There were only eight warriors, and that included Little Hawk and Willow Boy, who would have been counted among the pony boys any other summer.

Much more worrisome was the bad habit the older men had of taking charge. Each decision caused a quarrel, and Wolf worried he wouldn't be able to defend the helpless ones if an enemy found them.

"They'll still be considering which man should strike the first blow when the Pawnees are riding off with the ponies—and the women!" Stands Long complained.

Corn Dancer didn't help matters. Each morning he rode off on his own or with a pair of youngsters, Sandpiper and Lark Wing. They would ignore the difficult work required to get the pony drags across creeks or rivers. They neglected the needs of the helpless ones. Instead they would be off shooting game and alerting any nearby enemy of their presence.

"We should never have allowed him to come," Wolf grumbled.

"It's not too late to order him from our camp," Stands Long noted. "There's no choice if you want to cross Platte River unseen."

Much as it pained him, Wolf saw the choice just as clearly.

"I'll ask Pony's Tail to speak to him," Wolf said, sighing. "That way there's less likely to be bad blood among us."

"It might be best," Stands Long agreed.

Sandpiper and Lark Wing were Pony's Tail's cousins. Their father, Thunder Colt, had once been a Fox lance-carrier, but he had fallen riding after Bull Buffalo two summers before. The Colt walked with difficulty, and although he was a great bow-maker, he rarely rode to war or went hunting anymore. Wolf Running found it hard to speak to a famous man about trouble. The words might be better received from a relation.

They weren't. The same morning Wolf told Pony's Tail that Corn Dancer was no longer welcome in his band, Thunder Colt and three other men broke their lodges down and turned eastward.

"We should never have followed a boy," the Colt complained. "I will decide what's best for my sons!"

"It's my fault," Pony's Tail told Wolf afterward. "I didn't realize how deep my uncle's wounds are. He feels he should be leading us, and he had no ears to hear my words."

"It's no one's fault," Wolf argued. "The Wihio have disturbed the harmony of the world. Nothing's as it should be."

A day's ride south of Platte River, four other lodges turned back. The people were worried Wolf and his young companions would not be able to protect them. Only three lodges continued northward. Besides the small lodge tended by Burnt Willow Woman and a somewhat smaller shelter that served as the young men's lodge, one surviving lodge from the Turkey Creek camp traveled north. That belonged to an old man, Sky Lance, and his wife, Summer Plum Woman. They tended two small grandchildren and relied on Wolf Running and his brothers for protection. Their four sons were all dead now, and a solitary daughter had climbed Hanging Road when the coughing sickness struck the Omissis camps near Horse Creek.

"Do you want us to turn back with the others?" Sky Lance had asked pointedly.

"Uncle, you can choose," Wolf told the white-haired old warrior. "I have only sent one man from our camp."

"He was no more useless to you than I am," the Lance argued.

"You haven't endangered the rest of us," Wolf said, laughing. "Besides, if we run across bluecoats, we may need your bow."

"It's yours!" Sky Lance insisted. "I hope my grandsons grow old enough to follow you and Snow Wolf. Yes, that would be a thing to see!"

Wolf grinned his thanks. He then set out ahead to find a place to cross the river. There were several suitable spots, but Wihio wagon camps occupied the three nearest ones. Wolf decided to wait for the wagon people to leave. Meanwhile he hid his people in a nearby ravine.

Those were difficult days. With so few fighters left, each man had to keep watch part of every night. It was impossible to have scouts out in every direction, and some nights Wolf was surprised by the pinpricks of light made by the cooking fires of soldiers or wagon people camped in the nearby hills.

"We have to get across soon," Wolf told Stands Long. "We can't remain here unseen forever."

"We'll cross tomorrow," Stands Long declared. "If we

have to run off some ponies to distract the wagon people, we can."

Wolf agreed, but inside he had grave doubts. If soldiers rode down on the pony drags when they were in midstream, it wouldn't be possible to save the helpless ones.

Next morning the wagons camped at Split Hoof Crossing left early. Wolf then rode ahead. The pony drags followed. Stands Long, Little Hawk, and Willow Boy kept watch in back.

"Heammawihio," Wolf whispered, "help me keep these defenseless people safe."

Burnt Willow Woman, sensing the approaching danger, insisted Morning Hawk ride with Wolf Running.

"Brothers should get to know each other," she argued. "He's too old to bounce along in a pony drag."

Morning Hawk was only five, but he was a talkative child, and like his brothers he appeared older.

"He can ride with me," Wolf agreed, extending his hand down. Morning Hawk gripped Wolf's wrist, and Wolf lifted the boy up behind him.

"Don't worry," the boy whispered. "If the Pawnees or the bluecoats charge, I'll jump off so you can untie your shield."

"You wait for me to tell you," Wolf said, grinning. "I'll find a good place where you can use your bow."

"It's only a boy's bow," Morning Hawk muttered. "I couldn't hurt anyone with it."

"No?" Wolf asked. "Willow Boy told me you were a great killer of rabbits and birds."

"Our brother doesn't always tell the truth," the Hawk said, laughing. "I hit a frog once, though."

"They're difficult targets," Wolf observed. "Always hopping about."

"Yes," the boy agreed. He then devoted a considerable part of the morning to describing his attack on the frogs. It was a welcome distraction, for Wolf was gravely concerned about making the crossing.

Afterward, when the pony drags were clear of the rutted wagon road, and Wolf led his little party into the hills beyond, they all appeared relieved.

"You did well, Wolf," Sky Lance told him. "Be glad the others turned back. It would have been much harder getting ten lodges across."

Wolf knew the old man was right. No sooner had their dust trail died away than a party of bluecoats galloped along. The soldiers studied the crossing and quickly detected a trail left by the pony drags. Any trace vanished in the trail ruts and the rocky terrain beyond.

"How do they know someone was here?" Stands Long whispered. "We saw no scouts."

"I can't be certain," Wolf replied, "but it may be because the others crossed today."

Wolf then pointed to three buzzards turning slow circles in the sky a morning's riding farther east.

"Corn Dancer," Stands Long grumbled.

"Maybe."

The instant he spotted the buzzards, Wolf knew he would investigate. It wasn't possible to ignore such a clear sign of trouble. He hoped it marked the demise of a Wihio ox or perhaps a dead cavalry horse.

Wolf helped Morning Hawk down and motioned Little Hawk and Willow Boy to hang back and watch the others.

"We should all go or all stay," Little Hawk argued. "Two can do nothing."

"We'll be back," Wolf promised. "I don't intend to make a fight."

He and Stands Long then wove their way through the low hills and ravines north of Platte River, taking care to conceal their movements as much as possible. They continued eastward for a time. Then Wolf spied wagon dust, and the brother-friends hid in a stand of cottonwoods.

A small wagon band rolled past. Wolf counted only seven wagons. Soldiers were driving, so perhaps the wagons carried ammunition. After the Wihio passed, Wolf led the way on. Just after midday he spied dark shapes on the riverbank ahead.

"Ponies," Stands Long noted.

"Dead ones," Wolf added.

They climbed a low hill and scanned the horizon for bluecoats. The only ones in view were the men escorting the westbound wagons. Wolf took a deep breath, waved to Stands Long, and started down toward the river.

There had been a fight there. The first horse they passed was a cavalry mount. Its heavy saddle and iron shoes told that much. Beyond, in the shallows, three naked bodies gazed eerily skyward.

"That wasn't necessary," Wolf growled as he jumped down alongside. Pony's Tail lay between his young cousins, Sandpiper and Lark Wing. All three were marked by the neat round holes left by Wihio rifle balls. Someone had cut away Sandpiper's ears, and Lark Wing's left wrist was badly cut. Either buzzards had been picking at the bellies or the Wihio had savagely mutilated the corpses.

"He wore a silver bracelet," Stands Long noted. "They had trouble getting it off."

Wolf could understand that. Bluecoats set great store by silver. But the ears? Also, it was clear that the bullets had robbed the young men of life. Why cut them up?

"Maybe Pawnees . . ." Stands Long began.

"Did you see any Pawnees?" Wolf asked angrily. "This wasn't done by Pawnees. Pony's Tail had yet to count his sixteenth summer! Those others hadn't yet plucked their chins!"

"Wolf?" Stands Long asked as his brother-friend turned with furious eyes toward the west.

"Ayyyy!" Wolf shouted. "Come and fight me, child-hunters! Test my aim!"

"Wolf, we have others to think about," Stands Long argued.

"I smell Corn Dancer," Wolf added, gazing southward. "He was responsible for breaking up our band. How did he do it? Taunt the cousins into making the crossing first?"

"Wolf." Stands Long pointed ahead to another shape.

They left their young friend's corpse behind and walked on. Soon they happened on other bodies. Thunder Colt was there. So were two women and three small children. It appeared as if the entire band had been caught in midstream and cut down.

"Corn Dancer!" Wolf howled.

The Dancer had vanished. One or two others were also absent.

"What happened to the lodges?" Stands Long asked.

"Swept away by the river," Wolf suggested. "Left behind. Who can say?"

"We can't stay out here," Stands Long said, grabbing Wolf's arm and dragging him to the bank. "Someone will spot us."

"Let them come," Wolf muttered bitterly.

"And what about your pledge? You promised to guard the helpless ones, remember?"

"I remember," Wolf said, swallowing. "I remember everything. Someone must pay for this! Someone will!"

When they rejoined the others, Wolf didn't speak of the massacre of Thunder Colt's family. His companions knew something was wrong, but they asked no questions.

"There are good springs in those hills there," Sky Lance called when the band finally left Platte River behind.

"That's not the place," Wolf told them. "We're headed elsewhere."

Wolf plodded along northward, past a handful of good camping spots. Finally, as darkness descended, Stands Long drew him aside.

"This is a suitable place, Wolf," Stands Long said,

pointing to a small lake. "The people are tired. We have to stop."

"Are we safe?" Wolf asked. "Can't you hear the Wihio soldier horns?"

"No," Stands Long said, frowning. "And neither can you. You have to rest. We all do."

Wolf didn't remember much of the balance of that evening. He ate nothing. Burnt Willow Woman placed a cool cloth on his forehead and watched over him with a mother's concern.

"Has he caught a fever?" little Morning Hawk asked.

"What's happened to you, Nah nih?" Willow Bow cried.

"All this time he's carried the burden for the rest of us," Stands Long told him. "Now it's our turn to watch over him."

"But what's wrong?" Little Hawk asked.

"I'll explain it later," Stands Long promised. "Let's leave him to find some rest."

That night as the dying embers of the cooking fire began to lose their glow, Stands Long explained about Pony's Tail. He kept many of the details to himself, though. Boys were often plagued by ghosts, and the unburied bodies weren't very far away. Stands Long suspected those spirits were already troubling his brother-friend.

"Will the bluecoats follow us into these hills?" Morning Hawk asked.

"Why?" Willow Boy grumbled. "Better to leave us alone. We're helpless now. We have no good winter lodge. We have some hides and robes, but winter's hard in this country. We'll all be freezing when the Hard Face Moons find us."

"No, we'll survive," Stands Long insisted. "Wolf will find a path for us to walk. You've trusted him before, and you're still alive. Trust him a little longer."

Wolf slept fitfully a day and a half. He was feverish, and he called out in the night for his fathers, for old friends, for Snow Wolf to drive away the enemy.

Snow Wolf did visit the dream, but only to whisper an old warrior song.

> "It's good we're riding this morning.
> The enemy is strong, but we're Tsis tsis tas.
> We'll run them, hah!"

A similar Lakota war chant flooded the air, and many painted warriors rode out of the hills, waving rifles and lances. Then the white wolf glanced out at Platte River with somber red eyes.

"Some things are past understanding," the spirit creature whispered. "Hold the helpless ones in your heart, Brother. Do what's necessary. Others will always be eager to follow you."

Wolf awoke with a strange sensation. His flesh prickled, and he felt a heavy weight resting atop his chest.

"Uhh," he moaned as he blinked his eyes open.

"Nah nih," Morning Hawk whispered. The child was curled up beside his brother; the weight had been the Hawk's small head.

"You were worried," Wolf observed.

"I have no father," Morning Hawk explained. "Only brothers. Shouldn't I be worried when you are sick?"

"I'm not sick now," Wolf assured the child. "I'm whole again."

"And the anger?" Stands Long called from the far side of the shelter.

"Not anger," Wolf argued. "It was never anger. Rage, yes. It remains. Not for long, though. Soon it will be released."

"You can't imagine there are enough of us to strike the enemy?" Stands Long cried.

"We won't be alone much longer," Wolf explained. "The Lakotas are coming."

Wolf Running relocated the camp a short distance to the west. He found a good place sheltered by tall cottonwoods and watered by a shallow stream. The horses grazed and regained their strength. The men and boys hunted elk and restored their spirits.

Summer was melting away into memory, and Wolf welcomed its passing. He couldn't recall a season so torn by conflict and death. For once, he welcomed winter.

They were camped at the stream five days when the sound of approaching horses drew Wolf's attention. He hurriedly assembled his young companions. Armed with their bows, they formed a thin line and waited to welcome friends or punish enemies. Fortunately Wolf recognized a friendly face and shouted a greeting.

"Hau, Curly!" he called. "Cousin!"

"Hau, Wolf!" Curly shouted in reply. "You're too thin. Have you lost the true aim? Bull Buffalo's been thick on Platte River this summer."

"As thick as Wihio?" Wolf asked.

"I worried they might have killed you," Curly said, dismounting. "We saw many dead two days ago. I recognized Pony's Tail among them."

"Other good men fell there, too," Wolf said, dropping his bow on the ground beside his feet. "Too many."

"It's a hard thing, seeing good men killed," Curly agreed. "But now we're all together once more. We'll have a feast and celebrate our reunion. My father will be glad you're here."

"I'm afraid we've come like poor relations to ask your help," Wolf explained.

"Who helped Little Thunder's people when the Wihio punished them at Ash Hollow?" Curly asked. "You've always been generous to me, haven't you? We're grateful you ask our assistance."

The Lakotas began dismounting and moving through the camp, greeting the weary Omissis people warmly and offering meat and tobacco.

"Many moons have come and gone since I tasted anything half as good as this," Sky Lance declared after smoking a pipe. "It's good to be among friends."

"My father will be glad you've come, for another reason," Curly added when he and Wolf Running walked off alone.

"What reason is that?" Wolf asked.

"The traders are reluctant to sell us lead and powder for our guns," Curly explained. "There's been a lot of killing. We tried to trade for some at Fort Kearny, and the bluecoats shot at one of our men. You know the traders at Fort Laramie. You can speak for us there."

"I know them," Wolf admitted. "That was before the bluecoats fought us, though. I can't promise they would help."

"Would you ride in and speak with them?"

"If you ask it."

"It's a lot to ask," Curly said, staring at his feet. "The white soldiers are detaining your people. Mine, too. I wouldn't like to think of you sitting in an iron box."

"I can't promise lead or powder," Wolf said, sighing. "But I don't expect to find myself in danger. Not from the Logans."

"That's good," Curly said. "We'll lead you to our camp tomorrow. Then you and I will ride to the fort."

Wolf nodded his agreement. It was good to be among powerful friends once more. He expected he would sleep soundly that night for a change.

23

THE OGLALAS WELCOMED the weary survivors of the long march north. The chiefs generously shared food, and women helped sew new lodge skins. As for the children, they mixed freely, and soon a jabbering of combined Tsis tsis tas and Lakota words floated up from the nearby riverbank.

Once Wolf satisfied himself his family was provided for, he told Curly he was ready to ride to the fort.

"Stands Long will want to come, too," Wolf said.

"Good," Curly replied. "I'm also bringing others. They'll hang back from the fort but be ready to help if there's trouble."

"Do you expect any?" Wolf asked.

"Where Wihio are concerned, there's usually some sort of trouble," Curly observed. "It's always best to be prepared for it."

The following morning Curly led Wolf and Stands Long out from the encampment to where the ponies grazed. Three Oglala boys had already saddled ponies for them. Six other

Oglalas waited nearby, ready to escort the younger men westward.

"It would be best for you to wear these blankets when we reach Fort Laramie," Curly explained, offering Wolf and Stands Long red trade blankets. "The loafers who stay at the fort wrap themselves in them. No one will notice you that way."

"And you?" Wolf asked.

"Mine's rolled behind my saddle," Curly told him. "They're used to seeing me there, though. The Wihio might not notice the difference between a Lakota and a Cheyenne, but there are others around who will. This late, the Crows will all be up north, but the army uses Pawnees as its eyes. A Pawnee would gladly betray you."

"If he does, he'd better be clever about it," Wolf warned. "I have a knife that's good for cutting pieces off Pawnees."

Once the plan was explained, Curly mounted a buckskin mare and waved the others along.

"Where's my white?" Wolf asked.

"Ride the spotted pony instead," Curly urged. "Anyone who has seen you on the white's certain to remember you. No one will pay much attention to you on this animal."

"He's right," Stands Long said as he climbed atop a second buckskin. "It's not a long ride. Any pony will do."

"Unless we're chased," Wolf grumbled.

"This one will carry you swiftly," Curly assured his cousin. "We won't have to run far. Help will be at hand."

The ride itself took four days. As they swung down onto the wagon road north of Platte River, they had to be careful. Wagon bands and freight companies spread out for miles along the river. Many of the people traveling late in the season lacked good guides, and they frequently emptied their rifles at any Indian who rode within range.

"Fools," Wolf growled when a woman fired her ancient musket at him one morning. "She'll hit nothing at this range. I should charge and scare some of the fat off her."

"We're close to the fort now," Curly pointed out. "Don't do anything to attract the soldiers' attention."

Wolf nodded. It would have been enjoyable to run that Wihio, though.

When they finally approached the fort itself, Curly pointed to the line of white tents near the main barracks. There were extra soldiers on Platte River.

"This explains the cattle," Stands Long said, laughing. "I hope they're hungry."

"What's this?" Curly asked.

Wolf gave a quick account of the raid on the cattle herd, and the Oglalas howled their approval. Curly then waved his men back. He, Wolf Running, and Stands Long Beside Him would go on alone. Each wrapped himself in a trade blanket before continuing.

Things had changed at the fort. Once, Wolf felt comfortable riding through the gate as an old friend. Now, sentries cast a wary eye toward the three approaching riders. Wolf followed Curly's example and hung his head. The bluecoat studied the three, recognized Curly, and waved them along.

"Good," Curly mumbled. "The door of the store's open. Go ahead and talk to them."

"Stay with Curly," Wolf told Stands Long. "I'll talk to the Logans."

"Here," Curly said, handing over a rawhide pouch. It was heavy, and Wolf knew there were coins inside.

Wolf rolled off his horse. He then wrapped the blanket around his shoulders and started for the store. A pair of soldiers stepped outside as he approached, and he turned his head from them.

"Fool loafers," one of the bluecoats said, spitting tobacco juice at Wolf's feet. "No-accounts. Ought to shoot the bunch of 'em."

"Hush!" his companion barked. "Some of 'em speak English, you know."

"I don't much care," the soldier insisted. "They know

what I think of 'em. Old Bull Sumner ought to've kilt the whole Cheyenne nation down in Kansas. Then he could start on the Sioux."

Wolf felt the rage burning inside, but he remembered where he was and why. Instead of returning the insult, he stepped past the soldiers and slid into the store.

"Oh, Lord, which one are you?" Andy Logan called from behind the counter. "I told you fellows we have all the hides we can sell in three years! We aren't trading for more of them."

Wolf silently placed the pouch on the counter. Andy opened it and emptied its contents on the counter. There were several gold coins and a few silver dollars.

"Now there's a switch for you," Andy observed. "Cash money."

A couple of wagon women were examining cloth on one side of the store, and Wolf hesitated to reveal himself to his old friends. The women might alert the soldiers.

"What are you wanting, friend?" Andy said, trying to peer past the blanket and identify who he was dealing with.

"Powder," Wolf whispered. "Lead. Some flints for the old guns."

Andy paled.

"I don't know that I understand you, friend," Andy said, banging on the storeroom door. "Walker, come out and speak to this fellow, won't you? You know I'm hopeless with them Sioux words."

"Sioux?" one of the women cried out.

"At least they're not the murdering Cheyenne," the second woman babbled. "Why, did you hear how they killed that poor Mr. Robinson out on the Platte? Scalped him, too."

Wolf ignored the women. Andy rushed over and suggested they might like the fabric for new dresses.

"It's very expensive," the first one said.

"Tell you what," Andy replied. "I feel generous. Cut you twelve yards for the price of six. Can't be fairer than that."

"It's a deal, Mr. Logan," the second woman said. She eyed Wolf anxiously as she counted out payment. Andy then cut the cloth and handed it over. When the females left, Andy closed and bolted the door.

"Wolf, you're turning up like a bad penny," Andy observed.

"Good to see you, old friend," Walker added as he stepped out of the storeroom. "You're taller. Thought you'd stop growing one of these days."

"The bluecoats did their best to cut me down," Wolf told them.

"I see," Walker said, touching the scar on Wolf's forearm. "You have to know Mr. Twiss was mighty mad when he heard about all that. Wrote some nasty letters to Washington."

"While he was writing letters, my father was dying," Wolf said bitterly. "I find it hard to believe anybody now."

"Even us?" Walker asked.

"You and I are brothers," Wolf said, pulling the blanket away from his face. "It's hard remaining at peace when the world is on fire, though."

"Yes, it is," Walker agreed. "Your Sioux cousins send you here for the lead and powder?"

"We wouldn't sell any to them," Andy explained. "The army's blaming traders for supplying the tribes with rifles."

"You gave me mine," Wolfe noted.

"Seemed a fair trade," Walker said, grinning. "A rifle for my life."

"You'll give me the powder then?" Wolf asked. "The lead?"

"You know, if you hadn't burned all the money that was in that government fellow's buggy, you could buy everything in the store," Andy said. "You did burn all of it, didn't you?"

"Might not even have been Cheyenne did that," Walker argued.

"Was, though, wasn't it, Wolf?" Andy asked. "Next time you come across paper money, save it. It's as good as these coins, you know."

"Not as good," Wolf objected. "If I brought paper money with me, you could easily discover where I got it."

"True," Andy agreed. "You're smart, Wolf. Now, about the powder and lead . . ."

"I figure this'll buy a couple of kegs and plenty of lead," Walker interrupted. "I'll throw in the flints. Sorry about your pa, Wolf. The brothers well?"

"Alive," Wolf answered. "For now. I thank you for the lead and powder."

"Use it against buffalo," Andy warned. "Not people. We hear of any wagon trains getting ambushed, we won't be as eager to trade with you."

"Why trade with me now?" Wolf asked.

"I don't suppose you'd promise me that lead won't end up in some soldier's gullet," Andy muttered.

"I'm taking it to my cousins," Wolf explained. "I can't speak for them. I can say this: I expect to fight the soldiers again. When they ride into our country and try to kill the helpless ones, I'll fight them. Many will."

There was a sudden commotion outside, and someone shouted, "Cheyenne! In the store!"

"Blasted Pawnees," Walker said, handing over a small bag filled with flints. Wolf took the heavy lead in one arm and grabbed one of the kegs in the other. Stands Long, meanwhile, jumped off his horse and clubbed the Pawnee senseless. Andy opened the door, and Curly dashed inside.

"We have to go!" the young Oglala shouted. "Now!"

Wolf motioned to the other keg of powder, and Curly took it in his hands. The cousins then marched out the door together.

"Be careful, Wolf Running," Walker called.

"You, too, Brother," Wolf replied. Stands Long somehow had the horses waiting. The three secured the supplies and mounted the ponies. By then soldiers were dashing around, shouting and grabbing their weapons.

"Ride!" Curly yelled, flinging off his blanket and kicking his pony into a gallop. Stands Long and Wolf weren't far behind.

The three young warriors sped past the fort's outbuildings and headed for the river crossing. Soldiers rushed out behind them, firing their rifles and shouting curses. At the river crossing, two sentries tried to block the escape, but the other Oglalas galloped up, firing arrows and screaming savagely. The bluecoats retreated to the safety of some nearby rocks.

Wolf thought that once they crossed the river, they would be safe. Curly obviously thought so, too. Neither figured the soldiers would pursue, but they did. Twenty cavalry under a young lieutenant left the fort shortly after Curly, Wolf, and Stands Long fled. Led by a pair of Pawnee scouts, the soldiers had no trouble following the trail left by Curly's small party.

Ignorant of the determined bluecoats, Curly led the way into some hills a short ride north of Platte River. There the young men made camp.

"You did well," Curly told Wolf as he examined the lead and powder. "We'll make many bullets and cartridges. The flints will also be welcome. We'll once again be able to fight the bluecoats."

"Is that what's coming then?" Wolf asked.

"I'm not hungry to fight anybody," Curly confessed. "But these crazy people come upon our camps, shooting women and little children! They punish the innocent and ignore those who cheat us and steal our possessions. Yes, war's coming. It's already started down south, among your people."

Before Curly could elaborate, a horn pierced the night. Soldiers shouted and charged blindly into the small camp.

"Ayyyy!" Wolf screamed, grabbing his bow. He notched an arrow and waited for a bluecoat to cross between the fire and himself. When one did, Wolf fired. The arrow pierced the Wihio's left side, penetrated both lungs, and dropped him, dying, to the ground.

Wolf readied a second arrow, but the Wihio seemed everywhere. They wrestled with the Oglalas and blindly fired off their pistols.

"Wolf?" Stands Long called.

Wolf melted into the darkness and backed his way to where his brother-friend hid behind a boulder.

"We should save the powder," Wolf suggested.

"We should save ourselves," Stands Long argued.

"First the powder," Wolf insisted. "The Oglalas have provided everything we've asked for. I have to return their favor."

"Wolf," Stands Long pleaded.

"It's necessary," Wolf explained. He then trotted back into the turmoil. His eyes had adjusted to the dark, and he was able to avoid the shadowy shades of the enemy as he rescued first one and then the other powder keg. He was searching for the flints when Curly tapped his arm.

"I have them," Curly explained. "The lead is also safe."

"We have to leave," one of the Oglalas called.

"It's all we can do," Stands Long agreed, leading two ponies over. Wolf tied the kegs to a third pony and passed its rope to Curly.

"What do we do now?" Wolf asked his cousin.

"Ride hard," Curly explained. "Keep Platte River on your right, and you won't get lost."

"It's a long way to the camp," Wolf observed. "If the bluecoats follow us . . ."

"They won't," Curly assured his young companions. "We'll run their ponies."

The Oglalas did scatter the Wihio mounts, but the animals didn't run far. By morning the bluecoats were again in pursuit, and Wolf was stretching his horse's endurance to the limit.

By some miracle, Wolf counted five of Curly's original six Oglala companions. Only one had been killed in the raid.

"It's unbelievable," Curly remarked as they galloped eastward.

"That only one was killed?" Wolf asked.

"No, that they're following," Curly said. "They'll only break down their horses."

"Before or after ours drop?" Stands Long asked.

The horses were clearly the problem. When Wolf spotted a line of wagons approaching around midday, Curly formed his companions into a line.

"Wagon horses?" Wolf asked. "They won't hurry us along."

"Not the wagon animals," Curly said, pointing past them to a small herd of graceful ponies.

"Ayyyy!" the other Oglalas howled.

Wolf frowned. There were preparations a man should make before attacking. None of them wore medicine charms. Those wagon people were certain to have rifles.

"What choice do we have?" Stands Long asked, pointing to the relentless column of dust approaching from the west.

"We'll ride past the wagons, then cut out the ponies," Curly explained. "Understand?"

The Oglalas nodded. Wolf and Stands Long also agreed.

"Maybe you should hold back and watch over the powder," Curly then suggested to Wolf.

"I'm not a pony boy," Wolf growled. "This isn't something new for me."

"Ayyyy!" Curly shouted. "It's good cousins ride together."

Curly screamed again, then charged. The others formed a solitary line and galloped toward the surprised wagon folk. Some sought cover while others fired off their guns. An Oglala went down, bleeding from wounds in the chest and neck. Wolf tried to reach down and rescue the man, but it was too late. The Oglala was already dead.

The wagon people fired erratically, though, and only the one man fell. Meanwhile Curly cut past the last wagon and raced toward a pair of boys who were watching the horses. One screamed and dashed for safety. The second, a reddish-haired boy of sixteen or so, fumbled with a pistol. Curly aimed his rifle and shot the boy at close range, killing him instantly.

Now the raiders circled around the ponies, discarding their weary mounts for fresh ones. Some took the time to remove saddles, but three simply leapt onto the Wihio horses bareback and sped away.

Wolf took his time. The wagon people were forming a circle up ahead, and they didn't seem interested in the horses. Suddenly Wolf heard a whine past his ear. Then a hot dart slammed into his left shoulder. He could feel something warm and sticky dripping down his side.

"Wolf!" Stands Long shouted.

Wolf turned in time to spy a tall, bearded Wihio fire a third shot from behind a large boulder. Wolf managed to duck, and the ball flew harmlessly past his ear.

"Ayyyy!" Wolf shouted, slapping his tired horse into motion. The animal flew across the ground, and Wolf leapt from it past the boulder and slammed the Wihio to the earth. The hairy face tried to grasp his discarded pistol, but Wolf had driven the air from the Wihio's lungs.

"I'm first!" Wolf shouted, touching his attacker's chest.

"No, please," the Wihio whimpered.

Wolf felt pain surge through his body. He drew a knife and cut away the tall man's forelock. The Wihio screamed out in pain.

"Leave him alone!" a boy perhaps twelve years old shouted, jumping out from the rocks.

Wolf had just a second to think. He turned his knife as the

boy jumped. The youngster fell on the gleaming blade, and it sliced deeply into the boy's belly.

"Jubal?" the tall Wihio cried.

Wolf gazed at the pitiful corpse of the boy. Why hadn't he stayed in the rocks?

"Kill me, too," the first Wihio pleaded. Wolf lacked the heart. He tossed the scalp aside and stumbled to his feet. Behind the rocks were a woman and four other children, none as old as the dead one.

"Wolf?" Stands Long called.

"Here!" Wolf answered.

Stands Long shouted a warning, and Wolf dove to the ground as the scalped Wihio grabbed his pistol. The last shots flew harmlessly past Wolf. Blood was pouring across the man's face, and he could see nothing.

"Kill me!" the crazed man pleaded.

Stands Long, not knowing the pistol was empty, fired an arrow through the Wihio's heart. He fell at Wolf's feet.

"You're hurt," Stands Long observed as he climbed down to help.

"We have to hurry!" Curly shouted. "The soldiers are coming on!"

"Ah, more Wihio," an Oglala said, spotting the woman and the children.

"Leave them," Wolf suggested. "They're defenseless."

"My cousins weren't as old when the bluecoats killed them in Little Thunder's camp," the Oglala growled. He climbed down from his horse and killed the woman. He then chased the little ones out toward his companions.

"Let's get away from this place," Wolf pleaded. "Now!"

"Soon," Stands Long promised.

Meanwhile the Oglalas made a game of running the children back and forth between them. Finally Curly shouted it was time to leave.

A girl of nine or ten stared up with pleading eyes.

"Mister, please don't hurt my brothers and sisters," she

said. "You kilt Ma and Pa. Jubal, too. Ain't no need to . . ."

"Run!" Wolf shouted, stumbling toward them. "Run!"

He waved his arms like a wounded eagle, distracting the Oglalas. The girl and one of her brothers raced to the safety of the wagons. The other two children stood there, frozen in terror. The Oglalas cut them down.

Stands Long brought a fresh horse out, and Wolf managed to climb onto it.

"That wasn't necessary," Wolf muttered.

"You said the same thing when we found Pony's Tail," Stands Long observed.

"Don't interfere with us again!" an angry Oglala shouted.

"Hurry us away from this place," Wolf said, slumping over his horse.

"I will," Stands Long pleaded. The brother-friends then galloped off eastward.

24

WOLF RUNNING HAD little memory of the three days that followed. His mind drifted across the hills and streams north of Platte River, and he often saw the pleading eyes of the Wihio girl. He also felt the warm blood of the dead boy on his hands. He saw Pony's Tail lying between his young cousins.

Wolf entered the Oglala camp on a pony drag. His shoulder throbbed, and he gazed out at the lodges with feverish eyes. Stands Long had cut the ball out, but it was Curly who bound the wound in moss and sweet sage to drive out the evil humors.

The Oglalas and Tsis tsis tas celebrated their young men's return. Immediately warriors began melting the lead and forming balls in their steel molds. Others replaced their rifle flints.

"We're strong again," Curly told his cousin. "It's your doing, Cousin."

"I've paid a price," Wolf replied. "I've lost the harmony of my world."

As the grasses began to yellow, the Oglalas moved north to their winter camps. The ponies were let loose to graze, and the Tsis tsis tas erected their new lodges in a small circle nearby. Other Omissis bands joined them, as did a large Suhtai contingent.

"Winter's come," Little Hawk told his older brother, "and we're still alive. We'll grow strong again with the summer sun."

First, though, the Hard Face Moons of winter had to be endured. In that northern country, the snows started early, and the drifts were deep. Everything froze. Ponds, lakes, even rivers. Hunters couldn't leave their lodges to stalk game, and everyone relied on the stores of dried beef and buffalo put aside during summer and fall.

"Bear has the proper idea," Wolf told Morning Hawk. "He goes to sleep when the snows come and lives off his fat until the earth warms."

"You and I would have a difficult time," the boy said, touching Wolf's ribs and then his own.

"It's hard to grow fat when a people has so many enemies," Wolf observed.

His brothers did their best to bring his spirit back to life, but Wolf was lost in a dark region. The snow and the long nights only made matters worse. Sharing old stories and singing warrior songs made the time pass, but it did nothing to lift the gloom from his heart.

"Naha', a worse time's coming," Brunt Willow Woman told him. "You have to be strong enough to find your way. Invite a dream and let Snow Wolf guide you back to us."

Wolf read the despair etched on his mother's face, and he starved himself to bring the dream. Snow Wolf failed to appear, though. Instead Wolf found himself in a nightmare of fire and killing. Bluecoats stood on a hill, shooting wildly as Tsis tsis tas and Lakotas swarmed below.

"No!" Wolf screamed as he felt hot lead tear at his sides. Stands Long roused him.

"It's not starving that's required," Stands Long said afterward. "We should take a sweat."

"In winter?" Wolf cried. "With snows half a man's height deep?"

"The Suhtai have built a sweat lodge," Stands Long explained. "We're invited to join them there."

Wolf tried to stand, but his wound still ached, and he collapsed into the comfort of his hide bed.

"We'll go later," Stands Long said, sighing. "Rest."

That winter, Wolf's seventeenth, was numbing cold. Old men who painted their winter counts marked it as the season of the great snows. Among the Tsis tsis tas, it was also remembered as the starving time.

What had once seemed an endless store of dried meat began to dwindle as more and more bands straggled into the winter camps. Some had only their clothing, and little enough of that. They had eaten their dogs and even their ponies. Corn Dancer arrived with a woman and three boys—the sole survivors from Thunder Colt's band.

"I warned against making the crossing," he insisted.

"You drew the soldiers when you shot off your rifle," one of the children, a boy of ten named Broken Tooth, complained. "You should have led the way. Instead you let the young cousins do it."

The young people turned on Corn Dancer with rare savagery, and he was shaken. Wolf turned away from them. He had discord enough in his life.

The newcomers quickly became beggars. The Oglalas took in some of the younger children, adopting them into their tribe. Others went from lodge to lodge, pleading for food.

"Give them some meat," Wolf replied to each request made of the young men's lodge.

"We'll starve ourselves," Corn Dancer, who had made himself at home there, complained.

"Go out and hunt then," Wolf grumbled. "Aren't we men of the people? How can we eat when children are hungry?"

Some of the older people had a different solution. Sky Lance and Summer Plum Woman placed their grandchildren in the care of a young Suhtai family and walked out into the snowdrifts. It was an honorable death, and an easy one. The numbing cold took one slowly, peacefully, onto Hanging Road. Wolf rose from his bed long enough to help his brothers prepare burial scaffolds.

"You're better," Burnt Willow Woman observed. "I was worried."

"I'm still drifting," Wolf told her. "There are things that needed doing, though."

"Yes," she agreed.

That night Morning Hawk joined his brothers in their lodge. The boy enjoyed the occasional visits, and his laughter warmed his companions like a fire. Morning Hawk ran about and wrestled and swallowed life whole. When he wrapped himself in an elk hide and slept between Little Hawk and Willow Boy, Wolf should have guessed something was wrong.

That night Burnt Willow Woman, too, stepped into the snowdrifts. Her heart had ached since Red Hawk's death, but she had busied herself with her sons.

"She refused to eat," Morning Hawk explained when he led his brothers to her the following morning. "She asked how she could take food when there were children starving."

"She was needed!" Little Hawk shouted.

"Nah' koa!" Willow Boy howled.

"She was fortunate," Wolf observed. "Her pain is gone. She chose the moment and the place of her death. How many do that?"

Wolf's own pain prevented him from helping with the scaffold. The cold aggravated his injury, and his left arm was becoming useless. He did make the mourning prayers, though, and cut his hair.

By the time the burial prayers and three days mourning had been concluded, another family had taken possession of Burnt Willow Woman's lodge. The belongings had been divided among the others. Even the dried beef was gone.

"It was for us to make the giveaway," Wolf complained.

"It's too cold to wait for you," Corn Dancer argued.

"Find another place to sleep," Wolf growled. "You're a bleeding wound, Dancer, and my thinking's not right. I might cut you down without considering the harm it would bring the people."

Corn Dancer laughed at the notion. He lost his grin when he recognized the fire forming in Wolf's eyes.

"I'll go," Corn Dancer said. He vanished into a crowd of others.

"We've waited long enough to undergo the sweat," Stands Long declared. "We're all of us troubled, but you're becoming crazy, Wolf! It's time."

Wolf started to argue, but his brothers dragged him along to the Suhtai camp. It was a considerable distance to walk in the cold, and they arrived stiff and lifeless.

"Morning Hawk?" Wolf asked, seeing his small brother shivering at his side.

"Aren't you my father now?" the boy asked. "I had to come, didn't I?"

Wolf had a second surprise. He had been led into Long Dog's lodge. Younger Dog greeted them warmly. Spring Fox and Rabbit welcomed him, too.

"You should have come earlier," Sun Walker Maiden complained as she examined his stiff arm. "It will take time, restoring that arm."

"Does it matter?" Wolf asked. "Maybe it's time that I, too, found a snowdrift."

"It's not for you to decide," Flying Squirrel said, entering the lodge. "Have you forgotten so much? We'll sweat and we'll dream. Afterward, we'll do what is necessary to put an end to this starving."

Wolf half believed the medicine chief. Flying Squirrel had always spoken well, and his words again made sense.

"The rocks are ready," Long Dog announced from the entrance of his lodge. "We'll go now. Remember, this is a Suhtai sweat lodge. We'll perform the ancient rituals."

The Omissis visitors nodded their agreement. Younger Dog then led the way to the nearby sweat lodge.

It was smaller than the lodges Wolf had erected, and the ceiling was low. Inside, a wonderful warmth permeated the place. Wolf discarded his clothing and entered in his breechclout. His three brothers followed. Long Dog and Flying Squirrel came next. Younger Dog went last.

Wolf couldn't understand many of the prayers. The old Suhtai words were beyond his knowledge. The warmth of the place and the sweet scents of sage drove his despair away. He drifted into a brief dream.

"Have heart," Snow Wolf urged. "Follow me!"

Little Hawk nudged Wolf back to life and handed over a pipe. Wolf smoked and passed it on. The pipe moved around the small circle three times. As he, his brothers, and their companions smoked and talked, Wolf felt the pain flow out of him.

That night Wolf slept well for the first time since the bluecoat battle at Turkey Creek. Snow Wolf walked with him in a dream. They crossed green valleys and deep rivers. They climbed mountains and touched the sky.

"Brave up," Snow Wolf urged. "You're a man of the people. The defenseless ones have no one else to rely upon. Nothing lives long, Brother, but if you fade away, many will go with you."

When Wolf awoke, Stands Long was waiting with their bows beside the door.

"We have nothing to eat," Morning Hawk said, crawling over to his oldest brother. "You have to shoot an elk."

"An elk?" Wolf cried. "Who's seen game nearby? The animals have gone south with the sparrows."

"Wolf?" Stands Long asked. "You spoke of the elk. Were you talking in a dream?"

"I don't know," Wolf confessed. "Snow Wolf scolded me, but I don't remember any elk."

"Do we go?" Little Hawk asked.

"Do we have a choice?" Wolf said. "If there's nothing to eat, we have to shoot something."

"Don't shoot a tree," Morning Hawk said. "They're frozen and difficult to chew."

Wolf wrapped himself in his warmest hides. His shoulder was stiff, and he doubted he could hold a bow steadily. Nevertheless he led Stands Long, Little Hawk, and Willow Boy out past the camp into the snowbound wilderness beyond.

The aching cold quickly tore at them, and they soon sank waist-deep into snow. Wolf closed his eyes a moment and tried to fend off the pain. At that instant he heard something move through the trees just ahead.

The others sighed anxiously as Wolf stared through the white mist. The grandfather of all elk emerged, leading three females.

"Forgive me, Uncle," Wolf whispered as he drew an arrow from his quiver. "Our needs are great."

Behind him, the others also whispered the hunting prayers. As if hearing, the great elk turned and exposed his chest.

"Hemmawihio, thank you," Wolf whispered as he raised his bow. The pain was intense, but he managed to notch the arrow and aim. He then released it. The arrow flew across the mists and struck deep and hard into the heart of the bull elk. The animal uttered a deep grunt and fell.

Little Hawk killed the second elk, and Stands Long dropped the third. Willow Boy plunged through the snowdrifts until he was three paces from the fourth. He then dispatched it.

Wolf butchered the bull himself. He set rib meat aside as an offering and began cutting the hide away. They wrapped the fresh meat in the hide and returned to their camp.

"Three elk lay in the forest north of camp," Wolf informed the criers. "Ask the others to help us butcher the meat."

Two criers spread out among the three camp circles, and a small army of Omissis, Suhtai, and Oglala women trudged through the snow with their butchering knives.

"Take some of the meat to Flying Squirrel," Wolf urged his brothers. "And to Long Dog. We should thank them for the medicine that allowed us to find the elk."

Stands Long agreed. He hurried to deliver the meat himself. That night the cooking pots sizzled with elk roasts. For once hunger was chased from the camps.

Wolf's brothers were glad to have full bellies, but they had a second reason to celebrate.

"You've come back to us, Nah nih," Willow Boy said. "There's no longer any reason to worry. You're here to lead us onto man's road."

Wolf frowned. He was weary of leading.

"You can only be what you are," Stands Long argued. "Don't run from it. Accept what's coming and do your best for all of us."

Wolf nodded his agreement. It was a daunting task, but what choice did he have? None.

Wolf led his brothers and the other young men on other hunts, and the starving came to an end. Other days he rested on hides in Long Dog's lodge while the Dog and Sun Walker Maiden worked their fingers into the muscles and tendons, freeing Wolf's arm from their hold.

"See how much easier it is for you to hold a bow," Sun Walker told him each day. "We'll restore your old power. Have patience."

Wolf did. He endured pain and overcame doubt. Eventually the ice lost its hold on the land, and the sun brought new life to the world. Wolf's shoulder mended.

The Tsis tsis tas prepared to conduct the New Life Lodge ceremonies in the southern country once again, and the Omissis and Suhtai left their Oglala cousins and started south.

"We would never have seen summer without your generosity," Wolf told Curly before departing.

"A man's obliged to help his relations," the young Oglala replied. "Be careful crossing Platte River. Maybe we'll hunt Bull Buffalo together."

"Maybe," Wolf agreed.

The summer camp spread out on both banks of Beaver Creek, but there were far fewer lodges now. Fewer people as well. What the bluecoats had been unable to accomplish, the cold of winter had. Even the living were weak and thin. There were many absent friends.

Wolf Running and Stands Long Beside Him entered the New Life Lodge to hang by the pole a second time.

"This time we're suffering for the welfare of the people," Wolf told his brothers. "And to drive the bad feelings out of our hearts."

Afterward they led the scouts after Bull Buffalo. The hunters were younger that year, but they found many strong bulls to hunt. There would soon be hides for new lodges and meat to make even the frailest child fat and content.

Only afterward, when the hunting had been concluded and the camps began to break apart and set out on their own, did Younger Dog approach.

"We've hunted," the young man observed. "There's food in our lodges, and the children are again playing the hoop game. It's time young men turned to more serious matters."

"Yes?" Wolf asked, confused.

"Courtship," Younger Dog explained, handing over a newly carved flute. "My sister would welcome your attentions. Ne' hyo says it would be good to have another brave heart in the family."

"I have obligations," Wolf argued.

"You'll soon have more of them," Younger Dog replied. "It's time you two were married. The women are sewing a new lodge. Don't disappoint everyone."

Wolf accepted the flute. That afternoon he met Sun Walker Maiden at the river, and they spoke of the future.

"Go, speak with my father," she urged. "He knows your heart. Offer him ponies. It's time we began our life together."

"I'm a poor man now," Wolf explained.

"You have the brown stallion taken from the Wihio wagon people," she pointed out. "It's a good horse. Ne' hyo would accept it."

"A single horse?" Wolf gasped. "It's not right."

"There are men who would offer you others," she added. "Speak with my father. Make the bargain, Wolf."

Wolf did approach Long Dog's lodge. The path had become familiar to his feet, but he had difficulty making his feet move that evening.

"I've been expecting you," Long Dog said when Wolf arrived. "Maybe we can walk?"

"It's a good idea," Wolf agreed.

The Dog led the way past the Suhtai camp circle to a low hill. He stopped there and spoke of the Suhtai ways.

"In many ways, our habits are older and more sacred than those of the other bands," Long Dog said. "We hold strong medicine, and we insist our men walk the sacred path."

"It's best," Wolf agreed.

"I wouldn't welcome all men into my family," Long Dog continued. "Some don't take their responsibilities to heart. Many others are lazy."

"You wouldn't be disappointed in me," Wolf declared.

"I know that. There's the problem with the horses, though."

"I'm a poor man," Wolf said, sighing.

"I'm a proud man, Wolf. I can't give my daughter away like a worthless hide. You deserve a more valuable wife. I insist on three ponies. Good ones."

"I only have two, and the white's broken down. I need a good mount," Wolf noted.

"Come back and speak to me again when you have the horses," Long Dog suggested. "I know men who would offer some to you, but be careful. A man who depends on his friends' generosity loses part of his heart. A man has to have pride."

"Yes, he does," Wolf agreed.

He returned to young men's lodge with a stone for a heart. It was a sad thing, being so close to what he wanted and yet unable to have it.

"Wolf?" Stands Long called.

"She's a fine woman," Wolf said, sighing. "Her father wants three ponies."

"We'll get them," Stands Long boasted.

"I won't ask others," Wolf insisted.

"Ask?" Stands Long cried. "Ask? Who asks Pawnees for anything?"

"Pawnees?"

"A day's ride east of here," Stands Long explained. "Hunting Bull Buffalo. There are many good ponies in their herd, too. Let's go and take some of them to Long Dog."

"Ayyyy!" Wolf howled. "Let's do it!"

25

TALK OF RAIDING the Pawnee horse herd made its way through the Omissis camp, and small bands of raiders formed up and rode eastward. A handful of young Elks carried a pipe to Wolf Running in hopes of enlisting his leadership. But Wolf declined.

"Everyone knows you're going," Little Hawk complained afterward. "You could take the others along."

"Don't the Elks have chiefs?" Wolf asked. "Lance-carriers? I intend to strike hard and fast. We'll run twenty ponies. That will be enough for our needs. If we ask five or six others to go along, we'll need to drive off many more. You can't hide a large herd. The Pawnees would discover us."

"You won't hold us back, will you?" Little Hawk asked.

"You and Willow Boy can come. Stands Long, too. I'll arrange for Morning Hawk to stay with Sun Walker Maiden. The boy likes her."

"Maybe Younger Dog would come with us then," Little Hawk suggested.

"That would be fair," Wolf agreed.

Wolf set off later that afternoon with his small brother. Long Dog agreed to take charge of the boy.

"My brothers suggested your older son might like to come," Wolf said as he prepared to leave.

"He left before you arrived," Long Dog explained. "As we talk, he's probably readying his pony."

"Younger Dog has big ears," Sun Walker Maiden explained. "He always knows what's happening."

Wolf laughed at himself. He and Stands Long were probably the last to know of the proposed raid. The boys had planned it days ago.

What Little Hawk and Willow Boy didn't understand was that Wolf never set out without making the appropriate prayers. Other bands rode out as much as two days before Wolf was ready.

"He'll find the Pawnees, though," Stands Long declared. "Snow Wolf will guide him."

Actually Wolf Running hoped to avoid Pawnees. It was their ponies he was after. He ignored the scouts who suggested there were Pawnees camped on Platte River or on the Little Blue. Instead he located the buffalo herds and waited for hunting parties to approach.

"Warriors always ride their best ponies when they chase Bull Buffalo," Wolf explained. "It's the best I'm looking for."

"Long Dog will expect good horses, after all," Younger Dog declared. "You wouldn't want to insult my sister. Her sharp tongue would make you suffer."

All that first day, riding from the Omissis camp and heading out onto the buffalo range, Younger Dog entertained them with stories of his family. The smaller brothers were constantly tricking Sun Walker Maiden, and she cleverly avenged herself each and every time.

"Watch her with hawk's eyes," Younger Dog advised. "Check your bed for burrs and listen for rattlesnakes."

They made a camp of sorts on a hill overlooking a small herd of buffalo that first night. Wolf allowed no fire, and the young men chewed dried strips of buffalo meat to chase their hunger away. Wolf kept watch over his brothers and the ponies half the night. Stands Long stood guard the other half.

As dawn broke over the buffalo, Wolf spotted the Pawnees. There were seven or eight in the hunting party, but they drove close to fifty ponies along.

"There are others nearby," Wolf warned. "Keep alert."

The Omissis then painted their faces and tied up their ponies' tails. Each quietly sang a brave-heart song and prepared to strike the enemy.

"Listen carefully," Wolf told the others. "Stands Long and I will charge the pony boys. Once we drive them back, we'll hold off the others. You three have to drive the ponies along toward camp. Once you start them running, keep after them. Don't stop until you're safely among our friends again."

"What if you are attacked?" Younger Dog asked.

"Stands Long and I will know when to fight and when to run," Wolf assured the young man. "It's most important you run their ponies. Without fresh mounts, the Pawnees can't catch us."

The boys nodded, but Wolf noticed their hearts weren't in it.

"Promise me," he insisted. "I can't do anything if I'm worried you are in peril."

"Stands Long?" Little Hawk asked.

"I'll keep him safe," Stands Long vowed. "Or he'll watch me. Ah, we'll watch each other."

"We're brother-friends, after all," Wolf noted.

In truth, he didn't expect danger. He intended to wait until the Pawnees spread out toward the buffalo. That was the time to run the ponies.

It began well. The older Pawnees broke off in pairs and

charged the herd. The younger ones rushed ahead, eager to watch their fathers. Then Wolf Running and Stands Long Beside Him whipped their horses into a gallop and descended on the pony boys, howling like demons.

Two of the pony boys turned away and raced toward the hunters. The third, a boy of fourteen or fifteen, notched an arrow and fired it toward Wolf.

"Ayyyy!" Wolf shouted as he knocked the arrow aside with his shield. Before the young Pawnee could fire a second time, Wolf slammed his shield against the youngster's chest. The Pawnee flew backward, tumbled over his horse's rump, and fell facedown on the prairie.

"Ayyyy!" Wolf shouted as the pony boy frantically scrambled for safety. "I'm first!"

The coup encouraged his companions. Little Hawk raced among the Pawnee ponies, waving a blanket and turning them westward. Willow Boy and Younger Dog closed in on the flanks and kept the herd together.

"Ride!" Wolf shouted to the others. "Run them!"

"Ayyyy!" Stands Long howled. "We've done it."

It was too early to celebrate, though. While the hunters charged individual bulls, and the pony boys escaped, three other Pawnees now appeared at the crest of a nearby hill.

"Scouts from another band," Stands Long observed, pointing to them.

"Yes," Wolf agreed, staring at the Pawnees. Each was painted in reds and yellows. The tallest of the trio wore a bonnet made of thirty eagle feathers. His chest was scarred, and one eye was permanently closed.

"He's fought before," Stands Long noted.

"The others, too," Wolf added, pointing out the coup feathers tied in their hair.

"Well, we've fought, too," Stands Long boasted. "How do you want to go about it? Charge or wait?"

"The longer we put off a fight, the better chance the others have of getting the ponies away," Wolf argued.

"These Pawnees may find help," Stands Long pointed out.

"They may need it," Wolf growled. He put his bow aside and took out his rifle. He hadn't used it since the Turkey Creek fight, but he'd recently cleaned and oiled it the way Walker Logan had shown him. He loaded the gun, aimed at the tall Pawnee, and fired. The concussion tore the air. The ball missed the tall man but struck the Pawnee on the right just below his left ear.

Wolf turned his head away as the Pawnee's head exploded like a melon. The other Pawnees were spattered by bone and brain, and their horses reared and bucked. The tall Pawnee then took out his own rifle and returned the shot. His was an old gun, though, and the ball fell well short.

"They'll charge now," Stands Long said, stringing his bow.

"I would," Wolf said, stowing the rifle and pulling out a stone-tipped war club.

"If they were smart, they'd reload their guns and close the range," Stands Long suggested. "You might reload your own rifle."

"No, they'll charge before I could get it done."

Wolf was right. The two Pawnees howled and kicked their horses into motion. Screaming and racing down the hill, they separated. Wolf waited for the tall one. Stands Long notched an arrow and exchanged fire with the other. The Pawnee arrow struck Stands Long's shield. Stands Long's arrow pierced the Pawnee's chest and killed him.

Wolf nudged his horse into motion, and the tall Pawnee pulled up short. The Pawnee threw his rifle away and pulled a lance from behind his saddle.

Wolf grew cold. It was a medicine lance, painted with powerful signs. Three scalps dangled from the far end. There was something else, too. Ears!

"So," Wolf muttered, recalling the corpses at Platte River. The bluecoats hadn't been alone that day.

"Hah," the Pawnee said, laughingly touching the trophies. The taunt wasn't necessary. Wolf recognized the Pawnee as an experienced fighter. The lance alone was proof. He understood about the scalps. But those ears . . .

"Brave up," Wolf sang. "Nothing lives long. Only the earth and the mountains."

The Pawnee uttered a piercing scream and drove his horse onward. Wolf nudged the white to one side, braced himself, and received the lance thrust with his shield. The tough hump hide deflected the blow, but the steel point scarred Snow Wolf's nose. The force of the blow jolted Wolf and nearly unhorsed him.

Wolf recovered in time to deliver a blow of his own. He made a feint toward the Pawnee's head, then clubbed his knee just below where his shield offered protection.

The Pawnee grunted with pain, and he tried to slap his horse into motion and avoid a second blow. Wolf dodged a lance thrust and clubbed the Pawnee's shield arm once, twice, three times. The arm hung at an odd angle, and the shield dropped to the ground.

"Ayyyy!" Wolf howled as he lifted himself off his horse and dove at the tall Pawnee.

The one-eyed warrior tried to turn, but Wolf was light on his feet. He pounded the bigger man's chest and hammered the medicine lance from his fingers. The defenseless Pawnee rolled off his horse and tried to recover the weapon, but Wolf leapt on him again.

The scarred old warrior glanced around him. For the first time a trace of fear entered his surviving eye. Wolf made a move with his shield arm and then clubbed the Pawnee's chest again. This blow drove the tall man to the ground.

"I'm first!" Wolf shouted, crushing the enemy's skull with a fierce blow.

"Ayyyy!" Stands Long shouted. "You've killed him. Hurry. Let's go."

"Not yet," Wolf said, drawing out his knife and turning to

the Pawnee. "You left a boy to walk the other side with no ears to hear the birds sing," Wolf barked. "I leave you with no eyes to see him come for you."

Wolf cut out the lifeless eye.

"Remember this day, Pawnees," he spoke to the dead. "Go back to your country and leave the Wihio soldiers to find their own trails."

"Wolf!" Stands Long called anxiously.

"Yes," Wolf agreed as he grabbed the medicine lance. "It's time to go home."

If the Pawnee hunters had the energy to pursue, the sight of their dead argued against it. The tall one's mutilated face was enough to frighten anyone. And there was no hope of catching a well-armed band of Omissis who could change mounts a dozen times and still have fresh horses left to ride.

Wolf and Stands Long caught up with their companions a short time after the fight. Together, they escorted the stolen ponies westward. They rode all afternoon and continued after darkness fell. Wolf sometimes slowed the pace, but he was intent on returning to the camp. He didn't want the captured ponies straying.

As they rode, Stands Long recounted the details of the fighting. At each coup, the young men howled at the moon.

They reached the camp in the middle of the night. Wolf drove the ponies into a ravine and roped off both ends to secure the horses. He and his companions then spread hides on the slope above and slept until dawn.

As the sun rose over the Omissis camp, surprised pony boys discovered the captured ponies. By the time Wolf rose from his makeshift bed, men gathered to hear the story.

"Look!" Spring Fox shouted. "Nah nih has captured the whole Pawnee pony herd."

"Ayyyy!" Rabbit hollered. "Our brother is rich in horses."

"Maybe you, too, will want to take a wife," Wolf remarked as Younger Dog's brothers raced toward him.

"How many ponies can I keep?" the Dog asked.

"There are fifty," Wolf counted. "Ten are yours."

"No, you killed the tall Pawnee," Younger Dog argued. "Half are yours."

"We're equals," Wolf insisted. "I only ask to choose the five I'll take your father."

"Agreed," Younger Dog said, grinning.

While others spoke of the raid or recounted Wolf's killing of the medicine lance-carrier, Wolf himself bathed in the nearby creek and dressed in his finest clothes. He then tied three feathers in his hair.

"We'll bring the ponies," Little Hawk said, motioning to Willow Boy. The brothers, too, had put on their best shirts and oiled their hair.

"It's fitting we go with you, Nah nih," Willow Boy said. "It's a brother's obligation."

Wolf was glad to have the company. He hadn't perspired half so much when facing the one-eyed Pawnee. After all, Wolf understood fighting. Dying even. Courtship and women remained a mystery.

With his brothers leading the five ponies, Wolf couldn't turn back. He didn't want to. He knew his life wouldn't be complete without Sun Walker Maiden. But speaking of it to her father was another matter.

Morning Hawk greeted Wolf at the entrance to Long Dog's lodge.

"You brought the horses," the six-year-old said. "Good. I was afraid I might have to stay here."

"You'll come and live in my lodge as a son would," Wolf told him. "Unless Sun Walker Maiden refuses me."

"She won't," Morning Hawk said, laughing. "The women are already sewing your lodge skin."

Wolf grinned. Long Dog then stepped out and greeted him.

"Five?" Long Dog asked, counting the animals. "Three would have been acceptable."

"For such a fine woman?" Wolf asked. "Any less than five would have been an insult to your family."

The surrounding Suhtai applauded the remark. Wolf had taken a first step toward establishing harmony with Long Dog's relations.

"I suppose you'll ask her if she'll agree to become my wife," Wolf added nervously.

"I suppose I should," Long Dog agreed. "I hope she doesn't turn you down. I'd hate to lose such good ponies."

"Or a brave-heart son," Younger Dog added as he led his brothers along. "Don't worry," he told Wolf. "She'll agree."

She did.

The preparations for the wedding feast required six days. Wolf passed the time restoring his shield and making arrows. Flying Squirrel took him aside and instructed him in the obligations of a husband.

"Your father or uncle should have been the one to speak to you, but they're dead," the Squirrel said.

"I'm glad you're offering," Wolf told the medicine chief. "I know some things, but others I can only guess at."

As he sat with Flying Squirrel, listening to the secrets of life unfold, Wolf felt like a small boy sitting at his father's side. When it was over, he was astonished to discover the world was not such a mysterious place after all. Marriage was only another road to travel. It had its preparations and complexities, too.

Wolf Running and Sun Walker Maiden were joined in the ancient Suhtai fashion, and Wolf devoted three days to learning the old prayers. There wasn't so much to say or do, but with so many watching, he intended to get everything right. Once Long Dog presented his daughter, Wolf pledged to provide for her needs. The prayers that followed invoked medicine to protect their union.

Afterward the people danced and ate and celebrated. Wolf joined in it all. He had traveled many days on man's road, but always before he had wondered if it wasn't all a fraud.

He was only a young man of seventeen snows, after all. With Sun Walker Maiden at his side now, he was truly a man of the people.

The old women who had sewn the lodge skin led them to the place. Friends had furnished the inside. Long Dog had given them good cooking kettles, and the Elks had cut fresh pine poles that would weather any storm. Wolf's brothers offered buffalo hides and water skins. Flying Squirrel had painted the outside with a glowing sun, many buffalo skulls, and a haunting white wolf.

"Enjoy yourselves tonight," Stands Long called. "Morning Hawk will join you tomorrow."

Wolf's brothers laughed.

"You won't mind too much?" Wolf asked his young wife.

"I would have missed having little boys about," she replied. "Soon we'll have children of our own to fill this good lodge."

"That's a warming thought," Wolf said.

"Did you ever think that first time we met on the water path that we would ever walk the world together?" Sun Walker asked.

"Think?" Wolf asked. "I don't recall thinking much that afternoon. I was too busy running into maidens and spilling their water."

"I knew," she told him. "From that day."

"You didn't," Wolf objected. "You couldn't!"

"I told you the Suhtai medicine's strong, Wolf. You're not the only one with farseeing eyes."

"What is it those eyes see, Sun Walker?"

"Many good days together," she said, holding him close.

"I hope we'll have them," Wolf told her. "There's been too much dying, too much killing. I told you the men in my family haven't known long lives."

"It's not the length that's important," she said, nodding at the Pawnee medicine lance. "I've heard you say it yourself. A man can only be what he is. Nothing more."

"Yes," Wolf agreed.

"You, my husband, are already a great man. You've counted many coups. I don't know how many friends you've rescued. Snow Wolf guides your feet. Your medicine is strong."

"Yes, the medicine is strong," he agreed.

"Very strong," she said as she pulled him down onto the soft buffalo hides.

But as he lay there with her, sharing everything a man could share, Wolf Running couldn't help wondering if his medicine was strong enough for what was coming. Was anything?